A DEBT FROM THE PAST

Recent Titles by Beryl Matthews from Severn House

BATTLES LOST AND WON
A DEBT FROM THE PAST
DIAMONDS IN THE DUST
A FLIGHT OF GOLDEN WINGS
THE FORGOTTEN FAMILY
HOLD ON TO YOUR DREAMS
A NEW DAY
THE OPEN DOOR
A TIME OF PEACE
THE UNCERTAIN YEARS
WINGS OF THE MORNING

Sunderland Libraries	
SROW	
K1456811007	
Askews & Holts	May-2013
AF GENERAL	£19.99
	PO-4891/5

A DEBT FROM THE PAST

Beryl Matthews

This first world edition published 2013
in Great Britain and the USA by
SEVERN HOUSE PUBLISHERS LTD of
19 Cedar Road, Sutton, Surrey, England, SM2 5DA.

Copyright © 2013 by Beryl Matthews.

All rights reserved.
The moral right of the author has been asserted.

British Library Cataloguing in Publication Data

Matthews, Beryl.
  A debt from the past.
  1. Hampshire (England)–Social conditions–19th century–
Fiction.
  I. Title
  823.9'2-dc23

ISBN-13: 978-0-7278-8302-5 (cased)

Except where actual historical events and characters are being
described for the storyline of this novel, all situations in this
publication are fictitious and any resemblance to living persons
is purely coincidental.

All Severn House titles are printed on acid-free paper.

Severn House Publishers support The Forest Stewardship Council [FSC],
the leading international forest certification organisation. All our titles
that are printed on Greenpeace-approved FSC-certified paper carry the
FSC logo.

Typeset by Palimpsest Book Production Ltd.,
Falkirk, Stirlingshire, Scotland.
Printed and bound in Great Britain by
MPG Books Ltd., Bodmin, Cornwall.

One

Hampshire, 1850

'I must go to Helen!' Elizabeth Langton was immediately on her feet, her face white with horror. 'Why did she not send word to us? She knew where we were staying while on this trip to buy new stock for the estate. I would have returned immediately.'

'Wait, my dear.' Lord Edward Sharland caught Elizabeth as she headed for the door and made his god-daughter sit down again. 'This happened four days ago, and if Helen had wanted our help, she would have sent word.'

'But why would she not do so? I am her friend, and she was a great support to me when Father died. I would do the same for her.'

'She knows that, Beth.' Edward pulled up a chair and sat opposite her, running a hand through his still abundant but greying hair. 'You know your friend has always been fiercely independent and will face the shame by shouldering this tragedy alone. We will do all we can to help her through this, but we must respect her wishes.'

Beth nodded. 'You are right, of course. Tell me what you know, for I cannot grasp why Lord Denton should do such a terrible thing. He was always laughing and joking.'

'That was but a facade. Helen's father liked to gamble – we all knew that – and evidently it got out of hand when his wife died two years ago. He hid it well, but he was in deeper debt than anyone guessed. In the end he could see only one way out.'

'So he shot himself, leaving his daughter to deal with the mess he has left behind.' Beth's deep blue eyes blazed with anger. 'How could he do such a thoughtless thing?'

'He was obviously a desperate man, and desperate men do not think clearly. I have been informed that Helen will not accept help from anyone, and she has kept it a secret for as long as possible. She has a strong character, and I am sure she will cope with what has to be done. Nevertheless, we are her closet friends and neighbours, and we should offer our help. If she turns us away, then we must accept that.'

'I understand.' She gave her godfather a sad smile. 'You have shown me that I must not rush in emotionally and upset her any more than she already is. I will go to her now. It will take me just a moment to change into a riding habit.'

Within fifteen minutes they were on their way. The Denton estate was only a journey of four miles, but Elizabeth was anxious to see her friend and urged her mount into a steady canter.

When they reached the mansion, she stared in disbelief. Furniture and small items such as pictures and ornaments were being carried out and loaded on to waiting carts by an army of workers. It looked as if Helen's beautiful home was being emptied of its entire contents.

She heard Edward swear under his breath and looked at him as she dismounted. 'Is she moving?'

'I think she's doing more than that.'

Beth didn't stop to discuss the subject but ran into the house. Her friend was standing in the grand entrance hall, now stripped of all its furniture, and talking to a man as he ticked off items on a list he held in his hand. She stopped, unable to believe what was happening. Helen was wearing a plain brown dress, one more suited to a servant, but her back was straight, and a tight control was being held on her emotions, the only sign of strain showing in dark smudges under her glorious green eyes.

When the man walked away, Beth rushed up to her and put her arms around her, kissing her cheek. 'I am so sorry, Helen. Why didn't you send for me? I would not leave you to deal with this on your own.'

'I know.' Helen gave a tight smile and then stepped back. 'But I do not want you to be associated with this scandal – or me.'

Frowning at the puzzling statement, Beth shook her head. 'We have been friends since childhood, Helen, so why would you say such a thing? And what is going on here?'

'Everything is being sold.'

'Everything?'

'Yes. It is the only way I can pay off my father's debts. I am determined to clear every penny of the debts, but it will take everything I own to achieve this.'

'They are that huge?' Beth whispered in disbelief.

'I'm sorry to say they are.'

'Let us help, Helen.' Lord Edward had joined them.

'No, thank you, your lordship. I have gone over the figures most carefully and am confident that I shall be able to pay off everything owing.'

Beth was devastated for her friend, but she knew that when Helen set her mind to something she always triumphed, no matter how hard the struggle. But this was asking too much of a young woman, surely?

'Will you be able to keep the house in Bath?' Edward asked.

'No. My father lost that in a game of cards three months ago. As soon as everything is sold I will need to obtain a position as a governess.'

'But you can't do that. You are a lady!' Beth was horrified.

'I shall not be using my title or the Denton name again. I fear that my family name has been disgraced beyond repair, and I must find employment as soon as possible.'

'No! No!' Beth grasped Helen's hands. 'Whatever your father did was not your fault. You have nothing to be ashamed of.'

Helen shook her head sadly. 'Word will already be circulating through society, and I will not endure the whispers behind fans or open snubs that will occur should I be seen in society again.'

''I am sure that won't happen. You are not responsible for your father's actions, and everyone knows that. You are well respected, Helen. Sympathy will be society's reaction, not scorn.'

'You have a higher opinion of people than I, Beth, and I do not want – or need – sympathy from anyone.'

'Even me?'

'Especially you, my dear friend. Sympathy or pity will not help me in the task I have before me. I need you to be strong for me.'

'Then I shall be.' Beth tried to smile, though that was almost impossible because it was breaking her heart to see her friend brought so low. 'You stood by my side when my father died so unexpectedly, and your steadfast nature helped me through. Now it is my turn to repay that debt. You must let us help. What can I do?'

'Very well.' Helen relented, knowing they were determined to stand by her and grateful for their support. 'There are two men going through the house valuing everything, so would you watch that they are doing the job properly? You have a good head for figures, and I cannot afford to be cheated.'

'I will see they put a fair price on everything.' Beth was relieved to be given the chance to help, but there was one thing she could not allow Helen to do. Before turning away, she said, 'And when you have finished this dreadful business, you are to come and stay with me. I will not have you living with strangers as a servant.'

'I have no choice. I will be penniless and will need to make a living somehow.'

Lord Edward had been standing by, listening to the young ladies talk, and now he stepped forward. 'Elizabeth is right. You should move in with her, and I will make you an allowance.'

'Oh, your lordship, that is exceedingly generous of you, but I cannot allow you to support me in that way.' For the first time Helen's voice broke with emotion.

'Indeed you can, for you will be doing us both a favour.'

'In what way?'

'In a month from now I have to journey to India. I have important business to settle and shall be away for six or more months. It would ease my mind considerably to know you are with Elizabeth.' He gave his god-daughter an affectionate smile. 'And I know she would be most grateful for your company.'

Helen looked at her friend, who was nodding enthusiastically, then back to Lord Edward. 'That is an extremely generous offer, Lord Sharland, but the only way I could accept would be if I came as Elizabeth's companion. I cannot allow you to support me unless I give something back in return.'

After a brief glance at Elizabeth, Edward nodded. 'You have your pride, Helen, and I understand that. You are hereby employed as my god-daughter's companion.'

'Thank you, Lord Sharland.' Helen bowed her head, relief threatening to spill over into tears.

'Splendid. That's settled, then,' Edward said briskly. 'Now, what can I do to help?'

After glancing at the chaos around her, Helen took a deep steadying breath. 'There is someone in the stables who is interested in purchasing the horses. I would be most grateful if you could deal with that for me. You are an expert on horses and know the value of each animal.'

'I will gladly see to that for you. Are you selling all of them?'

'They must all go.'

'Oh, Helen, not Honey, surely.' Elizabeth knew how much her friend loved her horse.'

'Even she must go, but make sure she has a good home, Lord Sharland.'

'You leave everything to me.' He nodded and strode out of the house.

The next few days were frantic and heartbreaking. Helen insisted on dealing with most of the sales herself, but she did allow Elizabeth to help her with the figure work. Beth watched as her friend meticulously began paying off the debts as soon as there was enough money available.

After only two weeks Helen had cleared every debt her father had left behind. When that was done, she only had small trunk of simple clothes to her name, all the more elaborate gowns having been sold, and only one piece of jewellery remained, a small emerald pendant her mother had given her on her eighteenth birthday.

Her friend was now destitute, but there was one thing Helen didn't know. Lord Sharland had purchased Honey, and she was already happily installed in the Langton stables, awaiting her mistress.

Helen had insisted that she handle the final winding-up of the estate on her own, and Beth knew that was because she didn't want anyone to see the distress that losing her beloved home was going to cause. She understood and respected Helen's request that they leave her until everything was settled. Now she waited anxiously for Helen to arrive.

Two

It was a lovely day, showing a hint that spring was not far away, and Helen gazed out of the library window at the scene she would never see again. She felt as if the heart had been ripped out of her piece by piece as each of her father's creditors had been paid. The last one had just left, and the new owners would be moving in tomorrow. All she had left was the money in her purse — three pounds, ten shillings and sixpence — but she had done it and could now hold her head up. She had acted honourably, and every debt had been paid in full, even though that had meant beggaring herself. Her future would have been bleak indeed if Lord Sharland hadn't made his generous offer to her. It was a huge relief to know she had somewhere to go, and staying with Beth would give her time to recover from this ordeal before deciding what she could do to earn a living for the rest of her life.

Nodding to herself, Helen turned from the window. Thankfully, she was so numb she no longer had any feelings, and that was a blessing because the future ahead was going to be very difficult. Although she was going to live with her friend, it would be as a paid servant, and she must accept that she would always be a spinster because, with such a scandal surrounding her family, no man of substance would offer for her now.

Had her father fully realized the extent of the disaster he was leaving for her to deal with and the life of poverty now facing her? No, she doubted that. He must have been in a very confused state of mind to take his own life. Helen sighed in sadness for her dear father. They had always known he had a tendency to gamble, but it had never got out of hand until her mother had died. It was then he had sought the gaming tables as a release from his grief. She should have been aware that he was losing badly, but she hadn't because he had hidden it so well. He had appeared to recover from his wife's death, always smiling and generous to her. Word of his suicide must have spread with lightning speed because within two days the creditors were demanding their money. Fortunately, he had kept accurate records of his debts, so she knew exactly who was making a legitimate claim, and who was not. When she had found the ledger, the extent of the amounts owing had been alarming, and it had soon become clear there was only one way to deal with it. And she had done just that. Now it was over.

Helen picked up the box containing all the receipts she had made every creditor sign, stating that payment had been made in full, so that no future claims could be made on her. She made her way upstairs to collect her meagre belongings, bracing herself to face her new future, determined to earn her keep as Beth's companion. It was going to be strange for both of them, but she would make sure she was of help to her friend, for she had had to face her own heartbreak and problems in the last year. Elizabeth's mother had died when she had been very young, and her father had tragically been killed only nine months ago in a riding accident. Lord Sharland had been made her guardian, and, with his guiding hand, Elizabeth had taken on the task of running the large estate, with great success. It hadn't been easy – Helen knew that – but her friend had faced the challenge with courage, and that is what she too must do. There was a new kind of life ahead of her, and what she made of it would be up to her.

Picking up her bag and tucking the box of papers under her arm, she walked down the stairs and out of the house. The frosty ground crunched under her feet as she walked towards the coach Beth had insisted on supplying for her. As they drove away, Helen never looked back.

Helen was here at last! Beth turned away from the window, ran out of the room and down the stairs. She had been so worried about her friend and had wanted to stay by her side to the very end of the distressing business, but Helen would not hear of it. Beth had understood, but it had been hard watching her friend become pale and withdrawn. But she was here now, and the peace of the Langton estate would soon work its magic and help her to recover. The staff had all been told that Lady Helen Denton was coming as Elizabeth's companion, and, at her own request, her title was no longer to be used. Most of the staff had known the two since they were toddlers, and it wasn't going to be easy to think of Helen as little more than a servant, but Lord Sharland had impressed upon them the need to respect Helen's wishes in this matter.

Helen was standing in the entrance hall, and when Beth hurtled down the stairs, Jenkins, the butler, blocked her way, the expression on his face warning her to be careful. As soon as she glanced at her friend, she knew he was right. It was only a week since she had seen Helen, but in that time the change in her was dramatic, and Beth's heart ached, for her suffering was all too evident.

'Your . . . er . . . companion is here, Miss Elizabeth.'

'Thank you, Jenkins,' she said softly as the smile on her face disappeared. She could see now that her friend had closed herself off, shutting out her feelings and emotions.

She stepped forward, her smile of welcome back in place. 'Oh, Helen, I'm so pleased to see you at last.'

At that moment Lord Sharland strode in. 'Ah, welcome, my dear. I'm delighted you are here. I shall be leaving for India earlier than expected, and Elizabeth is going to need you.'

'I'm happy to be here, your lordship, and I thank you for your kindness in seeing to the sale of the horses for me, and to Elizabeth for her help and support.'

So formal, Beth thought in dismay. Helen had always called her Beth, but she was obviously determined to take on the role of companion. This was going to take time, but, knowing the strength of her friend's character, Helen would eventually heal.

'Think nothing of it.' Edward smiled and beckoned to the footman. 'Stanley, take Miss Helen's case up to her room, please. It's the one next to Miss Elizabeth.'

'At once, your lordship.'

'Now, if you ladies will excuse me, I have business to attend to, and I am sure you have a great deal to talk about.'

'Will you be joining us for dinner?' she asked her godfather.

'Of course. I've already informed Cook.'

'Excellent. We shall look forward to hearing all about your plans for your trip to India.' Beth kissed her godfather and then turned to Jenkins. 'We would like a large pot of tea and some pastries in my sitting room, please.'

The butler bowed and hurried away to the kitchens.

Cook had obviously anticipated the request because a trolley arrived the moment they were settled. Once they had cups of tea in their hands, Beth looked closely at her friend and was swept with such sadness that it was difficult to hide. Helen had been through a terrible ordeal and it showed. 'Is it all finished, Helen?' she asked gently.

'Yes.' She managed a faint smile. 'Every penny of the debts has been paid, and I have the receipts to prove it.'

'I am relieved to hear that, but I wish there had been another way.'

'There wasn't.' Helen's expression was one of grief mixed with determination. 'The debts were so huge that everything had to be sold, and quickly; otherwise, I would have had people pounding on my door for the rest of my life. I couldn't have lived like that, Elizabeth. Now no one can make a claim upon me.'

'Of course I understand. You have always had a clear head – and courage.'

'And stubborn pride.' Helen grimaced and then changed the subject. 'I am grateful to be here, Elizabeth, but now you must tell me what my duties will be as your paid companion.'

'Well, as you know, my guardian will be away for many months, so I will need your help in running the estate. Your advice will be invaluable, and we shall be busy. Mr Greenway is an excellent manager, but Father taught me how to handle the business side, and I like to keep an eye on everything pertaining to the estate. But –' she looked at Helen straight in the eyes – 'the thing I need most of all from you is your friendship. You are a guest in this house, Helen, and a very welcome one.' Elizabeth put down her cup and took her friend's hands in hers. 'I know you need to feel you are earning your keep – and you will be, for this is a very large estate – but you have always called me Beth, so please do not change that.'

'Of course.' A hint of a teasing smile crossed Helen's face. 'I expect I would have soon forgotten to be so formal and slipped back into our old ways.'

'Of course you would.' Beth smiled in relief and relaxed for the first time. The signs were that it wouldn't take Helen long to recover from her ordeal. What she had just gone through would have destroyed many a young woman, but not her friend. She was made of sterner stuff!

'I will be delighted to help in any way I can, Beth, and to be kept busy is just what I need.' Helen shook her head sadly. 'When we were children running wild around the estate, we never imagined we would end up like this. We are both twenty years old and we thought that by now we would be attending balls and social gatherings with a string of young men vying for our attention. Instead, you are working constantly, and I am destitute. How did such misfortune come upon us?'

'We have both been dealt tough challenges,' Beth agreed, 'but we can help and support each other through this. We were always getting into scrapes, if I remember rightly, and nothing daunted us. It won't now, and I feel sure we have had our share of disasters. From now on it will be smooth going for both of us.'

'You are right. The past is behind us, and we must look to the future – whatever it may hold.'

Three

The last four weeks had been good, Beth acknowledged with satisfaction. It had been a blessing to have Helen beside her now that her godfather was away, and her friend had already regained much of her vigour and health. Beth smiled quietly to herself as she remembered Helen's joy at seeing her beloved horse in the stables, and it had made both of them weep a little. Lord Sharland had told Helen that the animal was hers to use all the time, but she must exercise her and look after her, which she was delighted to do. It had been a good moment. And so was this. They had a rare couple of hours to themselves and were enjoying a relaxing time together. Although it was still cold, there were hints that spring was on the way. Once March gave way to April, they could look forward to long summer days. Beth missed her godfather and hoped that his business would not take too long, but with the support of her estate manager she was quite capable of running the estate successfully. Her only concern was that her godfather had appeared tense and distracted before he went, and she had been worried that the trip would be too much for him, but he had just laughed and said that he had done it many times and would be quite all right.

'Come in,' Beth said when there was a gentle tap on the door, and, as her butler stepped into the room, she didn't move from her comfortable position, curled up in an armchair with a book in her hands. 'What is it, Jenkins?'

'Mr Crighton wishes to speak with you, miss.'

She frowned, beginning to unwind herself. 'I wasn't expecting him today, but perhaps he is just checking to see that we have everything we need while Lord Sharland is away.'

'He has another gentleman with him, but he did not offer his name.'

'Perhaps the lawyer has a new assistant.' Helen put down her book and left her seat. 'Will you change before seeing them?'

'Certainly not. I'll be down in a few minutes, Jenkins.'

He inclined his head and left the room.

'She began smoothing down her blue dress. 'I am quite presentable. Let us go and see what Mr Crighton wants, and then perhaps we can go for a ride. The weather is quite pleasant.'

When they walked into the drawing room, the first thing to catch Beth's attention was Mr Crighton's nervousness. 'How kind of you to call.' Before the lawyer had a chance to say anything, Beth smiled graciously at the man standing by the fireplace. She felt a ripple of unease as soon as she looked at him. He was in his late twenties, she guessed, tall and slender to the point of being on the thin side. His hair was black, but it was his eyes that disturbed her the most – they were pale grey and as cold as a frosty morning.

The lawyer stepped forward. 'May I introduce—'

The stranger cut the lawyer off in mid-sentence. 'I am your guardian.'

It took a dozen heartbeats for the words to register in Beth's stunned mind. The gentleman was a complete stranger, and he was talking nonsense.

'My guardian is my godfather, Lord Edward Sharland.'

'He died a week ago.'

Beth gasped in pain. Her eyes filled with tears, but she fought them back as she spun round to face Mr Crighton. 'This cannot be true!'

Seeing the lawyer speechless and distressed, she turned to face the stranger again. 'How did this happen?'

'He caught a fever on his business trip to India.'

'Why was I not told?' She raised her voice in a most unladylike manner, but she was too upset and angry to care. How dare this man come and break such devastating news in these cold terms? He appeared to be unconcerned by her outburst and was leaning casually against the mantelpiece, as if telling her that her beloved godfather was dead was all he had to do. She didn't miss the longing glances he kept making towards the drinks decanters, but she certainly wouldn't offer this individual any refreshment. Beth knew that she was sadly remiss in the social graces and should have asked him to be seated, but she was devastated and so angry.

He detached himself from the fireplace and strode across the room, then poured himself a generous brandy.

'Sir!' Beth was incensed by his effrontery. 'I have not given you permission to act so freely in my house.'

He sipped the drink, clearly savouring the taste, and then raised an eyebrow. 'You are no longer in control of the Langton estate. Lord Sharland has put everything into my hands until you reach the age of twenty-one.'

Helen, who had been standing quietly by the door, now moved to Beth's side and guided her to a chair.

She was shaking badly, but, having a strong nature, Beth soon had herself under control again, speaking in a clear voice. 'My father declared me his sole heir, and it was arranged with my godfather that I should have complete authority over the Langton estate.'

'Ah –' he sat down and crossed his long legs – 'but I am not your godfather.'

She realized that she still did not know who he was. 'You have not had the courtesy to introduce yourself.'

'I beg your pardon; I thought your butler would have informed you who was calling.'

'He merely said Mr Crighton was here with another gentleman.' She cast the dark man a disbelieving look. Jenkins had got that wrong: this person was clearly no gentleman!

He dipped his head in a parody of a bow but did not rise to his feet. 'I am Lord Sharland's son, James, and your guardianship has become my responsibility.'

'You lie, sir! He did not have any children or close heirs; that is why my father appointed him my guardian.' Beth was struggling to clear the confusion from her mind. Who was he? Why had she never seen or heard of him before? Her heart ached for her dear father. How upset he would be if he knew that she had been left to the mercies of a complete stranger – and not a very trustworthy one, if she had guessed correctly. His clothes were fashionable enough, but the man wearing them looked decidedly uncivilized.

The lawyer spoke for the first time, shuffling with unease. 'I am sorry, Miss Langton, but it is as Lord Sharland says. Your godfather came to see me before he left for India to make these arrangements. I tried to persuade him not to, but he would not listen to me.'

'I would like to see the legal papers, please, Mr Crighton.'

'You need not bother yourself with details, Miss Langton,' the stranger said, not giving the lawyer a chance to speak again. 'You have Mr Crighton's word that this is all legal.'

'I doubt that very much, sir. You need not burden yourself with me. My father trained me well, and I have been running the estate on my own quite efficiently, and I shall continue to do so.'

'I think not.'

'How dare you walk in here and threaten to take over my affairs!' She was on her feet again. 'If you are truly the Sharland heir and now my guardian, you are honour-bound to abide by the agreement made between my father and godfather. The running of the estate was to be left in my hands.'

'You are mistaken, Miss Langton. There is no legal document to that effect, and I only have your word for such an arrangement,' he added.

'I am not given to telling lies, sir! Mr Crighton must have the details.'

'I have seen all the documents, and they state quite clearly that your guardian is to have control over your affairs until you reach the age of twenty one.' The expression in his eyes was unreadable.

Helen drew in a deep breath and reached out to grasp her friend's hand, coming close to whisper one word: 'Caution!'

But Beth was too upset and angry to listen. 'Do not distress yourself, Helen; there has been some dreadful mistake, and I shall soon have it clarified.'

At that moment the butler entered the drawing room and addressed her. His normally impassive expression had disappeared and he looked disapproving. 'A carriage has arrived loaded with luggage, Miss Langton, and the man assures me that he was told to deliver it to this address.'

'That is quite correct.' His lordship rose to his feet. 'Ask the man to take it up to the master suite.'

'You will do no such thing!' Beth raised her voice; his arrogance was beyond the pale. 'What right do you have to move your belongings into my home?'

His sigh was weary. 'You do not reach twenty-one for another year, so until then I shall take over the running of the Langton estate and use this mansion as if it were mine.'

'You cannot! I forbid it.' She was more than angry by now; she was frightened.

His laugh was humourless. 'You cannot stop me, Miss Langton. From the moment I was declared your guardian, you ceased to have any rights over your father's property. It is effectively mine to do with as I wish for the next year.'

Beth felt ill, but she would not allow this obnoxious man to believe he had won. 'I demand proof!'

'I do not care for your inference that I might be a liar. I am now the legal master of this house and your affairs.'

For the first time in her life a feeling of helplessness washed through her, but her stubborn character would not allow her to give up. 'But why do you not stay at your own house? The Sharland estate is no more than six miles away; there is no need for you to move in here, surely?'

'From what I have been told, you are sadly in need of supervision, and I cannot do that while I am residing in the Sharland house. Anyway, the house will not be habitable for some months while renovations are taking place to turn it into a school. I intend to see that you no longer run wild.' He pursed his lips in disapproval. 'I would have expected you to still be in deep mourning for your father. I believe he died less than a year ago.'

'My father forbade it.' She was incensed by his attitude; what right did he have to judge her? 'He said life was for the living. He never did agree with the dowdy dress and long periods of mourning.'

'A remarkable man, then.'

'Yes, he was.'

He cast her one more disapproving glance and then strode out of the room. The butler remained, obviously bewildered and distressed. 'Miss Langton?'

She tore her angry gaze away from the retreating figure and gave Jenkins a quick explanation.

His usually impassive expression wavered for a moment. 'I'm very sorry to hear about Lord Sharland. What shall we do about this gentleman moving in?'

'Do as he says for the moment, Jenkins, and tell the rest of the staff what has happened. Then have the master suite made ready for him. We shall have to go along with this for the time being. There has been a grave error made here, but I shall soon sort it out, and then we shall have the pleasure of throwing him and his belongings on to the street. For I have no doubt that is where he belongs!'

'What a terrible thing to happen to Lord Sharland.' The butler shook his head in sorrow. 'He was such a kind man.'

'Yes, he was, and that makes this all the more unbelievable.' Her voice trembled as grief began to overcome her. With tears filling her eyes, she held her hand out for her Helen. 'I will retire, Helen, while we decide what is to be done.'

Before leaving the room, she faced the lawyer. 'I shall be calling on you, Mr Crighton, when I shall expect to see all relevant papers and receive a full explanation about this disgraceful arrangement.'

The lawyer bowed his head. 'I am holding a letter for you from Lord Edward Sharland, Miss Langton, and there are provisions in the will I must discuss with you and Lady Helen.'

'Why did you not bring the letter with you?'

'Er . . . I was ordered by Lord Edward not to let anyone else know about the letter.' He glanced nervously around the room to make sure they were alone. 'And he did mean no one.'

'Very well. We shall be at your office early in the morning.'

Once in the privacy of her room, Beth allowed the tears to flow freely, unable to believe that her dear godfather was dead and that he should have put the Langton estate at the mercy of this stranger.

There was a tentative knock at the door and her maid, Jenny, peered in. 'Cook said to bring you a tray of tea, miss.'

'Thank you, Jenny. That is most thoughtful of her.' Beth dried her eyes. It was not wise to allow grief to distract her from the seriousness of the situation. 'Jenny, will you ask Tom to come and see me, please.'

'Up here, miss?'

'Yes, and tell him not to let our visitor see him. Leave the door slightly open when you leave.'

The maid hurried away, and before Beth and Helen had a chance to finish their first cup of tea, a young boy slid into the room.

'No one saw me, miss,' he whispered.

'Good. Come in and shut the door, Tom. I want you to do something for me.' When the lad nodded, she continued. 'Go and find the estate manager, Mr Greenway, and tell him that I'll come to the grain barn in an hour's time to see him. We have urgent matters to discuss, but it is imperative that the new Lord Sharland doesn't know we are meeting.'

'Understood, miss.' Tom opened the door a crack, then slid through the door and disappeared without making a sound.

'That boy is going to be very useful, Helen, for I fear we shall have to move with stealth. Until I am able to sort this mess out, everyone here will have to obey that obnoxious man, but I shall watch every move he makes. I refuse to put the prosperity of my family estate at the mercy of a man I do not know. I am hoping that my godfather's letter will throw some light on this mystery, for I cannot imagine why he has done this.'

'Neither can I.' Helen was shaking her head. 'It is so unlike him to do such a thing, and I cannot imagine what the lawyer needs to discuss with me.'

'I hope we shall find some answers tomorrow.'

Watching the time carefully, they finished the tea, and then Beth said, 'Time to go, Helen. We'll take the back stairs via the servants' quarters; with luck, we should be able to reach the stables unobserved.'

Halfway down, they met the butler. 'Where is he, Jenkins?'

'Still in the master's rooms, miss. He's asked for hot water so he can bathe.'

'Ah, that should keep him occupied for a while. I'm going to meet Mr Greenway to tell him what has happened and work out a plan of action with him. The estate must not suffer because of this unfortunate turn of events.'

'You'll have to hurry, then, miss, because he's informed Cook that in future dinner will be served at seven o'clock and not eight. We'll try and keep him busy until you get back.'

'Thank you, Jenkins. If he asks for me, tell him that I am indisposed.'

'I'll do that, miss.'

The stables were not overlooked from the house and they ran the last few yards.

Tom was there with three horses already saddled. 'I'd better come with you, miss, in case his nibs turns up.'

As wretched as she felt, that almost brought a smile to Beth's face. Tom was only thirteen, with a lot of growing still to do, but he'd clearly taken on the role of her protector.

'Thank you, Tom. We shall be pleased to have you ride with us.'

The estate manager was waiting for them, anxious to hear what had happened. 'Young Tom told us the sad news about Lord Edward, Miss Langton, but he didn't know much about the stranger who's turned up.'

Beth quickly explained and saw Mr Greenway's face darken with concern. 'I don't like the sound of that. This estate runs smoothly and makes a steady profit. Your father saw to that and he taught you his ways. As soon as you could sit on a horse, you were by his side, asking questions. You've a good business head on your shoulders, and we don't want a stranger coming in and changing things.'

'That is also my concern, so I want you to come and see me if he does anything you disagree with.' Beth ran a hand over her tired eyes. 'Please tell everyone to obey him for the moment, while I endeavour to find a way to overturn this decision. I cannot believe my godfather would put me in such a perilous position.'

'Neither can I, but we'll do as you say and try to see he doesn't do too much damage. Do you know what experience he has in running an estate?'

'I'm afraid not.' Beth shook her head in dismay. 'I know nothing about the man. It has come as a complete surprise to hear that my godfather had a son. I didn't even know he had been married. I am going to look into his legitimacy very carefully.'

'Try not to worry too much, Miss Langton. I'll spread the word, and you can be sure that he won't be able to make a move without one of us seeing.'

'Thank you. I will meet you here at our usual time each week, and not at the house, so we can go through everything together. I shall still keep the accounts, whether this man likes it or not! Now, you must all be very careful, for he does not appear to be a man with any kindness in him, and I do not want to lose any of you.'

Helen came into the barn with Tom. 'We should get back. It would not do to be late for dinner. Until you have the full facts, it would not be wise to antagonize this man.'

Beth nodded, grateful for her friend's steady wisdom. 'You're right, Helen. We must not give any indication that we are plotting behind his back to be rid of him.'

Four

It was a relief when Beth saw that her unwelcome guest was not at breakfast. Dinner the night before had been an ordeal. She would have preferred to have taken a meal in her rooms but was aware that she must not show the slightest sign of weakness. Not only was she dreadfully upset about her godfather's death so soon after her dear father, but she was furious that this arrogant man had taken her place at the head of the table. Hiding her displeasure, she had tried to find out more about him by being as polite as possible. To no avail. Not one piece of information did she manage to glean from him.

The butler held her chair for her, and she asked, 'Where is he, Jenkins?'

'He came down two hours ago, Miss Langton, and has now left with Tom.'

Beth's frown deepened. 'If he's taken Tom with him, then there's no doubt he is going to inspect the estate.'

'Very likely, miss. He didn't say where he was going or when he would be back. Cook is uncertain what to do about lunch.'

'If his lordship does not turn up in time for lunch, then he will have to go hungry.' Beth was in no mood to be charitable. One thing she could not abide in a man was bad manners. And this one appeared to have them in abundance.

The butler's mouth twitched at the corners. 'I'll tell Cook you require lunch as usual, shall I?'

'Indeed. The smooth running of this house is my responsibility, and if he wishes to relieve me of that task also, he will discover he has a fight on his hands.'

Helen looked at her with concern. 'I don't think it would be wise to upset him. We know so little about him.'

'Little!' Beth's laugh lacked humour. 'We know *nothing* about him, and as soon as we have eaten we will visit Mr Crighton and demand some answers.'

★ ★ ★

The lawyer shuffled the papers on his desk, showing his unease, clearly not relishing this unpleasant task. 'I assure you, Miss Langton, that it is legal. Your godfather left a sealed package with me to be opened upon his death. In it he stated that his son, James Sharland, was his heir, and if he died before your twenty-first birthday, his son was to take over as your guardian.'

'This is the first I have heard of such a person.' She was becoming more concerned by the minute, for she had not thought her godfather to be a secretive man.

'But what about my father's wishes – that I continue to run the estate, even if I had not reached my majority before he died?'

'That was only a verbal arrangement and it was never put in writing. Your father and godfather were certain one of them would survive to see that the agreement was carried out.' He lifted his hands in a helpless gesture. 'I did urge that it all be put into proper order, but they kept finding excuses not to do it.'

That didn't surprise her; they had always needed prodding to make them deal with the important things in life. Her father and godfather had been dear people, but they'd had the lamentable habit of procrastinating. 'Are you telling me that I have to be under this man's control for the next year?'

'Yes, unless you marry, of course, and then everything will go to your husband.'

'Never!'

He appeared saddened by her vehemence. 'I fear I have been lax in my duty towards you. I should have insisted the document be drawn up, but no one could have foreseen that Lord Edward Sharland would die so soon.'

Beth agreed, grief nearly overcoming her. 'And it has placed me in an untenable position. What will happen when I reach the age of twenty-one?'

'The entire estate will revert back to you, and your guardian will no longer have any authority over your affairs. Your father did at least set that all down properly, so you will only have to wait a year and you will regain control.'

'If there is anything left,' she said in despair. 'Can we prove that this man's claim of being my godfather's son is illegal? Is there no way out of this dilemma?'

'I have looked into this with great care, but there is none, I am afraid. Here –' he handed her some documents – 'these prove he is who he claims to be.'

'They could have been faked. And how do we know that he really is the person these documents relate to?' She was grasping at any tiny crumb of hope.

'I have checked. They are genuine, and to prove his identity your godfather left this with me.' He handed her a photograph. 'I'm so sorry, Miss Langton.'

Her heart began to race in panic as she studied the likeness. There was no doubt that this was the man claiming to be her new guardian. She was helpless, and it was not a feeling she was comfortable with, or would tolerate for long – and certainly not for the next twelve months.

'Tell me what you know about the new Lord Sharland?'

'Very little. As you know, we believed your godfather did not have children of his own, so when he died and I opened his letter, I was astonished. I thought it was just a formality, and the agreement made between Lord Edward and your father would stand, even though not set down in legal terms.' He raised his hands in a helpless gesture. 'But the Langton estate is a very desirable property, and I do not believe any gentleman would forgo the pleasure of running it for a while.'

'And why have we never known of his existence?' It was extremely hard to refer to him as a gentleman, for she was certain he was not one, but she was beginning to pray earnestly that there was some decency under his cold exterior. If not, she could well lose her inheritance.

'We do not know why your godfather kept him a secret.'

Beth frowned. 'Why was I not told the moment news of my godfather's death arrived?'

He looked apologetic. 'I did not know until your godfather's son arrived, and I was reluctant to tell you until I'd had a chance to check that this man was really the son of Lord Edward Sharland. You were still grieving for your father.'

Her chin came up in anger. 'Do you consider me a weakling, Mr Crighton?'

'No, no, of course not, but you are only just turned twenty . . .' His words tailed off. 'I have misjudged you: you have great inner strength, and I can see that now.'

'Indeed. And that is why my father was happy to leave the running of the estate in my hands. But do continue. Are you absolutely positive these documents are genuine?'

'There is no doubt. As an added precaution, I took him to see your godfather's mother, and she recognized him.'

'But her wits are addled! Any scoundrel would be able to convince her that they were related to the Sharlands.'

'I know she can be confused at times, but she recognized him as soon as he walked in the door. Before he uttered a word, she cried out his name and kissed him. And as I had all the necessary documents, your godfather's instructions in writing and Lady Sharland vouching for his identity, I could not delay handing over the estate.'

'And me with it.' Beth gave a frustrated sigh.

The lawyer nodded. 'He had letters written to him by your godfather, going back over ten years. I was allowed to read them all except one that had been written before Lord Edward left for India. I was told that its contents were not to be seen by anyone else. But . . .'

When he didn't complete the sentence, she prompted. 'But?'

'Oh, I do not know anything for sure.' He shrugged, looking self-conscious. 'I have never heard your godfather mention that he had once been married or that he had a son, and I have the uncomfortable feeling that there is something not quite the thing about him.'

'On that point we do agree!' she declared with some force. 'Now, you mentioned a letter for me?'

'Yes, yes, of course.' He handed her a sealed envelope.

She slit it open quickly, her hands shaking with emotion. After reading the short letter through twice, she handed it to Helen, and her friend frowned as she read it as well.

'But it tells you nothing!' she exclaimed.

'May I ask what is in the letter?' the lawyer asked. 'No personal details, of course, just the main points.'

'My godfather says that his son has promised to sort out a family problem, and the best way for him to do that is to become my guardian. He will need to reside at my house until I am of age. He apologizes for the inconvenience and worry this will cause me.' Beth sighed in exasperation and disappointment. She had been hoping for some answers in this letter, but she was more confused than ever. 'I do not understand why my godfather could not have explained what this is all about; then at least I would know what to expect. All this secrecy is not at all like him.'

Mr Crighton looked at her sympathetically. 'It appears that he was a secretive man. He knew he had a son, and yet he never mentioned him to anyone, not even me.'

'You are right, of course, but that is hard to accept.'

'There is one more thing I must inform you about. Lord Sharland leaves the bulk of his estate to his son, but there is a bequest of ten thousand pounds to you, Miss Langton, and a thousand for Lady Helen. These amounts will be paid to you as soon as the estate is wound up, but that may take some time.'

Both girls gasped, and Helen was wide-eyed with shock. 'That is extremely generous of him.'

'He was a kind and generous man, and a very wealthy one.' The lawyer smiled for the first time since they had arrived. 'I am relieved to be able to give you some good news.'

Back in the carriage and on their way home again, Beth struggled with a feeling of defeat. It seemed as if there was nothing she could do, but that was hard to accept. She turned to Helen who was sitting quietly, her hands tightly clasped together. 'My father and godfather have left me in dire straits by their failure to make the proper legal arrangements for me, and I will have to fight for my future. But I shall not allow that stranger to ruin the Langton estate or deprive me of my heritage.'

With determination clear in every move of her slender body, she turned to her friend. 'I know, after your own experiences, you must be fearful that I could also end up penniless, Helen, but my godfather has made sure neither of us will be left without money of our own, and together we will survive this next year.'

'I cannot believe Lord Sharland has left me such a substantial sum of money. It will help my situation immensely. At least when I have to seek a position somewhere, I shall not be penniless.'

'That is good news, indeed, and means you will not feel it so necessary to leave me too quickly. It will be a great comfort to have you by my side until this mess is sorted out.' Beth smiled, happy for her friend. 'Now, let us return home and decide on our strategy, for I would have the new Lord Sharland out of my house! If my godfather had wanted me to accept this situation willingly, then he should have given me more information!'

His first inspection of the estate had shown James that it was well run, and the accounts he'd studied during the night showed a healthy profit. Although Elizabeth Langton was young, she had been well trained by her father. It had also been made abundantly clear by everyone he had met that they all respected her and were fiercely protective towards her.

He rested his arms on a five-bar gate and gazed across the field, watching the herd of cows contentedly cropping the lush grass. It did not concern him that he was viewed with resentment and suspicion. That was the way it had to be if he was going to carry out his father's instructions. What he was going to need was help, and there was no better friend than Daniel. He'd send for him this very day. He did not relish the task before him and wondered why his father hadn't dealt with this long ago. And why the devil hadn't he told him about it when he'd discovered he had a son? It would have been easier to deal with then, but the chances of resolving this mess after all these years was remote indeed.

Suppressing a sigh, he turned his attention to the estate manager who was standing beside him. 'That will do for this morning. It will take me a week or so to become familiar with the estate. Carry on as you are for the moment, but you need not bother Miss Langton with anything now. Bring any problems straight to me.'

'Yes, your lordship.' Henry Greenway's tone was sharp, showing his disapproval as he walked beside the man who was a complete mystery to everyone.

James noticed it but did not comment as they reached the horses. He was going to have to get used to being disliked; there was no way out of that. Taking the reins from Tom, he swung smoothly into the saddle and then waited for the lad to mount as well.

Giving only a curt nod to the hostile faces watching him, he headed back to the house.

'Where is Miss Elizabeth?' he asked the butler as soon as he walked through the door.

'She has gone to town, your lordship, but will be back any moment. Lunch will be served in half an hour.'

'Who is accompanying her?' he asked sharply.

'Her companion – Miss Helen.'

At that moment there was a clatter of horses outside and James spun round, heading for the door. He met Beth and Helen at the entrance. 'You must not leave this house without being properly escorted!'

Helen did not react to his sharp tone, but Beth glared at him in astonishment. 'It is none of your business what I do or where I go.'

'Everything about you is my business for the next year, and I will not have you wandering off without my permission.'

'Don't be ridiculous!' Beth tried to pass him, but he blocked her way.

'You will do as I say.' He moderated his tone a little. 'Tell me when you need to go visiting, or anything else young ladies do, and I will see that you are properly escorted. That is all I'm asking.'

'You are being overly protective, and it is quite unnecessary. My father and godfather trusted me completely to look after myself. And, anyway, Helen is always with me. I am not used to reporting my every move.'

'I am aware of that, but you will do so now.' He moved aside to let her pass, and as he watched them walking up the stairs to their rooms, he realized that this wasn't going to be as easy as he had thought. Elizabeth Langton showed great strength of character, and he was still puzzled by the companion, Helen. She did not fit the role of servant. He sincerely prayed that Dan would be able to get here quickly because there was no way he could watch her and the estate every moment. And he had to be free to absent himself at all hours, night or day.

With that thought uppermost in his mind, he went to the study to pen the letter to Daniel Edgemont.

★ ★ ★

It was an uncomfortable lunch, and Beth did not even try to make conversation, still offended by his high-handed attitude towards her. She just could not understand why he would want to know every time she went out, and there was no way she would abide by such restricting rules.

He left immediately after lunch, and Beth gave him an hour to see if he returned. When there was no sign of him, she sought out the butler. 'Where is he, Jenkins?'

'Still out, Miss Langton.'

'Splendid. Gather all the staff together – in the kitchen, I think – and we shall hold a council of war.'

Jenkins nodded approval and then hurried away.

'Act with caution, Beth.' Helen voiced her fears, hoping to stop her impetuous friend from acting too hastily.

Beth smiled wryly. 'You know caution has never been one of my virtues. Now, let us devise a plan whereby his lordship is watched at all times.'

Helen did not look convinced and fell silent again. This was what Beth liked about her: she never argued or tried to push forward her opinions.

Beth marched into the vast kitchen to find the staff already assembled. 'You are all aware of the situation?'

They nodded, watching their mistress with anxious expressions.

'I have visited the lawyer, and there is little we can do legally.' She looked at each one of them with affection. 'You have all served the Langton family for a long time.'

'And we shall continue to do so,' Mrs Howard, the cook, declared. 'You are the mistress of this house, and I shall take my instructions only from you.'

'That's right.' Jenkins joined in. 'We could make life unpleasant for this man.'

'I could make sure his water is always cold.' The chambermaid giggled.

There followed a long list of ways to annoy their unwelcome guest, and Beth held up her hand to stop them. As much as she would enjoy seeing him inconvenienced, she must not allow her loyal staff to get on the wrong side of his temper, for she was certain that he would not hesitate to exact punishment for the slightest misdemeanour. He appeared a most disagreeable person. 'I am deeply touched by your loyalty, but I would not wish to see you dismissed. I believe there is a safer way to deal with him.'

'You tell us what you want,' the footman told her, 'and we'll do it, Miss Langton.'

'We should start by making him feel welcome,' she stated.

There were mutterings of disapproval at this declaration.

'Begging your pardon, Miss Langton,' the housekeeper said, 'but we are all worried that we might lose our positions now you are no longer in control of the estate. Might his lordship bring in his own retainers?'

'No! I shall not allow any of you to be replaced, and I shall keep control of the everyday running of the household. I do not think he will thwart me in that.' Her mouth set in a stubborn line. If he did, then the atmosphere in this peaceful home would become very stormy indeed. 'However, I want you to be very careful that you treat him with all outward respect. Do not allow your dislike to show —' she paused for effect — 'too much.'

The staff gave each other knowing looks.

'My plan is to make him relax, make him feel his position is secure. In that way we can hope he will leave us alone and we shall be able to go along in our normal manner.'

'Ah.' Jenkins smiled in satisfaction. 'I understand now what you're saying. If he thinks he's safe, he could drop his guard, and then we might be able to find out who he really is.'

'Exactly! How very astute of you,' she told her butler. 'We do not know one thing about his character. Is he honest, dishonest?'

'A rogue, I should say,' muttered the footman. 'Don't like the look of him at all.'

Beth continued, ignoring the disgruntled murmurings from her staff. 'Is he partial to the drink? Does he gamble heavily?'

Cook paled and had to sit down. 'Mercy me! What has come upon us? He could lose the estate on a turn of the cards. It does happen — as we all know.' She cast Helen a sorrowful glance. 'But we've never had a gambler in this house before.'

'We do not know that he does play at the tables, Mrs Howard,' Beth soothed the cook, 'but what I am saying is that we don't know what his habits are. There are many ways he could cast us into penury, but if we work together, we may be able to stop him before things get out of hand.'

Cook fanned herself with her apron.

'Mr Greenway —' Beth turned to her estate manager — 'will you keep a sharp eye on what he is doing, and report to me immediately if you think something underhand is going on?'

'You can rely on me,' he told her. 'He won't be able to take so much as an apple without us knowing. He will be watched every moment. My first meeting with him was interesting. He appeared to have a good knowledge of plants, and he examined the soil as if he knew what he was doing.'

'That is encouraging and eases my mind somewhat. Now, Jenkins, has he brought his own valet with him?'

'No, which is very strange. When I asked him, he said he would only need help occasionally, and that Stanley here —' he nodded to the footman — 'could serve as his valet when needed.'

Mrs Howard tutted. 'I've never heard of such a thing — a gentleman not having his own valet.'

'Ah, but is he a gentleman?' Jenkins asked.

Beth pursed her lips; she did not like what she was doing, but her future was at risk, and she had never been one to shirk an unpleasant task. 'What I am going to ask you to do is distasteful, but I cannot manage this on my own, and I can see no alternative.'

'You want us to spy on him,' footman Stanley declared with obvious relish.

Beth nodded and looked at the others. 'But I only want Jenkins, Greenway and Stanley to carry out this underhand task. I want the rest of you to go about your duties as usual, because if he dismisses any of you for incompetence, then I shall not be able to intervene on your behalf. Is that understood?'

All the females nodded, but they could not hide their disappointment at being excluded from such exciting goings-on.

'Now, I would ask you one more thing.' She turned to the men she had enlisted. 'Please be discreet, as I am going to need the support of every one of you.'

Beth glanced at the clock. 'I must not keep you any longer, so you had better all return to work. It wouldn't do for his lordship's dinner to be late, or he will become suspicious that we are up to something.'

As everyone scurried back to their respective tasks, she took her estate manager aside and spoke to him quietly. 'We shall need to keep a close watch on the accounts. I fear it most unlikely that he will allow me to continue doing them, and you will have more chance of checking them than I. Try to see that he does not take over the task without your help, because if he does, then we shall have lost control.'

Greenway frowned. 'I'll do my best, but even if he does, I shall keep my own records.'

'That is an excellent idea. Then if anything strange is going on, we shall be aware of it.' Beth smiled with satisfaction and left the kitchen, feeling more at ease. There were difficult times ahead, but at least she had retainers loyal to her, and Helen by her side.

Five

'Our meeting with Mr Crighton this morning did nothing to unravel this mystery. I cannot believe my godfather would have had a son and not told anyone about him,' Beth declared as soon as they were back in her private sitting room. 'But there is little more we can do about it at the moment.'

Helen nodded. 'I agree. You could employ a detective agency to investigate for you. There are such places, I believe. But such action would be distasteful and should only be used if the situation is desperate. Things are not at that state yet and, we must hope, never will be. You have acted wisely by being open with the staff. He will be closely watched now.'

'Yes, we must be vigilant and wait to see what he intends.' Beth gave a ragged sigh. 'And you are right about employing someone to investigate. I do not wish any of this to become public knowledge. All anyone outside this house needs to know is that, after the tragic death of my godfather, his son is now my guardian.'

'And he is as charming as his father.'

'That is taking things too far, Helen!' She couldn't help smiling at her friend's innocent expression. 'I would choke on the words.'

'Nevertheless, use wisdom and caution, Beth. I have a feeling that this man is not here just to take over as your guardian. There is something else going on, but it is too early to deduce what it is.'

'You have always been a good judge of character, and I value your opinion, Helen. I am so glad you are here, for I should be quite lost and frightened without you.'

'We will face whatever is to come together, as we have always done. You will not end up losing your home like me! And Lord Edward Sharland was an honourable man. He would not have placed you in this situation if he'd had the slightest doubt you would face ruin.'

'Of course he would not, and I must keep reminding myself of that. And he has left us both money, and that shows he was concerned for our welfare.' Beth's eyes misted with tears when she thought about the man she had adored. 'As he died so far from home and we cannot have a proper funeral, I shall arrange a memorial service in his memory. We cannot allow his passing to go unnoticed.'

'Indeed not. His many friends will wish to pay their respects.'

Beth was instantly on her feet. 'Let us make the arrangements now.'

The memorial service was quickly arranged, and they spent the rest of the afternoon writing invitations. There were many, and the task would take both of them some time.

When they went down to dinner, the butler caught them at the bottom of the stairs. 'His lordship has asked for the evening meal to be served in the main dining room in future, Miss Elizabeth, and the table be set just for two.'

Without saying a word, Beth stormed into the room, pulling Helen with her and muttering under her breath, 'How dare he!'

'We never dine in here,' Beth declared when she saw him standing by the window with a drink in his hand. 'This room is only used when we entertain, and Helen always dines with me.'

James Sharland held a chair for her to sit down, leaving Jenkins looking highly offended at having this duty taken from him.

'We shall use it in future,' his lordship told her peremptorily. 'It is a charming room.'

Helen was hovering uncertainly in the doorway. Beth beckoned her forward.

'See another place is set, please, Jenkins.'

'At once, Miss Langton.' He nodded to the maid who did this immediately, already having the setting ready.

He was wasting no time in making changes, she thought as mutiny simmered in her, but this was not the moment to argue. She must be patient, but she was not going to allow him to disrupt her routine too much, and she must make this clear from the outset.

He had tried to exclude Helen from the table but had not protested when she had insisted. A small victory, but that was the way she must handle this situation.

He was still holding her chair, so she gave a gracious nod of her head at this concession from him, sat down and smiled at the butler as he pushed past his lordship and placed the napkin on her lap with a possessive flourish.

'Thank you, Jenkins.'

He bowed and did the same for Helen, ignoring the gentleman who was seated at the other end of the table.

No one could have found fault with the way the first two courses were served, but Beth had the utmost difficulty in keeping her amusement under control. The staff fussed around her, making sure she had everything within reach, and would not so much as let her pick up the condiments, but when they attended the other end of the table, their attitude changed. Not enough to cause offence, but it was as if the new Lord Sharland did not exist, and the plates were removed with slightly bemused expressions on their faces.

Beth stifled a gurgle of laughter at their antics. It was as if they couldn't understand how the plates could be empty when there was no one there to eat the food. It was a performance worthy of a comedy play, and she suddenly realized that she was enjoying herself. Emboldened by the feeling, she said, 'I trust you will make yourself available to attend the memorial service for Lord Edward?'

'What memorial service?' His eyes narrowed as he looked at her.

'The one I arranged today. It is to be held in five days' time – two o'clock in the local church. I have already begun sending out invitations.'

'And you did not think to consult me first?'

'I doubted you would wish to burden yourself with the details, or indeed would even have the time. My godfather had many friends and they would wish to pay their respects to his memory.'

'Are you inviting everyone from this area?'

'Yes, of course.'

He bowed his head in acknowledgement. 'I will, of course, attend.'

It was a silent meal after that, and by the time the coffee had been served she was pleased at the way he had received the news of the memorial service. She should have consulted him, and he could have been angry, but he had said very little. That was a relief. However, she must have a word with the servants and ask them not to do this again, for she was sure that his lordship was not blessed with an abundance of good humour.

'I trust the food was to your liking?'

'The food, yes,' he told her, 'but the staff would be wise not to take this charade too far.'

She looked at him with wide-eyed innocence.

'Come now,' he chided, 'don't pretend you did not notice. I shall overlook it this time, but although I am a man of considerable patience, I do have my limits, and I shall not tolerate childish behaviour.' He paused. 'Is that clear?'

'Perfectly.' She stood up. 'We shall leave you to your brandy.'

'Sit down.' The order was softly spoken, but it was nonetheless an order it would be unwise to disobey. He was making her feel like a girl back in the schoolroom.

He lit a small cigar and she grimaced.

'Do you find the smoke distasteful?' he asked.

'There is a smoking room next door,' she pointed out.

'I prefer to remain here. It is quite the most agreeable room in the entire house.'

How dare he intimate that the rest of the house was a disgrace! It was all in good order; she had seen to that.

He drew on his cigar deeply, then tipped his head back and blew the smoke towards the ceiling. 'Why are you not married? Did you not *take* at your season?'

Her mouth dropped open at his bluntness, but she snapped it shut quickly before words of rebuke came spilling out. 'I have not had a season. My father was considering it before his untimely death. Since then I have been too busy running the estate to give it a thought.'

'You don't have to concern yourself with that now. I shall make arrangements for your come-out later this year. A season in London will be good for you.'

He wasn't going to get rid of her like that! 'You need not put yourself to all that trouble,' she told him as sweetly as possible. 'I do not want a season, and it would be unseemly as I am once again in mourning.'

He dismissed her objections with a wave of his hand. 'As your guardian, I feel it my duty to see you launched properly into society. You cannot spend the whole of your life in Hampshire, delightful though it is.'

'On the few occasions I have visited London, I found it quite disagreeable.' How was she going to get out of this predicament? Her mind started working furiously, looking for answers. 'And do you intend to be my chaperone?'

A fleeting expression of horror crossed his face. 'Indeed not! That is a job for a female, and I shall find you a suitable lady. You will need a new wardrobe; you are not dressed in the latest mode. Of course, it does not matter here, but you cannot possibly be seen in fashionable places dressed like that.'

She was furious! The dress she was wearing was one of her best, and she had always considered it quite fine. The deep violet colour was also eminently suitable for her present position. 'My father and godfather have recently died,' she declared. 'Would you expect me to be walking around in a red gown?'

'No, but in six months or so you will be able to wear more becoming shades. We shall keep the mourning period in mind when the dressmaker is summoned, but it is a blessing that your father forbade you to wear black – it would not suit you at all.'

'That will cost a great deal, and I would prefer you did not spend my money on such fripperies.'

'The cost of your season will come out of my own coffers.' He extinguished his cigar. 'Don't look so surprised. I do have funds of my own; after all, I am the Sharland heir.'

That was something she still had grave doubts about, but if he was an impostor, then he had managed to fool a great many people so far.

He tipped his head to one side and studied her carefully, then stood up. 'Yes, we should be able to make you quite presentable.'

She watched him stride away with murder in her heart.

The horse arriving at great speed had the grooms rushing to take care of the lathered animal.

Waiting for his friend to dismount, James stood there, shaking his head. 'That's no way to treat a fine animal, Dan.'

Daniel Edgemont jumped down and greeted James, smiling broadly and hardly out of breath. 'I intended to come in a few days' time anyway, but your summons sounded urgent. What's up, Professor? Have you found some rare plant, or perhaps an interesting ruin?'

'Nothing like that. I have a rather large problem, and I think it will be to your liking. I know how you relish a touch of danger.' James studied his friend's impassive expression. 'You knew my father well, and I suspect you are already aware of the task ahead of me, but come inside and I'll fill in the details.'

James took Daniel to the study, closed the door firmly after refreshments had been brought in, and began to talk.

When he'd finished telling Dan what had happened, his friend stared at him in astonishment. 'Damn it, James, your father had no right to force such a duty on you. You never even met the man until ten years ago.'

'That wasn't his fault. He didn't know of my existence until just before my mother died, and he did try to make up for that. My mother's family were very cruel and selfish in the way they acted. He was a kind man and I liked him.'

'That's as may be, but you are due to take up a position at Eton next month. It's something you've worked hard for. What is going to happen now?'

'I've already sent in my refusal. They'll give the teaching position to someone else.'

Dan swore fluently. 'You should have torn those papers up and walked away from this. You have a life of your own to live – that's if someone doesn't put an end to it rather quickly.'

'It's no good you raising your voice at me, Dan. I promised my father I would deal with this. What would you have me do? Just shrug and walk away?'

'No, of course you wouldn't have done that.'

'I know you helped my father in the past, and you could do nothing about it because the man had disappeared. But it was my father's belief that he turned up again quite recently.'

'I still believe you should have refused. You are jeopardizing your whole career by making such a foolish promise. More to the point, you have no experience in this field.'

'That's why you're here. To watch my back and find out how we need to handle this problem. I made a binding promise to look after Elizabeth Langton, and I will not go back on that commitment. He also left this for you.' James held out a sealed letter for Dan.

When he had read it, Dan placed it in his inside pocket, saying nothing about its contents.

'Aren't you going to tell me what he says?'

'No. So, what is this young lady like?' Dan sat back, a look of resignation on his face.

'Strong-willed, clever for one so young – and she hates me with a passion.' James stood up. 'Come, I'll show you to your room and have hot water sent up so you can bathe.'

'Who do you think it is?' Helen asked, as she sat with Beth in her private sitting room.

'I really have no idea. His lordship did not even have the manners to ask if he could invite a guest to stay, or ask me to greet him when he arrived.'

At that moment there was a tentative knock on the door. When Helen opened it, Tom Sparks sidled in. 'Beggin' your pardon, miss, but Cook said I was to come up at once and tell you what I'd heard when I took the horse from the gent. In a right state it was. Must have been riding like the wind.'

'Come in, Tom, and shut the door.' Beth waited impatiently as Tom stood in front of her, screwing his cap up in his hands. 'Did you find out who the man is?'

'His lordship called him Dan, and they seem pleased to see each other.' Tom shuffled, a look of deep concentration on his face. 'And this Dan called him . . . er . . . professor . . . yes, that's the word.'

'Professor?'

'Yes, miss. And Cook said I was to tell you what else he said, though it didn't make sense to me.'

'Go on, go on.' Beth couldn't wait to hear more.

'Well, he joked about getting here so quick when his lordship told him off about the way he'd treated the horse. Then he said something like "Have you found a rare plant, or some old ruin?"' Tom paused while he tried to remember exactly what was said. 'Then his lordship said no, but he had a problem that would interest this Dan as it could be dangerous. That's all I heard, miss, because they went in after that.'

Beth opened her purse and gave the lad a coin. 'Thank you, Tom. If you hear anything else, you must let me know at once.'

'Cor, thanks, miss.' His eyes shone when he looked at the coin in his hand. He opened the door carefully, peeked out and then disappeared silently.

'What on earth do you make of that?' Helen asked. 'What are they doing that could be dangerous?'

'I think Tom's imagination might be embroidering the conversation a little, for I cannot believe there is anything dangerous around here. But the mystery deepens, Helen.' Beth began to pace the room. 'From that conversation, I would take him to be an academic. But that cannot be . . . though Greenway did mention that he seemed to know a lot about plants and soil.' She shook her head as if trying to clear it. 'No, I think it must have been some private joke they share. But I must say I'm quite looking forward to meeting this friend who has hurried to be here.'

Helen didn't look as if she felt the same, but she said nothing.

Six

They did not see their unexpected visitor until dinner the next evening. He had been placed next to Helen at the dinner table, and this gave Beth a good chance to view the man carefully. She had to admit that she liked what she saw. Whereas James was dark and unapproachable, Daniel Edgemont had sandy-coloured hair and clear blue eyes that sparkled with amusement. There was an openness about him that was lacking in his friend.

For the first time the conversation flowed easily, and Beth took the opportunity to see if she could find out anything about him. 'Where are you from?' she asked casually, a smile of interest on her face.

'My home is in London, but I move around a lot.'

'And what do you do?' she asked.

'This and that.' He smiled and then turned his attention to Helen.

He's just as much a mystery as his lordship, she thought, frustrated. Realizing that she wasn't going to be given any information about these two men, she relaxed, determined at least to enjoy a pleasant, lively meal for a change.

Even Helen was smiling and laughing at Daniel's amusing tales as he explained about the different things he'd seen and done in various parts of the country. But it was all small talk, and Beth was quite taken aback when James laughed. The transformation was startling and made her wonder if there was a different man under the stern exterior.

Only time would tell, but now they had two men to watch.

'Have Mr Edgemont and his lordship risen?' Beth asked Jenkins, when she and Helen came down the next morning.

'Yes, Miss Langton. His lordship demanded breakfast at dawn.' The butler looked scandalized. 'Put Cook into a real spin. No gentleman would appear before ten o'clock.'

'Where are they now?'

'Went out as soon as they had eaten. I did ask when we could expect them back, but was only told that they would be "some time".'

'Splendid! If he isn't here, then I can't seek his permission to go out, but it would be wise to ask the footman to accompany us. That should help to avoid a scene.'

'Very well, miss. Shall I order the carriage ready in an hour?'

'Yes, please, Jenkins.' She turned to her friend, a determined expression on her face. 'We shall pay a visit to the elderly Lady Sharland and see if we can get to the bottom of this mystery.'

'How is her ladyship today?' Beth asked as they were escorted into the parlour.

'In fine fettle, Miss Langton.' The butler smiled. 'She is still too confused to grasp that her son has died, which we can be grateful for, but there has been an improvement of late. She will be delighted to see you, as always.'

He opened the door, announced her and then withdrew. Helen curtsied to her ladyship, found herself a seat in the corner and managed to look as inconspicuous as possible. Something she had become very good at.

'Elizabeth!' The lady remained seated but held her arms out in welcome. 'How thoughtful of you to visit.'

Beth kissed her cheek with real affection; she had always been very fond of her godfather's mother. 'I am sorry not to have come sooner, but—'

'I know, my dear, you have had little time for the social round. Such a burden has been placed on your young shoulders since your dear father died.' She squeezed Beth's hand and appeared mightily pleased about something. 'But you have someone to look after you now, and that must be a great relief to you.'

'It is indeed,' she lied. 'I am sure . . . Oh, I am sorry, but I cannot recall what relationship James Sharland is to you?'

'Such a dear boy.' Lady Sharland's eyes took on a blank look.

'Yes, of course.' Beth shook her head in mock confusion. 'I do declare that I cannot remember my godfather ever mentioning that he had a son.'

The lady laughed. 'You wait until you reach my great age – then it becomes difficult to remember anything. I am four and eighty, you know?'

'I am sure your memory is still sharp,' she teased. 'After all, you recognized his lordship even though he had been away for some time.' She knew she was taking a chance with this, but as no one had seen or heard of him before, it was logical to conclude that he had been living some distance away.

'Edward did bring him to meet me.' Her eyes took on a faraway look. 'That was a long time ago, but I knew him as soon as he walked in the door; he was the image of his father at that age.'

'Really? I have never seen a likeness of my godfather when he was a young man.'

'Fine man.' The elderly lady frowned and then picked up the bell that was on a small table beside her and rang it. 'We shall have tea.'

'Thank you. That would be very welcome.' Beth sat back and sighed inwardly. This was not getting her anywhere; the lady was being most evasive. To be honest, she disliked trying to trick her into revealing something about James Sharland, but what other choice was there?

Then Lady Sharland looked Beth straight in the eyes. 'It broke his heart, you know.'

'What did?'

'So cruel . . . They took her away and he never saw her again. So cruel . . . He never forgave them.' Lady Sharland smiled brightly. 'But it's all right now.'

'Yes, of course it is.' Beth wanted to question further, but the lady was clearly slipping back again.

'Terrible to lose your child.' Tears filled Lady Sharland's eyes 'Shouldn't still be here . . . should have gone to my maker long ago.'

Beth sat beside her and took hold of her hands. So she was aware that her son had died. 'It must be very hard to bear.'

'What is, dear?' Beth saw that her eyes were blank again, and it was obvious that she would not get any further information out of her ladyship.

It was another hour before they took their leave.

'Well, did you manage to glean anything from that?' Beth asked Helen when they were back in the carriage.

'Her ladyship is rather muddled in her thinking, and it was difficult to keep up with the sudden twists and turns of conversation.'

Beth smiled. 'Yes, she played the role of a forgetful old lady well, but I don't think her wits are as addled as she would have us believe.'

Helen didn't look convinced.

'Didn't you notice how she changed the subject whenever I questioned her about my new guardian?'

'I do admit that I found it frustrating. I had hoped we were going to find out the truth, but I am not sure we can believe anything she has told us.' Helen pulled the shade down when she noticed the wind blowing Beth's hair.

'She did not tell us anything, except to mention that someone had been taken away.'

'She is confused and doesn't know what she's saying,' Helen stated with certainty.

'I wonder?' Beth mused. 'There is quite clearly a skeleton in the Sharland cupboard. I did not consider my godfather a secretive man, but he must have been, for he guarded his past with great success. However, although her ladyship was very clever, we did gain some useful information.' Beth pulled the shade up again and ignored Helen's sigh.

'Did we?'

'She told us that he resembles his father, though I do admit that I cannot see the likeness.'

'I agree there is little resemblance to Lord Edward, but I have watched him closely and have noticed similarities in the mannerisms and character. But what does that tell us, and can we believe Lady Sharland's ramblings?' Helen asked.

'We shall have to assume that what she told us in her lucid moments was the truth.' Beth signed deeply. 'But why all the secrecy?'

'I don't know, Beth; it all sounds very confusing to me.' She shook her head in disbelief.

'Helen, it is clear that we have a mystery here, and I intend to find out the truth! Now, let us call at the book shop. There is a new title I wish to purchase.'

'The place looks deserted.' Dan surveyed the rambling mansion, frowning.

'My father moved the staff to the London house before he left for India. There's only a caretaker and his wife here now. Mr and Mrs Becks have been informed that I am coming. That's him coming across the yard.'

'Good to see you, your lordship. Are you stopping for a while? The wife can soon prepare you lunch.'

'We're only here for a short time. I've just brought my friend, Mr Edgemont, to have a look around the place.'

Becks nodded to Daniel. 'Pleasure, sir. Would you like refreshments, your lordship?'

'That would be welcome.'

They watched the retainer make his way back to the house, and James said, 'Come on, Dan, I'll show you around.'

'It's a bit of a monster,' Dan remarked when they walked into the enormous entrance hall. 'What on earth are you going to do with it? And that's one of the finest staircases I've ever seen.'

'Hmm, impressive, I agree. It's solid oak, and the sweep as it branches off in two directions at the top is elegant.'

'How many bedrooms does this place have?' Dan was turning round and round, taking in every aspect of the hall.

'Enough.'

He stopped and faced his friend again. 'Enough for what?'

'I'm going to turn this into a school for bright but impoverished children.'

'What? They'll wreck the place.' Dan studied James intently and then shook his head. 'You're serious.'

'Very.' Enthusiasm lit up his face. 'Why should only the titled and wealthy have a good education? I'll set up a scholarship for boys aged between ten and twelve. Anyone will be able to apply, and if they show promise, they can come here without charge.'

'You're crazy, James. That will cost a fortune!'

'I've got one and I'm going to put it to good use.' He grinned at Dan. 'Of course, I'm going to need help. You'd make a first-class riding and sports master . . . and perhaps a course on the law.'

A look of horror crossed Dan's face. 'You want me to work?'

'It will do you good and I'll pay you a fair wage. It won't be as dangerous as being a spy.'

Dan gave a snort of disgust. 'You're intending to fill this place with young boys – and you think that won't be dangerous? And are you going to pay yourself?'

'Don't be ridiculous, Dan. This school is going to be free for the boys I choose. I won't be earning an income.'

'Exactly! If you're working for nothing, then so am I.'

There was a slight pause before James asked, 'You'll do it?'

'How long before you can get it running?' Dan asked, without answering the question.

'Workmen are moving in this week, and I should be able to take in the first pupils at the start of the New Year. Ten at first, and if it's a success, we can increase the numbers slowly. I've already got some fine teachers working on selecting the first intake of boys.' James held his breath as he saw Dan trying to come to a decision. It was a revolutionary scheme and he couldn't ask for a better man by his side.

Dan pursed his lips. 'I'll give you six months, James. That's the best I can do.'

'I'll take it. Thank you, Dan.'

'I still think you're crazy. This is going to take a lot of our time, so we'd better get this business of yours cleared up as soon as possible.'

They turned sharply when they heard a sound behind them. It was Mrs Becks, and she indicated the trolley of refreshments. 'Where would you like this, your lordship?'

'Oh, in the library, please.'

They made their way to a huge room full of shelves from floor to ceiling crammed with books. It was only when they were settled that James noticed the boy with Mrs Becks. His eyes were fixed on them.

Seeing he'd been noticed, Mrs Becks drew him forward. 'This is our grandson, Charlie. I hope you don't mind him coming here, but he loves the books and wanted to see them again. The late Lord Sharland used to let him come and read whenever he wanted to, but we've stopped him doing it now. He has something to ask you, my lord.'

James beckoned the boy forward and waited.

Charlie looked him straight in the eyes and said, 'I would like your permission to come here to read the books, please. I'm very careful with them and never take them away. I'll put everything back in place and not make a mess.'

'You are proficient at reading?'

'Yes, my lord.' He gazed at the shelves with longing. 'It'll take me years to read all of these. I have books at school, but that's no good to me any more. It's all baby stuff. They said they can't teach me much more, so I'll have to leave soon.'

'How old are you, Charlie?' James was impressed with this bright lad.

'Eleven last month.' He looked downcast. 'I don't want to leave. I like learning, even if I've heard it all before.'

'Very well, Charlie, you may come here whenever you want to, and I'd like you to make a list of the books you read and let me know what you think of them.'

His face broke into a huge smile of relief. 'I'll do that, my lord. Can I look now?'

'Of course.' James smiled as the boy hurried over to the shelves, and then he turned his attention to the grandmother. 'There will be workmen arriving this week, Mrs Becks. They will be connecting the well outside to supply extra water to the house. I hope there will be enough.'

The boy turned from the book he was holding in his hand. 'That ain't the only water. There's a spring in the field out the back.'

'That's just a muddy bit of ground, Charlie,' Mrs Becks said dismissively.

'There's a spring there, Gran. That's why it's always muddy.' Charlie put the book back on the shelf and came to stand in front of James. 'You get the men to dig there and they'll find water.'

'Show us.'

James and Dan followed the boy outside to a small, rough field, surrounded by a wooden fence. They squelched their way over to the wettest part, and James stooped down to scrape away some of the soil. When even more water began to seep to the surface, he stood up again. 'I think you're right, Charlie. I'll get the men to sink another well here.'

The lad was staring at the once shiny boots, shaking with silent laughter. 'Oh, your lordship, them boots are covered in mud.'

'That's nothing,' Dan told him. 'I've seen him covered from head to toe in dirt when he's been digging in some ruin or other. He doesn't care.'

'Is that what you teach?' Charlie was clearly quite at ease with these gentlemen who didn't mind getting dirty. He approved of that.

The men glanced at each other, realizing that the boy had heard them talking in the hall. James answered. 'I do teach archaeology, but really I'm a botanist.'

'Cor! I've read that word somewhere. Is it about plants and things?' When James nodded, Charlie turned his attention to Dan, giving him a curious look. 'You really a spy?'

Leaning against the fence, James waited to see how his friend would deal with that question.

'I'm not supposed to tell anyone,' Dan whispered, making a great show of checking the area to make sure they weren't overheard.

'His lordship knows,' Charlie whispered back.

'Ah, well, he's my friend, and we help each other out when we can.'

Charlie could hardly contain his excitement. 'Can I be your friend? I can help. I notice things and I've got a good memory.'

'I can believe that.' Dan turned his head to wink at James. 'What do you think, Professor? Shall we recruit this young man?'

'He'll have to keep this a secret. Can you do that, Charlie?'

The boy nodded vigorously.

Dan gripped Charlie's hand and shook it. 'That's a deal, then. Now, you can help us by keeping your eyes open for anyone acting suspiciously around here.'

'Ah, are you looking for someone?'

Dan nodded. 'You let us know the moment you see anything.'

'I'll do that.' Charlie tipped his head to one side. 'Oh, Gran's calling me.'

As Charlie tore away, Dan pursed his lips. 'Do you think he'll keep all that to himself?'

'I doubt it, but if he does blurt it out, I expect people will just think it's a young boy's over-excited imagination.'

'You might be right, but it won't hurt to have us talked about. It might force our quarry out into the open.'

Seven

'Where have you been?' James asked in a stern voice as soon as Beth entered the drawing room.

'I have been to order a book I wish to read – that is all.' The lie came with ease, which was a skill Beth didn't know she possessed. She sat down and smiled. 'You left early so I could not ask your permission, but we took the footman with us. Did you have a pleasant morning? Shall we have the pleasure of your company at lunch?'

He cast her a suspicious glance and nodded, clearly not fooled by her agreeable manner.

'Splendid!' Not a bit put off, she beamed as if she had just received very welcome news. 'We have much to discuss.'

'Oh?'

She ignored his taciturn manner. 'Indeed. I would deem it an honour to show you the estate and point out the plans for this year.'

'I'm sure the manager can do that.'

'Of course he can – he is very efficient, and you will find his advice invaluable.'

When his lordship raised his eyebrows, she added quickly, 'Until you are thoroughly cognizant with the running of such a large and productive estate, of course.'

'Of course.'

'And as I am at a loss for something to do this afternoon . . .' Her smile was becoming fixed; he was making this very difficult for her, but she did not doubt that it was his intention to do so. She would have to step with care, for he would not be an easy man to fool.

'Very well,' he agreed suddenly. 'You may ride with me.'

'I shall look forward to it.' With her smile still in place, she turned to Dan. 'And will you be coming with us, Mr Edgemont?'

'I'm sorry to say I have some exploring of my own to do this afternoon.'

'Of course. It is a pleasant day for riding.'

Dan's mouth twitched at the corners. 'Indeed it is, and I have an animal that needs a great deal of exercise.'

Beth nodded and took in a silent breath to steady herself. She had to find out if she could still keep some control over the estate. 'Would you like me to go through the book-keeping with you?'

James narrowed his eyes. 'I am quite proficient at keeping accurate records.'

'I am sure you are, but—'

He surged to his feet. 'Do not overdo the obliging female, Beth; the role does not become you.'

Then he strode out of the room, leaving her volcanic with fury. How dare he address her in that familiar manner!

'It is not necessary to bring your companion with you,' he said, watching Helen mount her horse.

'She comes everywhere with me, and always when I am in the company of a gentleman.'

'I am your guardian, and therefore a chaperone is not required.'

She looked him straight in the eyes. 'But I only have your word for that.'

He tipped his head back and laughed, which was such a shock that she nearly slid from her mount. She felt quite overcome by his smile. The transformation was breathtaking, but she did not have time to dwell on it as he moved off at a trot and cast a glance back at her.

'Are you coming?'

She spurred her horse into action, and for the next two hours she showed him the Langton estate with a great deal of pride. It was impressive and she adored every acre of it.

He never said much – just an occasional nod or grunt – but his eyes swept over every field and building, examined the cattle, and then he rode on. For the first time since meeting him, she realized that there was a sharp, intelligent mind at work behind those cold eyes, and it was soon clear that he already knew a great deal about managing an estate.

When they stopped by a large, empty field, he dismounted.

'Why is this ground not being put to use?' he asked, as he helped her from her horse.

'Nothing will grow in it. We have tried many things but without success. We cannot even use it for grazing.'

'Hmm.' He vaulted the fence, bent down and took a handful of dirt, running it through his fingers.

Beth leant over the gate. 'As you see, the soil is too poor to do anything with. It is the only field on the entire estate we have been unable to put to good use.'

With long easy strides he began to walk across the enclosure, stopping now and again to examine something, and then he turned and came back, through the gate this time.

'I agree that it is a scrubby piece of land, but not useless; there is a small stream running past that copse of trees. We shall put pigs here,' he declared.

'Pigs!' She was horrified. 'But we have only ever had cows, sheep and goats,' she protested.

'Then it is time you expanded, and this is the perfect spot.'

'I don't think we need to go to all that expense.' The last thing she wanted was for this man to start making sweeping changes. 'The estate is running at a profit, and I do not consider it wise to jeopardize that with a risky scheme.'

He gave her a cold glance. 'It is not your decision to make.'

'It is my property and my future!' She was incensed by his attitude. 'And I will not allow you to ruin it.'

With one smooth movement he lifted her up and tossed her back on to her mount. 'For the next year you do not have a say in the running of the estate. That is my task and I will not have a piece of land going to waste when it could be put to good use.'

Then he swung himself back in the saddle and gave a derisive smile. 'You have had your own way for far too long, Elizabeth, and you will just have to learn to trust me.'

'How can I do that when you appear out of nowhere and proceed to take over my life?' Her horse sensed her agitation and began to prance.

Helen, who had been waiting in the background, came to her side as Beth's voice became raised in fury.

Beth ignored her beseeching expression, begging her to caution.

'Who are you, anyway?' she demanded. 'Why did my godfather never speak of you?'

'Perhaps I am the black sheep of the family,' he told her, without a flicker of emotion.

'Humph! That I can believe, and if that is the case, then it does not bode well for me.' She was so angry now that it was impossible to stop the suspicions pouring out. 'Where have you been hiding for years? Have you been living abroad in disgrace? Have you committed some heinous crime?'

His mouth compressed into a straight line, and his eyes glowed with anger. 'I am legally your guardian, and that is all you need to know.'

She watched in impotent fury as he galloped away.

The next day – and still seething – Beth sought out her estate manager. 'Pigs!' She waved her arms about in horror, just missing Greenway by a fraction.

He took a step back to avoid the unintentional blow to his middle region.

'You know I have an aversion to the beasts.' She gave a delicate shudder and curled her lip in disgust.

'That is true, but . . .' Greenway hesitated for a moment as if gathering his courage to speak to the furious girl in front of him. 'It is all the land is fit for, and I have often considered it myself, but your father would not hear of it because of your dislike of the animals.'

She instantly became still and opened her eyes wide in astonishment. 'You believe this to be a good idea?'

'I don't know his lordship's plans yet, but it could make sound business sense.' He took another step back, just to be on the safe side.

'I see.' She had the grace to calm down and try to look at the scheme dispassionately. Greenway was a loyal man, and she respected his judgement in matters pertaining to the estate. Indeed, she could never have managed since her father's death without his guidance, and she looked upon him as almost one of the family.

'In that case, will you talk to him about it?' She gave him an imploring look. 'I don't want him making changes unless it is for the benefit of the estate and everyone who lives and works here.'

'Leave it with me, Miss Langton. I'll seek out his lordship at once and see what plans he has for the field.'

'Thank you.' She gave a wry smile. 'You must forgive me for my outburst, but this situation has been thrust upon me, and when I consider what damage he could do in a year, it throws me into a panic.'

'I understand. We are all living on tenterhooks, wondering what he is going to do. If only we knew more about him.'

'He is certainly a mystery. I would ascertain his age to be around thirty, and yet it is as if he never existed until my godfather died.'

'That is true, but –' the estate manager gave a conspiratorial smile – 'there are plenty of us trying to unearth the truth, and he cannot keep his past hidden for ever.'

'I agree. However, I cannot help but fret.'

'Don't you worry yourself too much, Miss Langton. If he starts to act with disregard for the welfare of the estate, then we shall find a way to trim his sails.'

She laughed. 'That will not be easy, I fear, for he does appear to be in complete command of his ship.'

'For the moment, yes, but he must have a weak spot below the water line, and we shall find it eventually.' Greenway walked out of the room with a determined expression on his face.

The needle stabbed into Beth, and she muttered under her breath, placing the punctured finger in her mouth. The man sitting opposite her did not appear to have noticed her exclamation of pain; he was still engrossed in his reading.

She studied him through lowered lashes and sighed. The hostility between them was unnerving, and it was all her fault: she should never have spoken to him so accusingly yesterday. She was being unwise to allow her anger to show too much. Mr Edgemont had not returned for dinner, so they were alone – apart from Helen, of course, who was always with her, much to her relief.

'Lord Sharland.' She spoke quietly, but he looked up immediately. 'I wish to apologize for my outburst. I have spoken to

Greenway about your suggestion of making that field over to pigs, and he thinks the idea has merit.'

He put the book aside. 'I have discussed it with him; we are in complete agreement.'

'When will you go ahead with the scheme?' It was no good her fighting against it if her estate manager was also in favour of the plan.

'There is a little work to be done before purchasing the animals. They must have huts to protect them from the elements, but that should take no more than three days.'

'You have not wasted any time,' she told him, not able to hide the distaste she felt.

'Greenway tells me you have a fierce dislike of the beasts.'

'Indeed I have! When I was a small child, I came face to face with a sow. She chased me, and when I dropped my doll in terror, the disgusting animal ate it.' She struggled to keep a serious expression but was not very successful. 'I have never forgiven the breed.'

A deep, rumbling laugh came from his lordship. 'Do not be concerned, Elizabeth; they will be well away from the house and you need never see them.'

His tone was friendly, and he appeared more relaxed than she had seen him thus far. Emboldened by this, she decided to complete her apology. 'I was very rude to you yesterday; I do beg your forgiveness. I have an unruly tongue at times,' she admitted.

'I have already forgotten the incident.' He gave another brief smile and picked up his book again.

She took a deep breath and made pretence of returning to her sewing, but in truth she loathed the task and resented this forced inactivity. Running the estate had kept her busy from dawn to dusk, and she had loved every minute.

Tears of self-pity clouded her eyes, and she blinked them away. It was not the slightest good her riling against the situation; she needed to keep her composure and not enrage his lordship. If she did not keep her wits about her, then disaster could creep in without her noticing it, and she must not allow that to happen. But it was so very difficult, and, to be truthful, she was frightened. She had believed that her father and godfather had all matters concerning the estate and her future in prime order. It was distressing to discover that that was not the case.

The door opened, and Jenkins came into the room. 'Sir Peter Gresham has called to see you, my lord.'

The book was tossed aside, and for a fleeting moment his expression was thunderous, but he was soon in control of his emotions again. 'Tell him I am not at home.'

Without another word, he stepped through the open door into the garden and strode away from the house.

'Well!' Beth was astonished at such conduct. 'What do you think that was about, Jenkins?'

'I would say his lordship has no liking for the gentleman,' he remarked dryly.

'So it would appear, and that I can understand, for I also find Sir Peter a rather unpleasant person, but one has to be polite.' She frowned. 'I was not aware that his lordship had any acquaintances here?'

'Nor I,' the butler said with a thoughtful expression. 'Apart from his friend, Mr Edgemont, he appears to be a solitary man.'

'That is the impression I had gained – you would have expected the whole district to come visiting as soon as word got round, but Sir Peter is the first one to call since he arrived.' She settled herself elegantly in the chair and gave a mischievous smile. 'You had better show him in; I shall entertain him myself.'

Jenkins quickly checked that Helen was in her usual place on the window seat and then bowed. 'I shall see that refreshments are served in five minutes.'

Beth smiled to herself as she waited for her visitor to be shown in. This was the first time she had ever felt any pleasure at the prospect of meeting the gentleman. It was a novel experience.

She rose to greet him. 'How good of you to call, but I'm afraid Lord Sharland is unavailable.'

'That is disappointing, Miss Langton, as I so wished to see him today.'

'Perhaps you would allow me to take his place; it is an age since we met.' She smiled and simpered, hating herself for acting like this, but she wanted to keep him here and find out why he had called.

'Thank you; that is most gracious of you.' He waited until she was seated again and then sat down.

'I would not like to think that your visit was completely wasted.' She gave that smile again and hoped it did not look like a grimace. 'Ah, here is tea.' She poured and handed him a cup. 'Have you known Lord Sharland long?'

'We have never met, but when I heard he had arrived, I thought I should pay a visit.'

'He will be sorry to have missed you,' she lied with aplomb.

Sir Peter sipped his tea and then put the cup on the table. 'He is your guardian, I understand.'

'Yes, indeed.' She smiled brightly again, but her instinct was urging her to be careful what she said. 'He is a charming man and full of wonderful ideas for expanding the estate. After the unexpected death of my beloved godfather, I am fortunate to have such a wise guardian.'

He nodded, but she did not miss the glint of curiosity in his eyes.

'That was tragic, and I hope you will forgive me for calling so soon after your great bereavements?'

'You are welcome, sir.'

He smiled, sat back and crossed his legs. 'I was not aware that the late Lord Sharland had any direct heirs?'

'Really?' She tried an innocent look. 'He is a much-loved relative. He has lived abroad for many years – and that is why you have not heard of him before – but he has returned to shoulder his responsibilities.'

Beth was aware of a feeling of danger. She had never liked this man – she had heard he was violent – and, for some inexplicable reason, she felt it imperative to protect his lordship. Which was ridiculous because he was clearly very proficient at protecting himself.

'I see.' He appeared to relax. 'That would account for the fact that no one seems to know him.'

Now it was time to change the subject. 'And how is your sister?'

'Distressed!' He held his cup out for more tea. 'Our London

residence was broken into two days ago, while she was asleep in her bed.'

'How terrible!' She poured and handed the cup back to him, hoping her expression was suitably outraged. The sister was no more likeable than the brother. 'I trust she suffered no hurt?'

'She was unharmed and did not know anything about it until the servants rose to go about their chores.'

'That is indeed a blessing. Did the thieves take anything of value?'

'No, that was the strange thing: nothing was missing. But the house had been thoroughly searched.' He glowered. 'By an expert.'

'That is most distressing,' she sympathized. 'What do you think they were looking for?'

'We do not have the faintest idea.'

He was lying; she was sure of it. 'Ah, if nothing was taken, then it is clear that they did not find what they were looking for.'

'No, they did not!'

The certainty in his voice told her that he knew what the intruder had been after. How exciting! Another mystery.

He smiled and stood up. 'I must not take any more of your time, Miss Langton. Will you tell Lord Sharland I am sorry to have missed him and hope I shall have the pleasure of meeting him very soon.'

'I shall tell him, and please give my regards to your sister.'

'Well, well,' Beth murmured when they were alone again. 'What did you make of that, Helen? I cannot remember Sir Peter ever visiting us before.'

'Strange indeed. He was clearly disappointed at not finding Lord Sharland at home.'

'That was the impression I had as well. He could hardly sit still long enough to be polite.' Beth pursed her lips thoughtfully. 'And the way his lordship practically ran out of this room made it clear that he didn't want to see Sir Peter. I do believe you are right to suggest that there is more to this than a stranger taking over as my guardian.'

Both girls nodded and poured themselves another cup of tea.

'The mystery continues to grow, Helen. I find it very curious that his lordship should not want to meet Sir Peter – and that Sir Peter's London home has been recently broken into, but nothing taken. It feels as if there is a connection there.'

Helen pursed her lips. 'And Mr Edgemont has been missing for a while.'

'Indeed!'

Eight

James appeared just in time for dinner that evening and was even more uncommunicative than usual. They were well into the second course when Beth broke the silence. 'Is Mr Edgemont not joining us this evening?'

'No, he is still out . . . visiting.'

'Oh, does he know people who live in the area?'

'He knows a great many people.'

The expression on his face told her quite plainly that the subject was closed, so she didn't probe any further. 'I entertained Sir Peter Gresham in your stead this afternoon, and he appeared most interested in you.'

That did gain his attention. 'And what did you tell him?'

'I could not say much because, in truth, I know very little about you, so I lied shamelessly.'

'Really?' The corners of his lordship's mouth twitched.

'Yes, I do not like the Greshams and I told quite a few untruths.' She looked at him through lowered lashes as if ashamed of her conduct, but she doubted that her poor acting ability was fooling him.

'Such as?'

'I told him you were a charming man and I was fortunate to have you as my guardian.' She sighed and fanned herself with her napkin. 'I cannot understand why I should have told such a blatant untruth.'

The corners of his mouth twitched again, but otherwise his expression did not change. 'And did he want to know my relationship to the Sharlands?'

'He did.' She glared at the infuriating man; he was finding this far too amusing. 'But I had to wriggle out of answering that, because although you have told me you are his son, and the lawyer assures me that you are, and has papers to prove it, they could be forgeries.' She heard Helen draw in a sharp breath but ignored it. She had always spoken her mind and had no intention of changing now. 'I got around it by saying that you were a close relative and had been abroad for many years.'

'That was very inventive of you. Almost as inventive as you consider me to be.' His eyes regarded her intently. 'Did he believe you?'

'I don't know. It was hard to tell what he was thinking, but we had better get our stories straight before you meet him.'

'I have no intention of making his acquaintance . . . yet.' He sat back and folded his arms. 'However, you had better tell me exactly what was said.'

She gave a full account of the conversation. As she drew to a close, he was smiling broadly.

'I don't think this is anything to laugh about,' she declared indignantly. 'I have behaved in a most improper manner and I cannot understand why I should have acted in this way.'

His smile spread, and he stood up, came to her, then bent down and touched his lips to her cheek. It was no more than the touch of a butterfly wing, but she was startled that this cold, stern man should show gentleness. It was quite out of character.

'Why did you do that?' she gasped, taken completely by surprise.

'To thank you for trying to protect me.' He went back to his own place and started to eat again. Then he looked up. 'But it was not necessary; I am quite able to take care of my own affairs. And you can be assured that I shall not tell anyone that you are such an accomplished storyteller.' He drained his wine glass and stood up again. 'Now, if you ladies will excuse me, I have something to attend to.'

When they were sure he had left the house, Beth said to Helen, 'So much secrecy and it is quite driving me to distraction.'

Helen nodded. 'It is frustrating, I know, but you must learn to guard your tongue. You as good as accused him of criminal activity, and I do not feel that is wise.'

'I know I have an unruly tongue, but I cannot hide my feelings. His conduct is unacceptable, and I am sure he is up to no good.'

'That could well be so,' Helen agreed, looking pensive, 'but all will be revealed eventually, and you must bide your time. A year is not too long, and then this will be over. I could not help noticing that he is attractive when he isn't frowning. Has he said any more about your coming-out season?'

'No! And I most certainly will not agree to such a foolish thing. You know I cannot abide all that fussing. It is demeaning to put oneself on show just to catch a husband.'

'I know you don't agree with it, but if you had a husband, you would be free of his lordship.'

'And I would have another man taking over control of my affairs. I will not have it, Helen.' Beth shook her head vigorously. Then she noticed the expression on her friend's face. 'Oh, I'm so sorry, Helen. You should have had a season; you would soon have found a charming husband, I'm sure. We are the same age, and you have been forced to take on a position of a companion, but I want you to know that I consider you as I always have – my friend. However, my godfather listed you among the estate staff and you will therefore continue to receive your allowance.'

'That is very kind of you, but I am uneasy about the arrangement, Beth.' Helen gave a worried frown. 'Lord Edward assured me that my allowance would be coming out of his pocket, but now he is no longer able to do that I feel as if I shall be a drain on your estate. That isn't right, and he was kind enough to leave me a sum of money, so I should be finding a way to make my own living.'

'But you are not a drain!' Beth looked at her friend in alarm. 'You must not even think about leaving. Please, I need you! I cannot cope with what is happening without you by my side.'

'I would not consider leaving you until this mess is cleared up and you are once again secure, but I cannot allow you to support me for the rest of my life. After my father gambled away our fortune, I could have ended up in a very sorry situation, but you kindly took me in. I have no hope of finding a husband now as I have nothing to offer in the way of property or wealth.'

'Nonsense! You are a charming young lady; many men would be proud to have you as their wife.'

'I doubt that, but even if what you say is true, we do not meet any young men.'

'No, you are right.' Beth suddenly felt unhappy about their isolation. 'I have been thoughtless. My entire attention has been taken up with running the estate, but as soon as our mourning period is over, we shall have to change things.' She smiled encouragingly at her friend. 'We shall open up the ballroom and have a large, glittering function.'

'That would be lovely,' Helen agreed, giving Beth a searching look. 'There is more to life than business.'

'I'm sure you are right, but for the moment there is little we can do.' Beth put down her napkin and stood up. 'Let us retire to my sitting room.'

'Pstt!'

Beth stopped with her foot on the bottom stair and peered round the banister. Tom's head was sticking through the door leading to the servants' quarters. He beckoned and then his head disappeared.

'I wonder what he wants?' Helen couldn't help smiling at the young boy's antics.

'Let's find out.' Beth opened the door and looked in. 'It's all right, Tom – his lordship is out.'

'Don't want anyone else to hear,' he said excitedly, shutting the door firmly. 'I've got news. It was my day off today and I went to see Charlie Becks. He told me his lordship and Mr Edgemont went to the Sharland estate yesterday. He heard them talking, but they said he wasn't to tell anyone what he'd heard. As we're friends, he thought it would be all right if he told me. You'll never guess what they are.' Tom looked expectantly at her.

'I have no idea, Tom. What did your friend tell you?'

'Well, as I told you before, Mr Edgemont calls his lordship "professor". He really is a teacher, miss, and is going to turn the Sharland house into a school.'

James had already mentioned this, and Beth could see that her godfather's rambling house would make an excellent school. 'He really must be an academic, Helen.'

'He sounds like one.'

'There's more.' Tom could hardly contain himself in his eagerness to pass on the next bit of news. He moved closer and lowered his voice. 'They're both spies and probably going to use the school as a cover for something.'

It took Beth a few moments to compose herself, for she had the urge to burst into amused laughter. When she was fully in control again, she asked, 'Is your friend sure about that?'

'Yes, miss. Mr Edgemont asked Charlie to keep an eye open for anyone acting strange around the place. He's to tell them at once if he sees anything suspicious.'

'Did they say who they were looking for?'

Tom shook his head. 'Oh, no, that's a secret.'

'Of course.' Beth smiled at the lad. 'Thank you, Tom; you'll let us know if you hear anything else?'

'I will, miss.' He hurried away, looking very pleased he'd been able to pass on this exciting news.

When Beth and Helen had reached the sitting room, they looked at each other and then burst into laughter.

'Spies!' Beth could hardly contain herself. 'Oh dear, I do believe Mr Edgemont has been telling the young boy a tale. I can well believe that his lordship is a teacher, for he has an air of authority about him, but spies . . .'

'It does seem unlikely, but you must admit that they are indeed very mysterious gentlemen.'

Beth nodded, serious now. 'And we still need to keep an eye on what they are doing. It would be sensible if we could find out something about Mr Edgemont's family.'

'But how would we do that?'

'I don't know; I will have to think about it. If we can find out if he knows anyone in the area, then we could start there. We shall sleep on it, Helen.'

Her companion began to laugh again. 'I do believe we are also turning into spies!'

What was that? Beth sat up in bed and tipped her head to one side, listening intently. There it was again! A stair had creaked, and now a door was closing with a soft click as if someone was taking great care not to be heard.

'Helen,' she called quietly. 'Are you awake?'

'Yes . . . is something amiss?' A muffled reply came from the connecting door to the next room.

'It sounds as if someone is creeping around the house.'

There was a rustling sound from the other room, and then an exclamation as Helen walked into something in the dark.

'What are you doing?' Beth asked in a whisper, slipping on her wrap.

'I'm trying to find the candle.'

'Do not light it! We don't want the perpetrator to know he has been discovered. There is enough light from the moon for us to be able to see.' The last thing she wanted was to alert the intruder. She wanted to find out who was creeping around her house. And it *was* her house, whatever that odious man said!

Helen stumbled into the room, clutching a candlestick in one hand and a flint box in the other. 'Do you think it is a thief like the one who burgled Sir Peter Gresham's house?' Helen asked in a hushed whisper.

'Let us find out.' Beth's eyes were accustomed to the gloom by now. She took the candlestick from Helen, removed the candle and swung the heavy object. 'This will make a splendid weapon.'

'Shall I awaken the men?'

'There isn't time for that.' She unlocked her bedroom door and made for the stairs. When she stopped to listen, Helen cannoned into her.

'Sorry.'

'Shush!' She started down the stairs, Helen's restraining hand on the back of her robe.

Helen whispered in her ear. 'You must not confront the fiend yourself. We *must* awaken the men.'

At the foot of the stairs she stopped to listen again. Yes, it was unmistakable: someone was moving around with great stealth. She indicated towards the study and Helen shook her head frantically, trying to pull Beth back up the stairs. This was making things difficult, and if they were not careful, the thief would be away before she could find out who it was. 'You go back,' she whispered.

Helen shook her head again and held on to Beth even more.

Beth released Helen's fierce grip and moved towards the study. Even fear could not lessen Helen's loyalty to her, and it was clear that wherever Beth went, she was going too. It was only to be hoped that she would remain silent, for if they were discovered, then it could be dangerous for them.

They were just about to approach the study door when it opened. They dived behind the stairs for cover, watching the man leave by the front door.

Giving him a moment to get away from the house, the girls

hurried into the study and looked out into the garden. The moon was very bright now and she could see him quite clearly. He was tall, dressed entirely in dark clothing and wearing a cape and large brimmed hat that shaded his face.

'Oh, damn!' Beth muttered. 'I cannot see him with that hat on.'

Helen was bolder now the interloper was halfway across the garden. 'He has a horse under the trees.'

'So he has. That was well spotted, Helen,' she complimented, 'and I do declare that it is as black as his clothes.'

'It has a white mark on its head, though, and that is what I saw move. It could be the stallion from your stables,' Helen pointed out. 'See – the animal is facing us and is quite clear now.'

'Ah, yes, you are right. I wish he would move into the moonlight . . .' Her wish was instantly granted. The man mounted and lifted his face to look at the house for a brief moment before turning and making for the gate.

Beth and Helen hid behind the drapes for fear of being seen and sighed with relief as they heard him canter away.

'That was . . .' Helen could not contain her astonishment.

'Yes, it was James Sharland!' Beth put her weapon on to a small table and turned to survey the room. 'Now, what was he doing in Father's study?'

'I don't know.' Helen looked at her with imploring eyes. 'We should tell someone about this.'

'No!' Beth was adamant. 'I don't want this noised abroad until we know what is going on. After all, if he wishes to sneak out of the house at this late hour, then that is his business – for the moment.'

'Perhaps he has an assignation he wishes to keep secret.'

Beth controlled a laugh. 'I would say that was obvious, Helen. But what kind of assignation?'

'A lady?'

'Perhaps. Though I don't think this creeping around in the middle of the night is for a lover's tryst. I can't believe he is the kind of man who would care what others thought of him.'

'Oh, look!' Helen hurried over to the desk. 'This drawer is not properly closed.'

Beth joined her and pulled it open. There was a box in there and she knew what it contained.

'Has anything been taken?' Helen wanted to know.

She lifted the box out and opened it. It was as she feared; there was one empty space. 'There is something unpleasant going on. One of Father's pistols has been taken.'

'Perhaps he has taken it for protection?' Helen suggested. 'It is not a good time of night to be abroad.'

'I would hope that is so.' Beth frowned fiercely. 'But I don't think it is the reason; otherwise, James Sharland would not have been skulking around the house in this manner.'

'What do you think he is about, then?'

'Goodness knows, but I mean to find out!' Beth settled herself in a large leather chair and folded her arms. 'I shall wait in here until he returns. Then perhaps I will discover what he has been doing.'

'Oh, Beth, you cannot do that! You will be in great danger if he discovers you spying on him.'

'Nonsense, Helen; he would not harm me,' she stated with conviction.

'How do you know?' she asked. 'I am sure he would be angry, and I fear he could have an uncertain temper.'

'I am sure you are correct, but I believe he would do nothing drastic to jeopardize his position here at the moment. For some reason we are not yet aware of, he needs me and this establishment.' She even startled herself with this declaration, but some instinct was telling her it was true. 'I am sure that is why he has moved in and taken over.'

'Do you not think it would be wiser to awaken the men and ask them to watch for him?'

Beth shook her head. 'No, if he had not taken the pistol, then I might have considered asking them to try to find out what he is doing, but I would not like to place any of them in danger. I shall wait and see him return.'

Helen sat down, picked up the candlestick and cradled it in her lap, looking as if she would rather be tucked up safely in her bed. 'He was dressed in a very strange manner.'

'Indeed, and it was clear that he did not wish to be recognized.' Beth gazed out of the window at the small copse of trees where the horse had been hidden. 'I think we should call on Lady Sharland again tomorrow and hope she is more lucid. Perhaps we can glean a little more information from her, for I am convinced she knows more than she is prepared to admit.'

'I wish you wouldn't. You are far too bold.'

'Do not fear, Helen. Now, return to your bed. There is little point in us both losing a night's sleep.'

It was clear that Helen considered it very unwise to remain in the study, but, knowing her friend's stubbornness well, she shook her head firmly. 'I am not going to leave you alone.'

'I shall remain hidden, but you may leave the candlestick if you are concerned.'

Helen shook her head again, took a firm grip on the candlestick and sat down. 'I'm staying as well.'

Beth nodded, grateful to have Helen with her. 'I had thought you would find much-needed peace and tranquillity here so that you could heal after your terrible ordeal, but it seems that you have dealt with one disaster only to find yourself deep in this one of mine. I am so sorry, Helen.'

'There is no need to be.' Helen smiled confidently. 'This one will have a happy ending, I am sure.'

Beth had been dozing when a slight noise jolted her awake. Someone was creeping past the study window and making for the front door. A hasty glance around the room showed that Helen was not there, and Beth just had time to dive behind the drapes when the door opened and James Sharland came in. She heard the desk drawer open and then soft footfalls as he left the room. She let out a pent-up breath and peered cautiously around the drapes. The room was empty.

She was halfway to the desk when the door opened slightly, making Beth jump violently. When she saw Helen's face peering in, she let out a breath of relief. 'Oh, you gave me a fright. I thought he had come back.'

'No.' Helen eased into the room. 'He has gone upstairs to his rooms. I went to the kitchens to make us a hot drink. I was just coming back when I saw him return. I hid, hoping you had done the same.'

'I did.' Beth opened the drawer of the desk, pulled out the box and saw that it now contained two pistols.

'Oh, he has returned it,' Helen whispered.

Beth picked up the pistol and smelt it. 'It does not appear to have been used, so that is something to be grateful for.'

'Indeed,' Helen agreed. 'We don't want to find we have a murderer under our roof.'

'No, we do not . . .' Beth hesitated. 'But what *do* we have residing with us? I am beginning to wonder if young Tom might have told us the truth after all.'

Nine

James Sharland and Mr Edgemont were already at breakfast when Beth and Helen arrived. They rose to their feet and gave elegant bows.

'Good morning. I trust you slept well?'

'Yes, thank you.' Beth stifled a yawn; it had been half past four in the morning when she had finally made it to her bed again. 'I hope you had a comfortable and undisturbed night?'

'I cannot speak for Dan as he only arrived an hour ago, but I did not wake up once.' He smiled and sat down again.

How she managed to stop herself from challenging this statement she did not know, for she knew that he had not slept at all last night. But no one would ever have known because he looked fresh and rested.

'Forgive me for still wearing my riding clothes at your table, Miss Langton, but I have not had time to change yet.' Daniel gave her a charming smile.

She returned his friendly smile. 'There is nothing to forgive, Mr Edgemont. You must be very hungry after your ride.'

'Indeed.'

Helen was studying her eggs as if they were the most interesting objects she had ever seen. She remained silent, but Beth knew that she listened intently to anything that was said.

Jenkins came in and held a silver tray out to her. She took the heavily gilded card and gasped when she read it.

'My goodness! Sir Peter Gresham is to hold a masked ball – and we have been invited.'

'You sound surprised. Is it unusual for you to be invited to social functions?' his lordship asked wryly.

She glowered at him. 'No, it is not, but I have never known them do such a thing.' She turned to Jenkins. 'Who brought this?'

'One of his footmen, and he was agog with excitement. It seems there were strange happenings last night.'

'Really? Do tell me,' Beth said with an innocent smile.

'He said that they nearly caught someone trying to break into the house, but after the burglary at their London home, the Greshams have more men patrolling the ground now.'

'Was anyone hurt?' Beth asked, resisting the temptation to glance knowingly at her friend.

'No, but the footman said they caught a glimpse of him and he looked fierce enough to kill if cornered.' Beth heard Helen cough and did not dare to look at her friend. If this had been James Sharland, then he was playing a very dangerous game indeed!

Helen cleared her throat. 'Did he have any idea what the villain could have been after?' she asked.

'No. As he did not gain entry to the house, they have no way of knowing. They assumed he was a common thief after valuables.'

There was a brief splutter from the other end of the table, which was quickly turned into a cough.

The butler gave up trying to remain serious and let a grin spread. 'I think the incident has grown with each telling and probably bears little resemblance to the truth now. I expect they just saw a shadow in the grounds and thought it was an interloper. They were probably chasing a fox or some other animal.'

'I am sure you are right.' She looked pointedly at James as he helped himself to another plate of bacon and kidneys.

'And what do you think of this scoundrel?' she asked pointedly.

'A strange episode, but it doesn't seem as if any harm was done. Just someone having a little fun after imbibing too much brandy, I expect.'

She persisted with her questions. 'Let us assume it was a genuine burglary; what do you think he was after?'

His lordship looked at her with a puzzled expression. 'How would I know?'

'How indeed.' *But I'm sure you do know,* she thought silently, *for I saw you skulking off last night with one of Father's guns, and it would not take a genius to deduce that you were the burglar.* Keeping these thoughts to herself, she smiled sweetly at him and then turned to Jenkins. 'Is the footman waiting for a reply?'

'No, Miss Langton.' He bowed and left the room.

She picked up the invitation again. 'A masked ball. How very intriguing.'

'May I see the card?' His lordship held out his hand.

Helen took the card from Beth, got to her feet and took it up to him. She returned to her chair, never once looking at anyone, but Beth could see she was having a struggle to keep her features composed and not give away that they knew anything.

'Ah, but I cannot go.' Beth sighed in disappointment. 'And I am surprised they even sent it, since we are in mourning.'

James tapped the card on his fingers and gazed thoughtfully into space. 'But you said that your father forbade you to go into deep mourning, and I am sure Edward would have agreed with that also.'

Her head shot up. He had referred to his father as Edward. Was that a slip of the tongue? How she longed to discover the real identity of her mysterious guardian, for she was still not convinced he was who he said he was.

'I believe we should accept. If you went all in black, you would be unrecognizable.'

'Ah, but you said I would look dreadful in black, and, anyway, I should be unmasked at midnight,' she pointed out.

'Not if you leave before then.' He raised a brow in query. 'I think you would enjoy that – am I not right?'

'You are correct,' she admitted. 'I am curious to see the Gresham home because I don't believe anyone has been allowed past the entrance hall before.'

'Then you shall go.'

'Will you accompany me, my lord?' Her mouth curled at the corners. 'All in black?'

'If I come, Elizabeth, you will not recognize me.' He stood up, and both men strode from the room.

'Aha!' Helen whispered. 'I think we can guess who the robber was.'

'Of course he was, but what could he want so desperately?'

'It is very perplexing.'

'I agree. Come, Helen, we shall send an acceptance to Sir Peter and then call on Lady Sharland.'

★ ★ ★

'So what did you find out from your escapade?' Dan sat down and gave his friend an exasperated look.

'Nothing. I did not get near enough to the house to break in. I never expected to. My intention was to shake up a few people.'

'Humph! You've certainly succeeded. Are you telling me you risked gaol just for that?'

James sat forward, frustration showing on his face. 'I haven't got time to be subtle, so I'm shaking the tree to see what falls out. Have you discovered anything of use?'

'You mean, apart from finding out that I can't take my eyes off you for a moment?'

'You would have done the same thing, Dan, and don't try to pretend you wouldn't.'

'Probably, but I'm more experienced in things like that. Please wait until I'm around before you try anything as dangerous as that again.'

James nodded. 'Get on with it, Dan.'

His friend removed a small notebook from his inside pocket and flicked open the pages, reading silently for a moment. Then he looked up. 'Well, as you suspected, I'm sure Gresham is our man. He has a nasty reputation, and it is rumoured that he has extracted money from some prominent men who wish certain things to be kept secret. He is shunned by London society, and many believe he is seeking a way to be accepted again. Marriage would be his best way.'

'Ah.' James smiled in relief. 'That should rule out Elizabeth. Although she comes from a good family, she doesn't have a title, and that's the kind of prestige he would want.'

'But there is another lady in this house who does have a title. The so-called companion is really Lady Helen Martha Denton.'

There was a moment of silence as this startling piece of news was assimilated, and then James surged to his feet. 'What the hell is she doing pretending to be Elizabeth's companion?'

'I had a long talk with someone who knew the family well. It seems that after Helen's mother died some two years ago, Lord Denton started gambling to ease his grief, and it's the old story, I'm afraid. He lost everything he owned and shot himself in shame, leaving huge debts. His daughter set about paying off everything he owed, not satisfied until every farthing had been repaid. When she had finished, she was destitute. Helen and Elizabeth have been friends from childhood, and Elizabeth took Helen in to live here. Lord Edward wanted to give her an allowance, but the girl has her pride and insisted that she be taken on as a servant so she could earn her keep. Lord Edward and Elizabeth were horrified by such a thought but finally agreed that Helen become Elizabeth's companion. Evidently, Helen refuses to use her title and is fiercely loyal in her role as companion.'

'Dear Lord.' James was shaking his head. 'She appears such a timid creature, but that is just an act as well, isn't it?'

'Yes, I do believe so. She showed great strength of character in the way she insisted on repaying all of her father's debts.' Dan gazed into space for a while and then said, 'Why don't you take her into your confidence, James? I have a feeling she could be helpful.'

'I dare not at the moment, but I'll try to get to know her better, and then we'll see.' James glanced at the clock on the mantelpiece. 'I wouldn't be surprised if the ladies visited Grandmother again, so I believe we should do the same.'

'How good of you to call again so soon.' Lady Sharland held her hand out to greet Beth.

'I trust you are well?' She gave the lady's hand a gentle squeeze and sat down opposite her.

'I am in fine fettle.' She beamed. 'As you can see.'

'Indeed, you look in the best of spirits.'

'I am, I am.' She turned her head to look at the tall man striding into the room. 'And here is the reason for my happiness.'

James Sharland bent to kiss the elderly lady on the cheek.

'I do declare that I am being quite spoilt today. We must all have tea together.' She rang the bell to summon refreshments and then caught hold of his lordship's hand. 'All is well, James?' she asked, a worried frown creasing her brow.

'Of course.' He stooped down in front of her and smiled warmly.

'Is Daniel coming soon?' she asked in a whisper.

'I'm already here, Grandmother Sharland.' Dan also entered the room and kissed the lady's cheek.

'Oh, I'm so relieved you two boys are together again.' Lady Sharland's eyes clouded with tears. 'You will not be in any danger?'

'What a notion! Opening a school is not dangerous, Grandmother, though Dan believes otherwise.' James laughed and leant forward to say something in her ear.

He spoke too quietly that time for Beth to hear, but she couldn't help wondering what he had said because Lady Sharland was nodding vigorously. Beth could not take her eyes off the scene being played out. His lordship was displaying great affection for the elderly lady, and it was abundantly clear that she adored him. But why was she concerned about him being in danger? Did she know that he was creeping around at night with a pistol?

The refreshments arrived and further speculation would have to wait.

'James tells me that he is to arrange a season for you,' she said to Beth, looking quite excited at the prospect. 'I wish I were still young enough to accompany you, but you will like your chaperone – she is of the finest character.'

Beth glared at his lordship. 'I was not aware that arrangements were so far forward?'

'Oh, James.' Lady Sharland was looking from Beth to his lordship in a most agitated manner. 'Have I said something I shouldn't?'

He was immediately on his feet again, a comforting hand on her shoulder. 'Don't distress yourself. We haven't got round to discussing details yet, and, to be truthful, Elizabeth does not appear enamoured with the idea.'

'But you will love it, my dear.' Her expression had turned to one of longing. 'It is such fun to have all the young men hanging on your every word and fighting to secure the next dance.'

Beth could not imagine anything more dreadful, but she smiled. 'I am sure you are right, but I have been so busy running the estate that I have quite got out of the habit of being sociable.'

'I know, my dear. You have had a hard time, but you must put all that behind you now. James will take the burden of responsibility from you.'

Ah, but what else will he take from me? she wondered, as worry gripped her again. *He could do a great deal of harm in a year . . .*

'You leave everything to James; he will see you have a come-out to remember. I cannot imagine what your father and my son were thinking of, allowing you to remain at home and do work better suited to a man. They should have found you a husband long ago.'

Lady Sharland smiled at the man sitting opposite; he looked relaxed and slightly amused. 'Never mind; James will put everything to rights.'

Not while I have breath left in my body! Beth fumed. If he thought he was going to take away her home and have dominion over her life, then he was in for a very great fight!

'Helen should also be included in the social round.' James looked over at the girl who was sitting in the background as usual. He smiled.

Helen was clearly horrified, but Beth was smiling broadly. 'What a splendid idea, for I would not be able to endure the tedium of endless functions without you beside me, Helen.'

'Oh, I could not.' A look of determination crossed her face. 'It would not be proper.'

'Nonsense.' James swept away the denial. 'The matter is settled.'

Recognizing that there was no point arguing about it here, Helen fell silent.

As soon as was polite, Beth made her escape and stormed out to the waiting carriage. 'I wanted to talk to Lady Sharland to see if she would tell us anything of interest, but how could we with his lordship there?'

'It would have been difficult, I agree.' Helen did not sound like her usual placid self. 'Her ladyship appears very fond of both the gentlemen.'

'I have no doubt that he could charm any woman from eight to eighty with his elegant good looks and winning smile.'

Helen gave her a startled glance.

'Don't look at me like that, Helen. I am not including myself as one of those foolish females.' She folded her arms with a stubborn air. As far as she was concerned, the man was the devil incarnate. 'He is a rogue, and I wish he had never entered my life.' A tear trickled down Beth's cheek. She brushed it away with an exclamation of impatience. What was the matter with her? She had never indulged in self-pity. It was a useless emotion, but, to be truthful, she was becoming more confused each day – and not a little frightened.

Helen's hand settled over her tightly clenched one. 'Do not be overset. I know things seem bad at the moment, but the situation will right itself, you'll see, and I don't believe he is a bad man. He showed great kindness today, and Mr Edgemont appears to be a strong and trustworthy man. From what I have seen of the two of them together, he could be a restraining influence on Lord Sharland.'

Beth gave a wry smile. 'I wish I had a little of your tolerance and trust in providence, but I do admit to being worried. If he dispatches me to London, then I shall not be able to check that he does no harm to the estate or the people who depend upon it for their living.'

'But you have faithful staff who will keep you informed wherever you may be residing. And London is not far away.'

'Of course. I am being exceedingly foolish today – and in need of your sound reasoning.'

Raising her head, Helen showed a hint of pride and a determined set to her mouth. 'However, although I do believe he has a gentle side to him, I will not be bullied into joining you for a London season. I shall tell him so the moment I can have a private word with him.'

'Oh, but, Helen, I do so want you with me. How can I face that without you there?'

Helen was shaking her head. 'I cannot. It wouldn't be right, and I could not endure the gossip and pitying looks. The shame would be too great.'

'But the shame is not yours! You are being given the chance to take your rightful place in society, and that is very proper.'

'No, Beth, I will not agree to it!'

As she gazed at her lifelong friend, the tears began to flow freely. Grasping Helen's clenched hands, she smiled through the tears. 'Oh, Helen, will you please now drop this pretence of being my companion?'

'I'm sorry, but I can't do that while I am still taking money from you.'

Beth sat back, sadness showing in her eyes. 'Then joining in the London social scene might be a good thing. We must find you a wealthy husband.'

'And that is just what society will be expecting of me. I will not sink so low, Beth. There is little hope of me finding a good husband now, and I would never marry for material gain, even if I have to be a servant for the rest of my life.'

Beth dried her eyes and smiled sadly. 'I wish I had your courage, Helen.'

'That is something you have never lacked. Do not start to doubt yourself when things are rough. You will win through.'

'Yes,' she nodded, taking a deep breath. 'I have to.'

Ten

Sleep had been impossible for Helen. As much as she wanted to support Beth through this difficult time, the thought of appearing in society again filled her with dread. She had been close to collapse after dealing with her father's debts, and if it hadn't been for Beth and her godfather, she didn't know what would have happened to her. She owed her friend so much . . . but she would not endure this.

Drawing all of her courage around her, Helen made her way downstairs. Beth was busy arranging meals with Cook, and the gentlemen were in the library. If she put on her act of timid companion, then she might be able to convince his lordship that it wouldn't be right for a servant to accompany Elizabeth. She tapped on the door and waited.

'Come.'

She opened the door slowly and walked in, eyes down. 'I beg your pardon, your lordship, but may I have a word with you?'

'What is it, Helen?' he asked, studying her with a frown on his face.

She raised her eyes to meet his and clasped her hands tightly together in front of her, then looked down again. 'It would not be proper for me to accompany Miss Elizabeth to social events in London. She should have an older, experienced female with her.'

'I have already arranged that, and you will join Elizabeth as an equal.'

She gave him a startled look, certainly not expecting that! 'Impossible!'

A slight smile touched his lips at her sudden change of attitude. 'And why is that, Lady Helen?'

The use of her title was such a shock that it almost knocked her off her feet. She caught hold of the back of a chair to steady herself. After only a moment she had regained her composure and lifted her head to glare at the two men in the room. Her green eyes were as cold as a frosty dawn.

Daniel Edgemont was the first to speak, his voice gentle. 'Would you like a drink? Brandy, perhaps?'

'No, I would not!'

'Then sit down, please.'

'I prefer to stand, Mr Edgemont.' Helen turned her attention back to Lord Sharland. 'The fact that you know who I am will not make me change my mind. I have withdrawn from society and will not endure the gossip my return would most certainly cause. I presume you know what happened to my family?'

The men merely nodded.

'Yes, of course you do!' Helen glanced from one man to the other, angry to discover that they had delved into her past. 'Well, I am certain you are not what you appear to be, either. Just who are you? And what are you doing here?'

'I am James Sharland, an archaeologist and professor of history, and my friend is Daniel Edgemont . . .' James looked at Daniel, eyebrows raised. 'Tell Lady Helen what you do, Dan.'

He scratched his head, looking puzzled, and then shrugged. 'Anything I'm asked to do. As long as it's within the law, of course.'

The anger drained away from Helen as she studied their expressions of innocence. She smothered a laugh. 'I hardly think trying to burgle Sir Peter Gresham's home is within the law.'

'That wasn't me.'

'No, I don't believe it was, Mr Edgemont.' Helen turned her full attention back to his lordship. She was beginning to enjoy herself now. 'Did you find Mr Langton's pistol easy to handle?'

'Adequate,' James replied, without as much as a blink of his eyes. 'Are you in the habit of creeping around the house in the dead of night?'

'Only when we have guests who appear to be up to no good, your lordship,' Helen said sweetly as she sat down in a chair, indicating that she hadn't finished with them yet. She felt a profound sense of relief to be shedding her timid companion's act. It had taken a while to recover from the humiliation of paying off her father's debts, but that was all behind her now, and she would use her title again and lift her head proudly. She had nothing to be ashamed of. How good it felt to realize that at last. 'I believe it is time you told Elizabeth what you are both doing here, don't you?'

James and Daniel sat down as well, and James leant forward. 'I am Elizabeth's legal guardian for the moment, and that is all I can say. I'm going to ask you to trust us. I need Elizabeth to go to London, and for you to accompany her.'

'Elizabeth is afraid that if she leaves here, you will ruin the estate.' Helen frowned. 'It means a great deal to her.'

'I can assure you that will not happen.'

Helen shook her head. 'She only has your word for that, Lord Sharland, and we know nothing about you. Why should she believe you?'

'I understand your concerns, but I am here to carry out my father's instructions, and Daniel is here to help me.'

'And what are your father's instructions?' she asked boldly.

'That I cannot tell you at the moment, but once my task has been successfully completed, or Elizabeth comes of age, we shall leave.' James stood up and walked towards Helen. 'I am also going to ask you to convince Elizabeth that it would be helpful if she would carry out my instructions without question.'

'You are asking a great deal – and giving very little in return.'

'You can choose to believe that I mean Elizabeth no harm – or not. That is entirely up to you.' James turned away, indicating that this conversation was over.

Helen was now assailed by doubts. For some reason she really wanted to give him the trust he asked for, but how could she do that? She cast Mr Edgemont a beseeching look, but he remained silent. Suddenly, a feeling of dread swept over her. Was Elizabeth about to suffer a similar fate to hers? Oh, she prayed not! 'Is the Langton estate in financial trouble?' she blurted out.

'Not as far as I can see.'

She drew in a shaky breath. That had been a silly question; of course it wasn't. Beth looked after the accounts herself and would have known if anything had been amiss.

'Was there anything else you wanted to say, Lady Helen?'

The tone of his voice told her that she was dismissed, but she was going to speak her mind before she left. 'You have asked me to trust you, Lord Sharland, but, under the circumstances, that is something I cannot do. However, I will – reluctantly – go to London with Elizabeth.'

Without giving James a chance to reply, she left the room.

She made her way up to Elizabeth's private sitting room and found her checking over menus she had arranged for the next few days. She looked up and smiled. 'Have you been out for a walk now the rain has stopped?'

'No, I've been talking to his lordship and Mr Edgemont. They know who I am.'

'That is hardly surprising. Everyone here knows you are Lady Helen Denton, though I would not have expected the staff to talk to those two men.' A look of sadness showed in her eyes. 'You are the only one who tries to pretend you are a companion.'

'Well, that is over. When Lord Sharland called me Lady Helen, it was a shock, but it served to wake me up.' She smiled at her friend. 'I am grateful for the kindness of you and your godfather, and I accept the allowance settled on me – but only until the bequest from Lord Edward comes through, and then you shall have every penny back.'

'Oh, Helen, I do not want anything from you but your friendship and support.' Beth rushed over and hugged her friend. 'I have so longed to see you cast aside the role of servant! Welcome back, my dear.'

Happy to have their relationship again on a proper footing, Beth asked, 'And did you find out anything about those two mysterious men?'

'No, I'm afraid not. His lordship would only tell me that he is here to carry out some instructions left by his father, and to take over as your guardian. He asked me to trust him . . .'

Beth pulled a face. 'And what did you say?'

'I said I could not do so unless he told me what he was really doing here. He refused, of course. However, I did agree to go to London with you, so we shall be able to support each other, for there will be a great deal of talk and speculation about both of us, I fear.' She drew in a deep breath. 'I do admit to being relieved the pretence is over.'

'I am also happy it is, Helen. At least if we are together, we might be able to endure the social round, and it will be an opportunity for you to take your proper place in society again. Did Mr Edgemont say anything?'

'Hardly a word.' Helen frowned. 'For a moment there I wanted to believe they only had your best interests at heart, for they have strong personalities, but they are both so secretive and I could not do it.'

Beth nodded. 'I think we should still be very vigilant.'

'Oh, one thing I couldn't resist.' Helen gave a quiet laugh. 'I let his lordship know we were aware that he had been the one who was chased away from the Gresham house.'

'And what did he say?'

'There was absolutely no response at all, but he didn't deny it. And you are right, Beth: we must keep a very sharp eye on their activities.'

Beth was buoyant by the time she went down to lunch. Her friend was completely over the disaster she had had to deal with when her father had committed suicide. And, together, she was sure they could overcome whatever was happening here. Helen had shown enormous strength of character as she had struggled through the crisis thrust upon her. It was a great comfort to have her by her side, and she trusted her friend's judgement. She was well aware that she was going to have to gain control of her emotions if she was to survive this next year and still have a home of her own. She would *not* allow James Sharland to gain the upper hand!

'Lady Sharland seemed in fine health,' she remarked as the first course was served.

'She is much improved, and she does enjoy a visit from you.'

'And you.'

Lord Sharland nodded. 'She loves to have callers, and so few bother with her these days.'

'Conversation can be difficult at times,' Beth remarked, 'but she is a dear lady. Do you think she would like to come and stay here for a while?'

'I have already suggested it,' his lordship informed her, 'but she will not leave her own home and the staff who care for her so lovingly.'

'That is understandable.' Beth knew she should not ask the next question, but her curiosity was such that she could not resist. 'Why did she feel you might be in danger?'

He gave a blank look. 'Did she?'

'Yes. She asked you quite clearly.' She wasn't fooled by his expression; he knew what she was referring to.

'I'm afraid she gets rather confused at times and says the strangest things. You must not pay too much attention to her ramblings.'

'She seemed in perfect control of her faculties at the time,' she told him.

'Maybe – but her question made no sense.' He laughed. 'I can assure you that I am not in any danger.'

What a shame, she thought waspishly. She immediately reprimanded herself. She had never wished anyone harm in her life and, although sorely tried, she would not start now. She did not pursue the subject further, and when she looked back on the visit, Lady Sharland had said some peculiar things. No, difficult as it was to admit it, his lordship had the right of it, she decided. It had just been an odd remark from a confused mind. However, there was another matter to be raised.

'What about the lady who is supposed to be coming to help with our season – is that also imagination?' She hoped most sincerely that it was!

'No, Lady Trenchard will be arriving soon; I have instructed the housekeeper to make rooms ready for her.'

'Trenchard? I don't believe I know the lady?'

'You have never met her. She lives in Scotland and is making the arduous journey at my request.'

'Scotland!' Beth was astounded. 'Could you not have found someone already living in London?'

'Lady Trenchard is most suitable.' He poured himself another glass of wine, ignoring Jenkins, who was hovering and looked affronted at being deprived of the task.

'I hope she isn't travelling alone?'

'The man I have engaged to start our pig farm is accompanying her.'

Her mouth turned down in disgust. This was the first she had heard about bringing in another man, and the venture had now been elevated to a pig farm. 'Does he also come from Scotland, then?'

His lordship nodded.

'But where will you house him?'

'A room in the servants' quarters will suffice for the time being. There is space on that ground to build a cottage. Work will begin on the building next week.'

'How dare you authorize such work without consulting me!' she exploded, absolutely furious.

He gave her a level stare. 'Have you forgotten that I am your legal guardian and have complete control of the estate until you come of age?'

That was true enough. Her godfather had never interfered with her management of the estate, but, in handing over his duties to his son, he had tied her hands completely. She fought to control her temper, knowing she wouldn't get anywhere by shouting at him. 'Would it be too much to ask you to discuss your plans with me?'

'As you wish. Perhaps you would like to ride out with me tomorrow and I will show you where the cottage will be built?'

'I would like that. Thank you,' she added. Then the answer to one mystery suddenly became clear. 'Have you also been living in Scotland, and that is why no one appears to know you?'

'That is correct.'

His expression was shuttered, and she knew that an explanation would not be forthcoming. He had granted her a small snippet of information, but it was all he was going to allow. She continued with her meal, deep in thought. But it was a step towards finding out who he really was. He had the speech and manners of a gentleman, without a trace of an accent, so she had assumed that the answers would have been found in London, but that was clearly not the case.

She smiled. 'It was wise of you to arrange for your man to travel with Lady Trenchard, for she might need protection from a robber during the long journey.'

He tipped his head back and laughed out loud. 'It would be the robber who would need protection if he dared to hold up Alice. No man would be permitted to take anything from her – jewels or loved ones.'

'She sounds formidable.' Beth had never seen him so animated, or with such a look of affection in his eyes. It transformed him, and she could feel herself warming to him for the first time since his unexpected arrival. But she quickly banished the feeling. It would be foolish to drop her guard.

He flicked open his pocket watch and rose to his feet. 'If they have not been delayed, the coach should be arriving within the hour.'

The next two hours seemed interminable, for Beth was not pleased about having this unknown lady descend upon her, and she hoped he was not going to fill the house with his acquaintances.

At last a carriage pulled up at the door, and she hurried out to greet her guest. She had determined not to like Lady Trenchard, but she took to her immediately. She was tall, elegant and stately in her deportment, more than fifty years old, with deep chestnut hair, liberally sprinkled with silver, and vivid blue eyes. Beth caught her breath; she must have been quite a beauty in her day.

'You must be Elizabeth.'

Beth felt as if she had been thoroughly assessed in one brief, penetrating glance.

'You are right, James,' Lady Trenchard said to the man standing beside her. 'She is indeed very beautiful.'

Beth gave him a startled, disbelieving look, but his expression was well schooled, except for a slight movement at the corners of his mouth.

'Now, Elizabeth –' she paused – 'or do you prefer to be called Beth?'

'Beth, please.' She was quite overcome with the lady's strong personality and would not normally have given a stranger such liberty – lady or not!

'Beth. That suits you.' She took her arm. 'You may call me Alice. Now, show me to my room, for I am feeling quite fatigued after that dreary journey.'

She did not look at all weary, Beth thought as she led her into the house. The lady was alive with energy.

When they reached the stairs, Beth stopped. 'Oh, your lordship, where is your man you said was travelling with Lady Trenchard?'

'Jenkins took him to the back entrance and into the servants' wing.'

She did not miss the look of amusement that passed between Lady Trenchard and his lordship. They were clearly finding it very difficult not to burst into laughter. What was so amusing about a hired hand being taken to the servants' entrance? She could not fathom it.

After seeing her guest comfortably installed, Beth left her to rest and went to the kitchen. Jenkins and her estate manager, Greenway, were waiting for her.

'Have you settled his lordship's man?' she asked.

'Er . . . yes.' Greenway looked rather bewildered.

'What is it?' she demanded, sensing an atmosphere. 'What is wrong with him?'

'Well, he is no more than a boy,' Greenway told her.

'Oh, no,' Jenkins interrupted, 'he must be around twenty-five, but certainly no more than that.'

Beth was puzzled. 'That is rather a tender age to be an expert pig farmer, is it not?'

'That's what I thought.' Her manager held a chair for her to sit down. 'But I've had a talk with him and there's no doubt he knows the animals.'

'Well, that is something, I suppose. As long as he is competent, his age matters little.' She sampled one of cook's tarts and nodded approval.

'There's something else odd.' Jenkins tapped his fingers on the table, deep in thought.

'What is it?' she prompted.

'I might be wrong, but I would swear that he is a gentleman wearing a working man's clothes.'

'What is his name?'

'George Riley,' Jenkins informed her, 'but I don't think that's his real name. I haven't any proof of that,' he added hastily, 'but something about him doesn't seem right.'

'Oh, not another mystery man!' she exclaimed, shaking her head in dismay. 'Well, keep an eye on him, and let me know if you think he is not up to the job.'

It was half an hour before dinner, and Beth decided to meet this pig man.

He was in the kitchen when she entered. He leapt to his feet and bowed, keeping his eyes lowered.

'You must be Riley?'

He nodded, still keeping his eyes hooded, which she found annoying. She liked people to look her straight in the eyes.

'Look at me!' she demanded. Her estate manager had been right; this tall, elegant young man was no farm worker.

He lifted his head and she gasped when she saw the pale grey eyes looking at her. She turned and stormed out of the kitchen and into the drawing room.

'Do you consider me lacking in wits?' Beth demanded, hands on hips in fury.

His lordship put his glass down on the drinks table. 'No.'

'I am pleased to hear it.' She turned on Lady Trenchard. 'Madam, I do not take kindly to being deceived in my own home.'

'What is it, Beth?' She reached out, but dropped her hand when Beth moved back.

'Do not pretend innocence! Dishonesty is the one thing I will not tolerate.'

'We are quite at a loss to know what you are talking about.' James frowned. 'What has sent you into such a fury?'

'Shall we invite your relative to join us for dinner?' she demanded, nearly shedding tears of rage.

'Ah.'

'Is that all you have to say for yourself? I demand to know what is going on!'

'I'm sorry, James.' A quiet voice spoke from the doorway. 'She recognized me at once. We are too alike.'

Beth spun round and glared at the young man. 'Come in, Mr Sharland – or whatever your name is.'

'Alex Beaufort,' he told her in that same quiet tone. 'I am James's cousin.'

'I don't doubt that you are related to each other, for I could not mistake the unusual colour of your eyes, but I think you are both masquerading under false identities, and I am deeply hurt at being used in this manner.'

'We mean you no harm,' the young man assured her.

'Don't try to talk with her, Alex.' James came and stood beside his cousin. 'She is too angry to listen.'

'And is that surprising?' Her foot was tapping with impatience on the carpet. 'I demand an explanation for this ridiculous subterfuge.'

'My dear —' Lady Trenchard stepped forward — 'please don't upset yourself. It can all be explained.'

'We will tell her nothing!' James snapped.

Beth was now beyond all reasoning. 'You will all leave my house this instant, or I shall have you removed by force.'

'You will do no such thing.' His lordship came menacingly to within a few inches of her. 'I am still your legal guardian.'

'Please, Miss Langton—'

She did not allow the young man to say anything else. 'Take your cousin and this lady, and leave now!'

'We cannot do that.' James was clearly at the end of his patience.

'We shall see about that!' She turned towards the door, but he caught her arm in a fierce grip.

'I have almost a year and can do a lot of damage in that time,' he warned. 'If you reveal this to anyone outside of this room, then I shall cast you into penury.'

'Oh, James!' Lady Trenchard whispered in distress.

The threat terrified Beth, for she knew he meant it. No matter how angry she was, she mustn't do anything to jeopardize the estate. 'I see I have little choice in the matter. I do not indulge in tittle-tattle, sir, and you can be assured that I shall not utter one word of this to anyone, and neither will Helen.'

Beth shook her arm free of his grip and turned to her friend. 'Come, Helen, we shall dine in my room and leave these people to their devious intrigues.'

Eleven

There was a knock on Beth's door, and Helen opened it.

'Would you ask Elizabeth if she would allow me to talk with her?'

'Let Lady Trenchard in,' Beth told her friend. She had slept little during the night, for her mind would not cease racing as she tried to make some sense of what was happening – but to no avail. The fact that he was filling her house with his family and friends was alarming. She felt under siege in her own home.

She rose when the lady entered and indicated a chair for her to sit in.

'Thank you. It is gracious of you to see me.'

Beth said nothing, noting that Lady Trenchard did not appear to have slept soundly, either.

'I have come to beg your forgiveness for our deception. I was not in agreement with this course of action, but my . . . James would not be swayed, and I could not allow Alex to make the long journey from Scotland on his own.'

Beth still said nothing. She was deeply hurt by their conduct.

'Ah, this is very difficult.' Lady Trenchard was clearly distressed.

'It can all be cleared up,' Beth said. 'All you have to do is tell me why this subterfuge has been necessary.'

'I cannot!'

'There does appear to be a rather tangled family history. Can you at least explain that to us?'

When the lady shook her head, Beth stood up and said briskly, 'Then there is nothing further to discuss.'

'Oh, please, my dear, don't dismiss me.'

'What else can I do, Lady Trenchard?' She sat down again, disturbed to see this normally composed woman so overset.

'I am pleading with you to trust James.'

'How can I do that? He has done nothing but lie to me from the moment he arrived. And I have grave doubts that he is really my guardian.' Beth gave a weary sigh. 'But how do I prove it?'

Lady Trenchard shook her head. 'He told you the truth about that. He is Edward Sharland's legal heir.'

'So everyone believes. And that is why I feel so helpless. He is a hard man and will, no doubt, carry out his threat to ruin me if I disobey him. I am at a loss to understand why I have been dragged into his devious scheme. I cannot believe this is what my godfather intended. He would never have placed me in this dreadful position. He wouldn't . . .' Beth's voice broke slightly with distress.

'I am so sorry it has come to this.' The lady studied Beth intently. 'But you are wise to be cautious, for he will carry through his plan, regardless of whom he has to hurt along the way.'

'And what is his plan?' Beth prompted, hoping she could still tempt her to reveal something.

'I am not privy to that information. Only he can tell you that,' she replied.

Beth gave an impatient wave of her hand. 'But he will not.'

'No.'

'Then we are at an impasse. It seems I have no choice but to await my twenty-first birthday and hope this fiend leaves me something to inherit.'

Lady Trenchard visibly flinched at the word 'fiend'. 'He has good reason for his conduct. My boys' lives have been blighted—'

'They are your sons?' Beth was astounded, for they looked nothing like her.

'I did not bear them, but I consider them my sons.' She stopped and tried to compose herself. 'May I have a glass of wine?'

Helen poured one after a nod from Beth and handed it to Lady Trenchard, then returned to her seat in the corner of the room.

'James was ten and Alex but a babe of two years when they came to me.' The hand holding the glass shook. 'Alex was too young to understand or miss the parents he had lost, but James knew, and the anger has been simmering in him until he has grown into a hard man.' She gave Beth a pleading look. 'He is not a bad man, but he will have justice done or die in the attempt. Nothing else matters to him. Alex is a gentle, loving boy, and I'm sure that, somewhere inside, James is the same, but I fear it is too deeply buried now.'

This was not the story Beth had expected to hear. It sounded as if he had suffered a terrible wrong. Doubts began to assail her – until she remembered the way he was treating her. Whatever he had come here to do, it was not right of him to threaten her. That could not be excused!

'They both have vast personal fortunes, but James refuses to marry until this has been cleared up, and Alex will do anything he can to help James. They are more like brothers, you see; in fact, that is how they think of each other.'

Lady Trenchard stood up with an exclamation of distress. 'I have said more than is prudent, but I do so want you to make allowances for his conduct.'

'Don't distress yourself.' Beth stood up, suddenly feeling very sorry for this woman who was so desperate to defend her boys, as she called them. What dark secret did their background hold? Even more perplexing was the obvious fact that her godfather was involved. 'Nothing will go beyond this room, but, in truth, you have not told us anything of import.'

The lady gave a weak smile. 'Will you make your peace with James?'

'I doubt that will be possible with his threat hanging over me, but I shall talk with him.'

James was in the study with Alex when she entered. The two men rose to their feet.

Beth did not waste any time. 'Lady Trenchard has begged me to make my peace with you, but I fear that will not be possible. However, she has tried to ease my fears.'

'And has she succeeded?' he asked, studying her through narrowed eyes.

'No. I cannot trust you. For some reason you are using your guardianship and this house for a purpose of your own, but I would ask you to remember that I am an innocent pawn caught up in your intrigue.'

Alex stepped forward. 'My brother means you no harm, Miss Langton.'

She gazed at the presentable boy as he referred to James as his brother, for it was clear that was how he considered their relationship. Alex's mouth turned up at the corners as if he was used to smiling, and the eyes, although the same colour as his cousin's, held warmth that was sadly lacking in the other man's grim expression.

'I fear he does.' Beth turned her attention back to James. 'It would ease my mind if you would explain what you are doing.'

'You do not need to know,' he snapped.

'In that you are wrong. If you carry out your threat to ruin me, then it is very much my concern, and the concern of everyone who depends upon the Langton estate for a living.'

'Miss Langton!' Alex exclaimed, stepping towards her again. 'My brother would not do such a heartless thing.'

'Yes, I would,' James snapped. 'I will crush anyone who stands in my way.'

'Oh, James,' Lady Trenchard sighed as she entered the room, 'there is no need for this. Elizabeth can be trusted, I am sure of it.'

'You know I trust no one in this matter, Alice, not even you. I will clear this up, no matter what the cost to anyone.'

'I believe you are a heartless man,' Beth told him, 'but we must try to behave in a polite manner towards each other, else it will soon be commented upon.'

'I agree. I don't want any gossip to bring attention to this house.' He gave her a studied look. 'Is that understood?'

'Perfectly.' She started to walk out of the room but stopped. The man was a beast and she did not see why she should dissemble any longer: she would speak her mind.

'In future, if you wish to creep out in the middle of the night, it would be more convenient for you to keep my father's pistols in your room, and then you will not have to sneak about like a thief.' She took a steadying breath and, with a flourish, turned and swept out of the room.

Waiting patiently outside the door and having heard the conversation, Helen gave a smile of approval to her friend. Beth's mouth was set in a straight line. 'I do declare that I enjoyed giving him that set-down. He is not going to have everything his own way, and he will soon learn that I am not some empty-headed female who will crumble before his forceful presence.'

Helen fell in beside her friend as she headed for the kitchen at full speed. 'I am sure he knows that already, for you have always shown a strong will, Beth.'

'Indeed I have.' She stopped so suddenly that Helen collided with her.

'Oh, I do beg your pardon . . .'

She caught Helen to steady her, a deep frown furrowing her brow. 'Father always said I was more like a son to him than a daughter. Do you consider me mannish?'

Helen gave a gurgle of laughter. 'No, you are beautiful and, with your delicate colouring, you are very feminine, but there is great strength within you. That is what your father meant, and that is why he was content to leave the estate in your hands.'

'I do hope you are right, but I pray that I have the same inner strength and courageous character to weather this storm as you did when your life collapsed around you. I am very frightened, Helen.'

'Of course you are.' Helen slipped her hand through Beth's arm, giving it an encouraging squeeze. 'We shall face this together. I do feel more at ease now Lady Trenchard is here, though, and I have the impression that she will try to curb his lordship from harming the estate. And she is very elegant. It could be fun choosing clothes with her guiding hand. We do both need a new wardrobe, and his lordship said he is going to pay.'

'Hmm.' Beth became thoughtful. 'Do you think his lordship was right about me wearing pastel shades?'

'Yes, you would look most fetching in them, though you have never cared much for fashion.'

'That is true.' Beth continued down the passage, a puzzled frown on her face. Why was she fussing about which colours would suit her best? It had never been a thing of importance to her, and it was all due to this foolish talk about her having a season. She would not give it another thought!

When they reached the kitchen, they found Jenkins, Greenway and the footman sampling some of Cook's tarts.

'Ah, good, you are all here.'

The men scrambled to their feet.

'Stanley, when you have been acting as valet to his lordship, does he talk to you?'

'No, Miss Langton, never says a word.'

'As I expected.'

'We haven't been able to find the smallest piece of gossip

about him, or Mr Edgemont,' Jenkins informed her, with obvious regret.

'Well, I have managed to glean one piece of information. His lordship is from Scotland, and that is why no one has seen him before.'

'Ah.' Greenway nodded. 'Then we are wasting our time.'

'Exactly, and I now want you to forget our plan to unearth his identity.' She picked up two tarts, handed one to Helen and proceeded to eat the other.

The men waited patiently for her to finish.

'The only thing we can do now is see that he does not harm the estate.' She smiled, hoping she appeared relaxed and at ease. 'In less than a year I shall have reached my twenty-first birthday, and then we shall be rid of him.'

'We will be vigilant until then, Miss Langton,' Greenway assured her.

'Thank you.' She went to walk out but stopped and looked at everyone in turn, making sure she had their full attention. 'I don't want his lordship to be discussed outside of this house. If anyone asks questions, you are to tell them that he is a fine man and is taking his duties as my guardian seriously. We will deal with this crisis ourselves, and as quietly as possible.'

Dinner that evening was a strained affair, although Beth did her best to lighten the atmosphere. From now on she was going to be pleasant to his lordship and Lady Trenchard. She could not help liking her, for she was a truly pleasant lady.

'Alice, I want you to take Elizabeth and Helen to London and get them both a decent wardrobe. You may leave in the morning.'

Beth's good intentions vanished. 'I don't need new clothes yet!'

He scrutinized her dress carefully, gave a delicate shudder and then raised an eyebrow. 'Really? I would consider it a matter of urgency. And you will need something suitable for your neighbour's masked ball, surely?'

'Did you not teach him manners, Lady Trenchard?' she asked sharply, not prepared to admit that she had forgotten all about the function.

'I fear he was not a boy one could mould easily.' Her mouth

twitched at the corners. 'I did try, but he has always had his own views of what is right and wrong.'

Beth shook her head in mock despair. 'It would appear that he has got the two confused.'

'No, James has a very clear understanding of what is right.'

'When you ladies have finished discussing me, perhaps we can see to the arrangements for your journey?'

Beth had expected him to be angry, but he appeared to be amused, and the cold eyes had a gleam of warmth about them, which she found disconcerting. And when Daniel Edgemont gave her a sly wink, she nearly spilled her wine. He was a man of few words, and she liked that about him, but she had no doubt that there was a sharp mind at work, never missing a detail.

'How long is this tiresome business going to take?' she asked, resigned to a trip to London. A few days away would not be too bad, and Helen was looking quite excited at the prospect.

'No more than two weeks.'

'I am not staying away from the estate for that long!' Beth cast a quick look around the room to make sure that no servants were present. 'I think we can forget this charade about me having a season, don't you?'

'It isn't a charade,' he told her, his eyes icing over again. 'I intend to see that you are not denied what every other young lady of breeding expects. My father should have seen to it before now.'

He sounded as if he cared – but, no, one look at his expression and she knew she had been mistaken.

'You will go with Alice and may return as soon as you have purchased a suitable wardrobe of fashionable clothes.'

Beth felt this was a concession, so she nodded. She would have the task finished in a few days!

'No more!' Beth exclaimed in alarm, as Lady Trenchard and Helen were trying to make her get ready for another shopping trip. 'I am never going to wear all these gowns.'

'It is no use you fussing, Beth. James has given me strict instructions on what you are to have, and I dare not return with only a few paltry dresses.'

'I don't consider fifteen outfits to be a paltry wardrobe!' Beth exploded. 'And what about all the accessories? We cannot move in here for boxes, and they keep arriving.'

'They are necessary, my dear, for both of you had very little,' Alice reminded her gently.

'I know. Father was always urging me to buy more, but it never seemed necessary, for we lived very quietly.' She gazed anxiously at the piles of boxes and parcels. 'This is costing a deal of money.'

'We have not spent half the allowance James gave me.'

Beth's mouth dropped open in astonishment. 'But we have purchased a new wardrobe for Helen, enough clothes for me to fill two dressing rooms, and you have also had gowns made!'

'Mere trifles, Beth.'

'They may be mere trifles to you, Lady Trenchard,' Helen said, shaking her head in dismay, 'but I refuse to let you buy me any more. I cannot hope to repay Lord Sharland for this expense. And I do not like being in his debt like this.'

'You must not feel like that, Helen. James left me strict instructions that you were both to be dressed in the highest fashion, and he has made enough money available to do just that. He expects nothing in return.'

'I don't understand why he is doing this.' Beth sat down and stared at Lady Trenchard. 'One moment he is threatening to ruin me, and the next he is spending a great deal of his own money to see us dressed in the height of fashion. I declare that I am becoming quite confused.'

'He is a complex man and therefore difficult to understand.' The lady sat opposite Beth and gave a gentle smile. 'He has been shocked to see such a beautiful and spirited girl locked into the task of running the estate and catering to the whims of two selfish men—'

'But it wasn't like that,' she protested. 'I am happy living as I do.'

'My dear, you must let me have my say. James abhors injustice of any kind and feels that neither you nor Helen has been given the opportunities other young girls expect. As your guardian, he considers it his duty to put the matter right.'

'But his conduct towards me is inexplicable. He insists that I have a season, and in the next breath he is threatening to cast me into penury.' Beth gave a helpless shrug.

'I know.' Lady Trenchard's expression clouded. 'But my James has a mission to carry out which means more to him than life itself, and if anyone stands in his way, he will show no mercy. Even to you, Elizabeth.'

'You know what the mystery is?' Beth asked hopefully.

'I am not able to give you that information, my dear, but I do know it is very important.' Then Alice smiled and stood up. 'We have one more purchase to make.'

The thought of just one last visit to the dressmaker heartened Beth. 'Very well, but I cannot think what else we need.'

'Why, have you forgotten Sir Peter Gresham's masked ball?'

'Ah, yes,' she chuckled, unable to contain her amusement. 'His lordship said I should go all in black.'

Lady Trenchard threw her hands up in horror. 'No, my dear, we shall see you have something quite splendid. And then we shall take a turn around the park, for it is a lovely day.'

It appeared as if most of London was intent on enjoying the fine weather. The carriage drew to a halt and Alice turned to Beth. 'There is a gentleman coming towards us. Do you know who he is?'

'That is Sir Peter Gresham.' She did not have time to explain further as he cantered up, dismounted and bowed.

'What a pleasant surprise, Miss Langton.' His eyes narrowed when he saw Alice and Helen, but he nodded politely and turned his attention back to Beth. 'We do not often see you in town.'

'We are on a shopping trip.' She smiled sweetly – or at least she hoped she did, for she could not abide this man. 'May I introduce Lady Trenchard?'

He bowed again. 'I don't believe I have had the pleasure of meeting you before?'

'No, my estates are in Scotland, and I don't often venture into this part of the country, but my niece is to have her season at last, and I have come to make the arrangements.'

This declaration jolted Beth. Why was she telling him a lie?

'Ah, I see the reason for the shopping. When will you be returning to Hampshire?'

'Tomorrow,' Lady Trenchard said, before Beth could utter a word.

'This is most fortuitous,' Sir Peter declared. 'I too am travelling on the morrow. Would you do me the honour of joining me in my carriage?'

'We have already arranged to go by train,' Beth declared, not wanting to spend such a long journey with him.

'But as you have been on a shopping expedition, you must have a great deal of luggage. I have ample room for any purchases.' He smiled encouragingly.

'Then that would save us having our purchases delivered to Hampshire. We would be happy to accept your kind invitation.' Lady Trenchard looked pleased. 'We are residing at the Sharland house.'

'Then I shall send a carriage for you at nine o'clock tomorrow morning.' He raised an eyebrow. 'I trust that is not too early for you?'

'Indeed not; we shall be ready.' Alice watched him ride away, and her expression changed from polite gratitude to one of distaste. 'So, that is Sir Peter Gresham.'

'Why did you tell him I was your niece?' Beth asked.

'Oh, it just came out, and it was the easiest way to explain my presence here.' She sat back with a satisfied sigh. 'We shall have a more comfortable journey home, anyway.'

'How much longer do we have to wait for him to finish luncheon?' Beth paced up and down outside the inn.

'But it has been a pleasant journey,' Helen hastened to assure her.

'And a long one!'

Alice came out of the hostelry and joined them.

'We have languished here for more than two hours.' Beth was at the end of her patience. 'And that is far too long.'

'I agree, my dear. I have given instructions for the carriage to be made ready, and I have told Sir Peter that we are ready to resume our journey,' she informed them. 'We shall allow him another thirty minutes and that is all.'

No more than ten minutes passed before the gentleman appeared, rather unsteady on his feet. The ladies were helped into the coach, and they were on their way at last.

There was still an hour's journey ahead of them when there

was a commotion and the carriage shuddered to a halt. The door was wrenched open and they were looking at a pistol.

'Out!' the highwayman ordered in a gruff voice.

They were all herded together, and another man rode from out of the trees, also brandishing a pistol.

Beth was mesmerized by the pistols, but not because of fear. Slowly, she lifted her eyes to the robber who had half of his face covered with a scarf and a black hat pulled down on his forehead. She turned her head to look at the other man and saw the same thing, but these eyes were sparkling with devilment, and he even had the nerve to wink at her. Beth stifled an angry sound. How dare they do this, and with her father's pistols!

Helen was clutching her arm but appeared unafraid; she had obviously recognized them as well. And so had Alice, who was clearly angry.

The shock had sobered Sir Peter up, but he looked terrified. 'We are not carrying anything of value. The ladies have been shopping in town and that is all we carry.'

The taller of the highwaymen gave him a contemptuous glance and then proceeded to make a thorough search of the carriage, tossing all the parcels on to the road. When nothing was found, he turned his attention to the ladies and ordered them to hand over their jewels.

Beth watched carefully to see exactly what they did. The highwayman she knew to be James Sharland took nothing from the driver or Sir Peter, although his gold pocket watch was clearly visible, but he demanded every piece of jewellery they were wearing. Helen removed a small pendant from around her neck. It was the only possession she had managed to save after her father's suicide, and it meant the world to her. James clasped her hands as he took it from her and then stepped back.

He pocketed the jewels and, with a nod to his companion, they rode away.

While they waited for the carriage to be reloaded, Helen opened her hand slightly to show Beth she still had the pendant. That was the first kind gesture she had seen from James Sharland since his arrival in her life, and it made her realize even more what a complex character he was. But she was pleased for her friend who had a hint of tears in her eyes, because it would have hurt her terribly to be parted from that treasured possession, even for a short time.

'Highwaymen!' Peter Gresham was ranting. 'You never have those rascals around now! Was this some prank?'

Alice had finished overseeing the loading of the carriage and came over to Beth, whispering in her ear, 'When I get my hands on those men, I swear I shall do violence!'

Twelve

There had been no sign of the men for the rest of that day, and as Beth was about to enter the breakfast room the next morning, she heard Alice's raised voice.

'You promised me that Alex would be here just to set up the pig farm – and you involve him in that madcap scheme! What do you think you were doing, playing at highwaymen like you did as children?'

A deep voice said something Beth couldn't hear.

'I'm sure you wouldn't have done it if you had known we were on the coach, but I am not interested in your excuses, James. I am disappointed in you. And what in heaven's name were you doing? What can you possibly gain by harassing the man in this way? You don't even know if he is the culprit. Edward couldn't prove it in nearly thirty years, so what hope have you? And I'm disappointed with you, Daniel. You are supposed to be keeping them out of trouble! Where on earth were you?'

There was another murmured answer.

Beth knew she shouldn't be listening to someone else's conversation, but she was consumed with curiosity after yesterday's hold-up. It was clear to her now that his lordship was after Sir Peter Gresham for some wrongdoing in the past, but what could it be? Was it something that could send James Sharland to prison, or even worse? But no, that couldn't be right because he was carrying out instructions left by his father, so it must concern the Sharland family. She chewed her lip, trying to sort out the confusing jumble in her mind. But if that was the case, then why had he moved in here and involved them in the dark secrets of his family?

Beth moved closer to the door, quite forgetting that she had been brought up a lady.

Then his lordship raised his voice. 'Dan is sure he is the one we're looking for, and I will find the proof we need, for all our sakes.'

'James –' the tone was softer now, almost pleading – 'you and Alex have me, and everything I own is yours. As soon as your father found out what had happened, he made sure everything was put to rights legally. Is that not enough?'

'Alice, we owe you a great debt of gratitude and I don't like to hurt you, but I must do this. I made a promise.'

Alice was obviously crying by now. 'I could not love you and Alex more if you were my own blood, but if you persist in this, you will be unmasked, and I shall lose you to the gallows. You will also ruin Alex . . . Edward had no right to place this burden upon you!'

When Helen joined her at the door, Beth put a finger to her lips and then led her out of the house.

'We shall have to forgo breakfast this morning,' she told her companion.

Helen nodded. 'Lady Trenchard sounded angry.'

'Yes, but I believe fear was the cause of her fury. They are harbouring some dark secret, and Alice is quite desperate for their safety.'

'What do you think it is all about, Beth?'

Beth sighed. 'I wish I knew, but the more I learn, the more I am fearful for the Langton estate and our future. My mind is in a whirl with speculation, but whatever his lordship is involved in, we cannot hope to remain untarnished by his activities.'

'He is treating you ill,' Helen declared.

'I agree, but if he is not paying heed to Alice, then I fear we shall be of little consequence to him.'

Beth cantered up to the estate manager, stopped and dismounted.

'Welcome home, Miss Langton.'

'Thank you, Greenway. How are things with the estate?'

'Everything is running smoothly. His lordship has made small changes – and all for the better, as far as I can see.'

'Really?' She was taken aback by the tone of respect in his voice.

'Yes, Miss Langton.' He hesitated for a moment, looking a little uneasy. 'I think we might have misjudged him.'

'In what way?'

'Well, he clearly knows how to run a large estate and appears genuinely concerned that it should show a profit. And Mr Beaufort, although young, is quite an expert on pigs, and farming in general.'

Beth silently cursed the two weeks she had been away. His lordship had clearly used this time to gain the respect of Greenway. 'That may well be so, but I want you to remain vigilant. I am still uncertain of his motives; it may well suit his purpose to appear the dedicated guardian for a while.'

'Of course, Miss Langton. You can rely on me.'

She nodded, knowing that she had planted a seed of doubt again. She would have to be satisfied with that for the moment. 'Have the pigs arrived?'

'They are due any time now. All is in readiness and the cottage is finished.'

'In that case, I had better have a look at it before the beasts arrive.'

It was an invigorating ride, and she grinned at Helen as they galloped along. It did not seem as if any great harm had been done in her absence. She was relieved.

'How wonderful to be back,' she called. 'I did so hate London.'

Helen smiled in agreement.

When they arrived at the field, the transformation was astounding; Beth hardly recognized it. 'My goodness, what a change!'

'And look at the fine cottage, Beth.'

They both dismounted and walked over to it.

'Indeed, a splendid building.' Beth tried the door, but it was locked, so she turned her attention to the field.

'What are those huts for?' Helen asked.

'I am not sure, but they might be for the animals to breed in, I suppose. I am afraid I am not familiar with the methods of pig farming, but I am pleased to see that they have constructed a secure fence all round to stop the beasts from roaming the estate.'

She left Helen peering through one of the cottage windows, trying to glimpse the inside, and walked into the field. As she approached the copse of trees by the stream, there was a rustling sound followed by a grunt. Beth watched in horror as an enormous pig appeared and glared at her with a belligerent gleam in its eyes.

With a screech of panic, she lifted her skirts and ran, but she had not gone far when she collided with something solid and had the breath knocked out of her.

'Easy, Elizabeth.' Strong arms wrapped around her. 'You are not in any danger.'

It wasn't the slightest good anyone telling her that, so she fought until she was able to get him between her and the pig. He was shaking with laughter as she clung to his broad back for safety.

'You may find this amusing, but that beast was about to attack me.'

'I doubt he would have,' said another voice. 'He arrived in the early hours of this morning and is just a mite fractious after his journey. He is wondering where his sows are.'

Beth peered round his lordship's shoulder and saw Alex herding the beast into one of the pens, helped by Charlie Becks, young Tom's friend. 'Greenway said the pigs hadn't arrived yet.'

'He wasn't around when Alex unloaded the animal. Oh, and we have employed young Charlie to help. He's a bright boy, and Alex wants to train him in all aspects of pig farming. We hope you approve?'

'Oh, yes, an excellent idea.' Beth could see the pleasure on the youngster's face. He was laughing as Alex talked to him, and it looked as if it was going to be a perfect arrangement.

'There you are,' Alex told her, still grinning broadly as he came over to them. 'You can leave the field in safety now.'

'Oh, good. Can I run?'

The brothers nodded and roared with laughter as she rushed out and shut the gate behind her.

She gave them a curious look as they strolled out of the field and joined her. 'You both seem in remarkable spirits after your escapade yesterday.'

'We do apologize if we frightened you,' Alex said.

'Oh, you didn't frighten me. I recognized the pistols at once and knew who the villains were.' She glared at James. 'I trust we are to be given our jewels back, or have you disposed of them already?'

'They are with Alice,' he informed her. 'It would have looked suspicious if we hadn't taken them. And I must thank you for not revealing our identities.'

'I only refrained from doing that because Lady Trenchard was with us. She was clearly beside herself with anger, and I did not wish to distress her further.'

James grimaced. 'I received the full force of her disapproval this morning.'

'And rightly deserved!' Beth exclaimed. 'Just what on earth do you think you are doing?'

'We are just trying to make Gresham feel besieged. And you gave *us* a fright,' Alex told her, grinning in amusement. 'We didn't expect you to be travelling with Gresham, and when we saw Alice there, I knew we were going to be in trouble.'

'You will be in a great deal more trouble if anyone finds out it was you. Sir Peter Gresham is an unpleasant man and he will already be trying to discover who the highwaymen are.'

'We are well aware of how powerful Gresham is.' His lordship spoke with bitterness; his earlier good humour had completely disappeared.

Beth looked from one man to the other. So it *was* something to do with the Gresham family, and that is why his lordship had avoided meeting him when he had called. Did they know each other? She was gleaning small pieces of information, but it was only making her more desperate to find out the true story. 'I perceive that you are playing a dangerous game, Lord Sharland.'

'It is not a game!' He spoke with menace.

'No, and I suspect that you do not care whom you hurt whilst carrying out your dastardly scheme.'

'I have already told you that I will not allow anyone to stand in my way. I made a solemn promise to my father, and I will keep that promise, no matter what I have to do.'

'Will you care for the casualties you leave in your wake?' Beth asked.

'No!'

She mounted, turned her horse and cantered away, tears clouding her eyes. During the last few weeks she had become fond of Alice, Alex was a likeable boy, and Daniel Edgemont had an aura of quiet strength about him. Even his lordship was an impressive man, and if he had not been so ruthless . . . She gave a mental shrug. It was useless trying to analyze her feelings towards him, for he was clearly a danger to her and everything she held dear.

★   ★   ★

'Helen, I want you to leave here.'

Beth's friend clutched the dress she was holding close to her body, and the colour drained from her face. 'I can't leave you!'

'It is for the best.'

'But what have I done to anger you?' Helen gasped.

'Nothing.' Beth made her sit down. 'I am concerned for your safety. I don't like what is going on here. It clearly involves Sir Peter, and I believe him to be a dangerous man.'

'Then you must come away as well.'

'No, I cannot abandon the estate and its workers.'

'I shall not leave you!' Helen stood up and straightened her shoulders. 'I know you are only trying to protect me from any scandal, but whatever is going on, we can face it together. We have been friends since childhood. You stood by me when Father killed himself, and now it is my turn to do the same for you.'

Beth smiled affectionately at Helen. 'I remember the time when you kept that fierce dog from reaching me and got bitten yourself.'

'We were nine years old, and I would do the same now.'

'I know, but I would be more at ease if I knew you were away from here.' Beth removed the dress from Helen's fierce grip and smoothed out the creases. 'You have suffered enough of late, Helen, and for that reason I shall find you somewhere pleasant to stay until this wretched business is over.'

Helen shook her head. 'I will *not* leave you.'

Beth sighed but knew it was useless to argue further. Helen's stubborn streak surfaced rarely; when it did, nothing would turn her. 'Very well, you may stay. To be truthful, I should be very frightened without you here.'

The smile of relief was dazzling. 'We shall do well enough, and your fears may be unfounded. His lordship has kept his dubious activities away from the estate so far.'

'I agree, but I have a premonition that it will not remain so.'

'Whatever happens, we shall face it together, Beth.'

'Of course we shall.' Beth tried to shake off her anxieties; she was letting her imagination run away with her. 'I admit that I do like Alice and Alex, and Daniel appears to be dependable, but we would be wise not to trust anyone.'

'They are very pleasant,' Helen agreed, 'but they are all

embroiled in his lordship's schemes and should be treated with caution.'

Beth smiled. 'How very sensible you are, and I am glad you refused to leave, for I should have missed you quite dreadfully, but I felt I should give you the opportunity to leave if you so wished.'

'Well, I do not wish! Nothing would have made me go,' Helen declared stoutly. 'I survived one scandal, and if another one should come upon us, then we shall weather that storm as well.'

There was a knock on the door and Helen opened it to reveal Jenkins.

'Sir Peter Gresham has called, Miss Langton.'

'Oh dear. Quickly, Helen, help me change.'

'Shall I tell him you will be down shortly?' the butler asked.

'Yes. Where is his lordship?' she wanted to know.

'Disappeared as soon as the gentleman arrived.' Jenkins smiled grimly. 'Just as before.'

'What about Lady Trenchard?'

'She is also unavailable,' he told her. He bowed and went back down the stairs.

Beth muttered in irritation. 'So they leave me to face him. I do believe they are cowards.'

Fifteen minutes later Beth and Helen entered the drawing room.

'I apologize for keeping you waiting, Sir Peter.'

'That is quite all right.' He smiled and watched while they sat down. 'My call was unexpected, but I was concerned after that scandalous business yesterday. I trust you are quite recovered?'

'Yes, thank you, sir; we are over our fright. Would you partake of some refreshment?'

He shook his head. 'Alas, I cannot stay. Is Lord Sharland at home?'

'I am afraid you have just missed him again.' She did not like the look of Sir Peter; he appeared rather agitated.

'Your guardian is elusive.'

'He has much to do at the moment.' She smiled in apology.

'And Lady Trenchard – is she also busy?'

'She is resting,' Beth lied, not caring for the derisive tone in his voice. 'The hold-up has unsettled her.'

His expression turned thunderous. 'I shall find out who those villains were; you can be sure of that. I already have my best men tracking them down.'

Beth's insides lurched, knowing that, if found, they would be traced to this house, but she managed to contain her panic. 'I expect they are well out of the district by now.'

'That will not save them! The country will be scoured for them. They cannot escape.' He slapped the whip he was carrying against his leg.

'Everyone will be relieved to see them apprehended.' How she managed to say that, she did not know. Her greatest fear now was that they would be caught and she would be accused of harbouring criminals. At that moment she hated James for placing them in such danger. 'Now the railways are so popular, I thought the days of highwaymen were long past.'

Sir Peter nodded and stood up. 'One would have thought so! I must leave now that I know you are all right. Our masked ball is next week; I trust we shall have the pleasure of your company?'

'We are looking forward to the occasion.'

'Perhaps we will be able to meet Lord Sharland at last.' Without waiting for an answer, he walked out of the room.

Beth let out a pent-up breath and sat down. 'He is becoming suspicious, I am sure of it. Let us hope he doesn't track down the highwaymen. If he does, then we shall be in dire straits.'

'There is one way to protect yourself,' Helen said gently.

'I know. I should go to the authorities and have them arrested.'

'But you will not!' His lordship strode into the room.

She was bristling with anger at his demanding tone. 'How do you know I will continue to protect you?'

He poured himself a drink, sat down and gave her a smile that did not reach his eyes. 'Because you cannot decide if I am really a criminal.'

'That is a preposterous notion!' she declared. 'There is no doubt in my mind that you are. I have seen you with my own eyes.'

'Ah, but have I harmed anyone or stolen anything?' He raised a brow in query.

She frowned at this statement. If he was involved in the burglaries at Sir Peter's homes and the highway hold-up, then it was true that he had not taken anything.

'Well?' he asked when she didn't answer.

'Now that I think about it, what you claim appears to be the case, but you have still acted unlawfully.'

He dipped his head in acknowledgement. 'But the law is not always right, my dear Elizabeth.'

She did not understand his answer, but the last three words made her glower at him. 'I am not *your dear Elizabeth*.'

'You must allow me a small dream,' he emptied his glass in one swallow and stood up. Then he strode from the room, his expression grim.

'What did he mean?' Helen came and sat beside her.

'I don't know. He seems to talk in riddles.' Beth chewed her lip anxiously. His words had held so much bitterness that they had touched her heart and made it ache in sympathy. It was almost as if he was sad about the hostility between them. Just for a moment he had let his guard slip, and she had almost blurted out that she did like and trust him. It was a complete mystery why she should feel like this, and she decided that the uncertainty was making her over-sensitive.

'He is correct in one thing,' she told Helen, 'I would not turn him over to the law, for I have the nasty feeling that if I did, then we would all suffer.' She gasped as the realization hit her. 'I do believe my wits are becoming addled. I am beginning to care what happens to him!'

Thirteen

'My goodness, what a crush.' Beth gazed around the ballroom in astonishment. 'And just look at the magnificence! No expense has been spared in decorating the place. The flowers alone must have cost a fortune.'

Alice nodded. 'And the whole of London society is here, by the look of it. More out of curiosity, I suspect, for the man has a bad reputation.'

'No doubt.' Beth moved aside to allow an exuberant couple to reach the dance floor. 'I have never seen so many jewels.' Then a thought struck her and she whispered, 'Is his lordship coming?'

'He is already here,' Alice told her.

'Where?' She scanned the crowds. 'I cannot see him.'

'No one would recognize him, my dear – not even you.'

'I will if he is wearing black,' she declared with confidence, 'and anyway I only need to see his eyes to know him.'

'He is not wearing black – quite the opposite, in fact. I have never seen him looking so bright.'

This she had to see! 'Do tell me where he is?'

'He is quite close to us.'

Beth frowned behind her mask. 'I still can't see him, and I would have thought his height would have made him stand out.'

'He has disguised that as well.'

'How can he? Is he walking on his knees?' she joked. 'And all three are above average height; they would stand out in any crowd.'

Alice laughed again. 'Daniel is a master at blending in unnoticed, and he has taught them well.'

'Ah.' So it was imperative that their identities remain a secret.

'If you are wondering whether he is going to steal a few of the magnificent baubles on display, then you can be at ease, Beth. He doesn't want them or need them.'

'Oh, I did not—'

'Yes, you did, and understandably so, after that last escapade.'

Beth sighed. 'You understand that I cannot trust him, or any of them, don't you?'

'I do, and I am not in agreement with you being kept on tenterhooks in this manner, but I am sworn to silence. Not that I have been told the content of Edward's will.' Alice sighed. 'And I too would do anything to help my boys.'

'Even if they are breaking the law?' Beth asked.

'Yes, the most heinous crime would not make me betray them.'

By that statement, Beth knew she would not be able to rely on Alice as a friend. 'I do admit to being all at sea with his lordship. One moment I feel I could like him, and the next I am terrified of him and what he might do.'

'You do well to be cautious, Beth, for although I love him dearly, I would not vouch for him behaving like a gentleman at the present time.'

'Alex is of a gentler nature, though.' Beth studied the crowds again. 'Is he also here?'

'They are both here, along with Daniel.'

There was so much concern in her voice that Beth cast a sympathetic glance in her direction. However much she told herself not to get too close to this woman, she could not help liking her. 'I can see you are very worried about them.'

'They are my life.' Her sigh was heartfelt. 'And I wish we had never left Scotland. It was wrong of Edward to place this burden on James. He should have dealt with it himself, but he did have a very bad habit of leaving tasks until tomorrow. And, with Edward, tomorrow never came.'

'I know, and my father was the same. That is why I find myself in this predicament.' Beth cast Alice a curious glance. 'You appear to know my godfather well.'

'Of course I do, my dear; he spent a good deal of time with us over the last few years. Didn't James explain that to you?'

'No, he didn't!' Beth could hardly believe this. Her godfather often disappeared for long periods, but she had always assumed he was dealing with his many businesses. 'Why did he never mention visiting you?'

'Because I was looking after his son and he didn't want anyone to know about us.' Alice patted her hand. 'I'm sorry, Beth. This is all very confusing for you, but I see no reason for secrecy now.'

When Alice turned her attention back to the crowded room, Beth knew the subject was at an end. Sensing the tension in the woman beside her, she asked, 'Is there to be trouble this evening?'

'No!' Alice smiled, clearly trying to banish her fears. 'We are here to enjoy ourselves like everyone else; that is the sole purpose of this evening.'

Beth sincerely hoped that was true! She studied the throng again but gave up after a while. If the three men were here, then she could not pick them out in the swirl of bright colours. His lordship always wore subdued basic colours, and she could not imagine him in anything else.

'Gresham has spared no expense,' Alice murmured.

'I agree, though I can't understand why he has given such a lavish affair. He doesn't have the reputation for entertaining or spending money.'

'Except on his home.' Alice brought her attention to the huge glittering chandeliers. 'Venetian glass, and paintings by every artist of note.'

'Perhaps he is trying to find a husband for his sister and is hoping to impress with his wealth?' Beth suggested. 'She has been a widow for many years, I believe.'

'If that is his intention, then he is wasting his time and money.'

Beth was taken aback by the bitterness in Alice's voice. 'She is no beauty, but she is quite presentable.'

'That is so, but no man of standing would have her, not even if Gresham gave this fine mansion as her dowry.'

'I would have thought the gentlemen would have been queuing for her hand if he did that,' Beth joked. 'Is there some great scandal attached to her that I do not know about?'

'Not that I am aware of. Now –' Alice led Beth and Helen into the banquet room – 'let us see what delicacies are on offer, for I am quite famished.'

Beth was enjoying the evening, much to her surprise. No one knew who she was, and she could relax and just be herself. Her life had been severely restricted for some time as she had worked to learn how to run the estate, never giving a thought to herself or what she might be missing. She smiled, knowing that if her father were looking down at the splendid scene, then he would be laughing with pleasure as well. She also hoped that her mother was with him again, for he had never fully recovered from her death. Beth could hardly remember her, but she had been aware of her father's grief at her passing.

'I don't think I can dance another step,' she declared, sitting next to Alice and Helen, and wiggling her toes with a sigh of relief.

'Is this the same girl who is adamant she doesn't want a London season?'

'Oh, I don't,' Beth declared. 'The sole purpose of a season is to search for a husband, and I would hate that, but here no one knows us, so we can relax and just enjoy ourselves. It is really quite agreeable – and wonderful to see Helen dancing and talking so happily.' She gave her friend a broad smile.

Alice laughed quietly at her response. 'You don't know who you have danced with – and clearly do not care.'

'Exactly. I am free to be myself, without anyone trying to assess my suitability as a wife.' Beth gave a delicate shudder. 'I can't think of anything more distasteful.'

'You will change your mind about marriage when you have met the right man.' Alice patted her hand. 'And I think that will not be long, for you are quite a beauty.'

'Have you spoken with *them*?' she asked from behind her fan, changing the subject. She did not enjoy talking about herself.

'I have danced with them . . . and so have you.'

Beth sat upright and dropped her fan in shock. 'I would have known. They both have distinctive eyes and those they cannot disguise.'

'You think not?'

'Of course . . .' She picked up her fan and started to cool herself with it, deep in thought. There was one partner who had made her feel most ill at ease; the closeness of his body and the way he held her, but the eyes . . .

Suddenly, Alice sat up, her body straight with tension as she stared at a couple on the dance floor.

Beth followed her gaze. 'Sir Peter's sister appears to have snared herself a gallant partner.'

'Be careful, my boy,' Alice murmured under her breath.

The words were almost inaudible in the revelry of the ballroom, but Beth just heard them and at that moment realized who the man was. He was the man who had made her feel uneasy in his presence. She had attributed that to the elaborate lion's mask he was wearing, but it had not been that at all. It was James Sharland!

'That is a very clever mask his lordship is wearing,' she said boldly. Really, she was becoming tired of all this subterfuge!

Alice let out a pent-up breath as the dance ended and the lion stalked to the other end of the room.

'You cannot see his eyes,' Beth persisted, even though Alice did not seem inclined to talk. 'Can he see where he is going?'

'The design creates an illusion. Everyone naturally looks into the animal's eyes, but James can see through another part of the mask.'

Beth scanned the crowd until she found what she was looking for, and her irritation turned into laughter. 'And his brother is the ape! But where is Mr Edgemont?'

'I don't know what mask he is wearing, and Daniel has the ability to remain unseen if he so wants. I am surprised you did not recognize James and Alex sooner; they are the only ones with their eyes disguised.'

'Will you tell me why that is so important?' Beth asked.

Alice put her glass down, looking at it suspiciously. 'I believe I have had more than enough of this excellent brew.'

'You were saying?' Beth prompted, hoping she would continue, for she had been about to reveal something.

Alice smiled and made an effort at a joke, pointedly changing the subject. 'It is a shame for two such handsome faces to be hidden, is it not?'

'I consider it most inconsiderate of them.' Beth joined in the banter. 'They are depriving all the ladies present the excuse to swoon at their feet.'

'And you, Beth – would you swoon at James's feet?'

She grimaced. 'Only in terror.'

Then Beth was whisked on to the dance floor again and she threw herself into having fun, something that had been sadly lacking in her short life so far. The next hour sped by and it was fifteen minutes to midnight when she came back to her seat.

Alice was preoccupied and watchful, as if waiting for something, and Beth knew it must be her boys causing concern. A quick search of the crowd showed her that the lion and the ape were nowhere to be seen. And she still had no idea what mask Daniel was wearing. She started to fume again. How dare they cause this gentle lady so much worry!

'What is the matter, Alice?' she asked.

'Nothing, my dear; I am fatigued, that is all.' She smiled. 'I am not as young as you.'

'They will be unmasking soon; is it that prospect making you tense?'

But she was denied an answer as the lion appeared from behind a pillar, walked casually past them, touched Alice on the shoulder and continued out of the door.

'Would you mind if we left now, Beth? I am afraid I am feeling unwell.'

'We shall leave at once.' Beth helped her up and was alarmed to feel her trembling. It was time his lordship had a good talking to, and she was in just the mood to confront him!

The carriage was waiting for them. Helen was already there, so they removed their masks and were just about to get in when Sir Peter appeared.

'Are you leaving so soon, Miss Langton?'

'It has been a most enjoyable evening, but I am afraid my aunt is indisposed.'

'I am sorry to hear that, Lady Trenchard.' He helped her into the carriage and made sure a rug was placed over her legs. 'I hope you will soon recover.'

She nodded graciously but appeared too ill to speak, so he turned his attention back to Beth.

'Lord Sharland did not attend, after all?'

Out of the corner of her eye she caught the slight shake of Alice's head. 'I apologize for his absence, but he was called to London on business early today.'

'I see.'

Beth climbed into the carriage with the sure feeling he knew it was not the truth.

'My sister would like to call on you now she is residing here again,' he informed her.

'She will be most welcome.' She signalled to the driver, needing to get away from him as quickly as possible before she told any more untruths.

As the carriage rumbled out of the gates, Beth breathed a ragged sigh of relief. 'I do declare that I am at a loss to understand why I keep telling lies for his lordship? It is not something I have been used to doing, so I hope he appreciates my dubious talent.'

'He does, my dear.' Alice spoke softly. 'Why do you think Lady Pemberton wants to visit?'

'Who is Lady Pemberton?'

'Gresham's sister. Didn't you know her name?' Alice asked.

Beth shook her head. 'I have not had any dealings with her as she has spent most of her time in London or Bath. I knew Sir Peter had a sister, but I was never interested enough to enquire further.'

Alice closed her eyes and laid her head back, effectively closing the conversation.

Beth knew that something had happened at the ball, because the evening had obviously been an ordeal for Alice.

She set her mouth in a stubborn line. Was that man aware of the worry he was causing everyone?

Once Alice was settled in her bed, Beth stormed downstairs. There was a light on in the study, and, after a quick knock on the door, she swept in.

The three men were sitting comfortably, each with a large glass of brandy in their hands. They stood up as she entered the room.

'Is Alice all right?' James asked.

'Yes, but she has had a difficult evening, wondering what the devil you were all up to!' She glanced around the room, feeling just in the mood for taking them on. 'And you might as well know that you were called to London this morning on unexpected business.'

The corners of his mouth twitched. 'That is very kind of you to supply me with an alibi.'

'Don't think I am doing it for your sake,' she snapped. 'Sir Peter was showing interest in you again, and Alice was distressed enough.'

'So you lied again.'

'Yes!' She stepped towards him. 'But I don't think he believed us this time.'

'That is a great pity.' He leant on the edge of the desk and sipped his drink. 'But he can't know for sure that I was at the ball tonight.'

Beth thought he looked quite smug, and that infuriated her. 'I don't know why I keep telling these untruths for you, but I shall not do it again. I demand to know what is going on.'

'Demand?' He took hold of her arm and pulled her towards him until they were face to face. 'Why couldn't you have been a docile little girl who would not have questioned my presence here?'

She shook herself free. 'Is that what you expected?'

'I must admit that I did.' He sighed. 'But my father omitted to tell me about your spirited nature.'

'Well, you must have been sorely disappointed, then! And I think you owe me an explanation.'

James eased back a step or two, but he was still close enough to tower over her. 'It is better you don't know anything; then you can't let anything slip about us.'

'And are you any closer to settling this matter, James?' Alice came into the room.

'We have made progress, and that is all I can say.'

Alice looked rather faint, and Beth helped her to a chair.

'Then I shall take Alex back to Scotland where he will be safe. I should never have brought him here. We will leave first thing in the morning.'

'He won't go,' James told her gently. 'He likes it here and wishes to see this thing through to the end.'

Alice stood up, holding on to Beth for support. 'Then I shall go alone. It would destroy me to watch you both throw your life away.'

'It won't come to that.' He spoke with confidence. 'We shall not be playing at highwaymen again, and if Gresham discovers it was us, he will not do anything about it. We are safe from the gallows, Alice, and we will succeed.'

'And if you fail, then . . .' The last word trembled and tailed off.

James kissed her cheek with affection. 'That has always been a possibility, and if that happens, then Alex will return to Scotland, and I will stay here and run my school. If you must go tomorrow, will you take Elizabeth and Helen with you?'

At the mention of her name, Beth's head shot up. 'We will not leave here!'

They both ignored her outburst.

'James, is it important to you that they are away from here for a while?'

He nodded.

'I am not going anywhere!' Beth raised her voice.

James's expression hardened. 'Then you will take the consequences.'

'Whatever they may be.' Beth turned to Alice. 'I will not leave my estate.'

'I understand, my dear. I would do the same thing in your position.'

'Stubborn females,' James muttered.

'Yes, James, we can be at times. I want your word that you will do all you can to finish this unpleasant business quickly.'

'You have my word.'

'Good.' Alice started to walk to the door, then stopped and turned round. 'Have you found what you were looking for?'

'We have something that may be of help. The next step is up to Dan.'

'Then you will do what you have to without delay, James.' She walked out of the room.

Beth gaped at his lordship. 'What in heaven's name was that all about? What have you been looking for?'

He stood in front of her. 'Your constant questions are a complication I can well do without.'

She watched him stride away from her, Alex right behind him, and she felt like crying.

The only other person left in the room was Daniel Edgemont, and she looked at him appealingly. 'You say very little, Mr Edgemont, but I am sure you are playing a very important role in this matter – whatever it may be. If I ask you one question, will you answer it for me?'

'If I can.'

'Are you dealing with a problem caused by my godfather – or my own father?' She wasn't quite sure why she had included her father, but she had a growing suspicion that this was something to do with her family as well. She could see no other reason for them moving in with her. After all, if this concerned only the Sharland family, they could have resided in their own property.

He thought about it for a few seconds and then said simply, 'As a friend of Edward, your father knew about his past, but he had no part in it.'

She nodded, relieved to have that confirmed, and she turned and walked out of the room.

Fourteen

'Please don't leave,' Beth pleaded. In the short time she had known Alice, she had come to look upon her with some affection and, more than that, as someone who could be trusted. Alice was a sensible and loving person, and the thought of her not being here during this troubling time was not something Beth wanted. The problem was she was becoming too fond of her unwanted guests, and, to be honest, she was feeling all adrift.

Alice slammed the lid of her trunk down and sat on it, looking dejected. 'I am a coward. You put me to shame, Beth. You realize something is about to happen which could prove dangerous, and yet you refuse to run.'

Beth sat beside her. 'Whatever is to come upon us, I must stay and face it. I am responsible for this estate and all who work here. I promised my father I would see that we prospered and the workers had secure jobs. I won't break that promise, no matter what I have to face.'

'Oh, Beth, what am I to do? I begged James to come and settle Edward's affairs and then return to Scotland, but he would not hear of it. This was the chance he had been waiting for to make an evil man pay for his past deeds, he told me, and an opportunity to fulfil his dream of opening his own school. Alex gave me no rest until I agreed to allow him to come with me.'

Another of Beth's suspicions had been confirmed. He was using his guardianship of her for some purpose of his own. It was a tangled web, but a few strands were now starting to unravel. How she wished to know the whole story, but she would not ask again. It would be revealed at the right time. She must contain her impatience and remain watchful.

Beth knelt on the floor beside the distraught woman. 'You must be brave for their sake. Whatever is going on, they need your support, especially James, for he appears to have taken a heavy burden on his shoulders.'

Alice looked at her in astonishment. 'Does this mean that you don't believe him to be a villain?'

'I have yet to decide, but I have seen he has a great affection for you, and I'm sure he would not let anything untoward happen to you or Alex. Will you tell me just one thing?' Beth asked.

'If I can.'

'Is James in danger of being sent to gaol?'

Alice let out a ragged sigh. 'He is not a criminal, though he is dicing with the law, but he sees no way around it. The only comfort I have is that Daniel is here. Although some things he is involved in are dubious, I do know for certain that he is on the side of the law.'

'Oh.' She was startled by this piece of information. 'Is he a lawyer?'

'He is connected to the law, and he also does some work for the police and the government at times, and that is all I can tell you.'

Beth nodded. 'If that is the case, then I think we must trust him to make sure this business doesn't get out of hand. We can do nothing but wait, and I believe we would all be comforted by your presence.'

At that moment Helen showed Alex in. For once, his ready smile was not present. 'Don't leave, Alice.'

She straightened up. 'Beth has persuaded me to stay. She has made me realize that my place is here – and we do have a season to prepare for.'

The smile was back, and he spun her round as if she were a girl. 'It will be all right; you'll see. Dan will not let anything bad happen to any of us.'

'I know, Alex, but what about James? Will he heed Daniel's advice?'

'He is aware of the risks, but he has waited a long time for this moment and is prepared for whatever happens.' He smiled gently. 'We cannot deny him this chance, for he will never rest easy until it is done. What that man has done must not go unpunished.'

'But it was such a long time ago, and I had hoped that it would stay buried. However, I feared this day would eventually come. Will you be safe in that remote cottage?'

'I am moving back into the house again.'

'The servants' quarters?'

'No, I must stay close to you, Elizabeth and Helen, James says.'

'That will be a comfort.' Alice smiled at Beth and Helen. 'Will it not, my dears?'

'Indeed it will,' Beth answered, though she knew the only way she would feel safe again would be if James left. 'What about those animals?' she asked, giving a delicate shudder. 'Who will look after them?'

'Young Charlie has taken a great interest and he is to care for them.' Alex gave an impish grin. 'He thinks they are beautiful and is most eager to take on the task.'

'My goodness, he has a strange notion of beauty,' she declared.

That broke the tension and they all started to laugh – even Helen, who was now happy to be herself once again. It was as if the mystery and hint of danger had woken her up and revealed the brave, steadfast friend Beth had always known. It was clear now that her friend had been playing the role of companion, but she had never lost her dignity and poise. After all she had been through, this could not have been easy, and it showed what a truly remarkable person she was. Beth was grateful to have Helen by her side and prayed she could show as much courage.

'Ah, it is good to hear laughter.' James looked in through the open door and smiled. 'Are you staying, Alice?'

'Yes, James. Beth has been very persuasive.'

He gave a slight bow to Beth. 'Thank you.'

'As I have become embroiled in this mystery, I would appreciate knowing if I am to lose everything. I believe you owe me that much explanation.'

He studied her for a moment and then sighed. 'I have already tried to assure you that you will not lose the estate, whatever the outcome of our investigation. If we fail, though, your reputation could suffer because of your association to me.'

Beth shrugged. 'That I can live with.'

'Do not dismiss it so lightly, Elizabeth, for it is a hard way to live.' He gave Helen a surprisingly fond glance. 'As Lady Helen has discovered.'

'That is true,' Helen agreed, returning his smile. 'May I ask why you have not tried to keep this investigation of yours away from Beth?'

'I had no choice. It was the only way I could get close to Gresham without arousing suspicion, and carry out my father's wishes.'

'I believe he is already curious about your identity,' Beth told him.

'He may have his suspicions, but I don't believe he is really sure I am who I am claiming to be, or if I am really here.'

James appeared relaxed and untroubled, but when Beth looked closely, she could see the lines of strain around his eyes.

'Miss Langton?' Jenkins appeared. 'Sir Peter Gresham and his sister have called to see you.'

'Help!' Alex exclaimed. 'Let us get out of here, James. Where's Dan? He mustn't be seen, either.'

'He won't return until later tonight.'

Beth watched them hurry away and turned to Alice. 'Will you join us?'

'No, my dear. Tell them I am still indisposed.'

'Very well. Will you come with me, Helen, for I have no wish to see them on my own?'

'Of course.'

'How kind of you to visit again so soon,' Beth said as they entered the drawing room, hoping her smile looked as welcoming as the one Helen was managing. 'You will take tea, or perhaps something stronger for you, sir?'

'Tea will be fine.' He glanced at the closed door. 'We were concerned for Lady Trenchard's health. Is she not joining us?'

'She sends her sincere apologies, but she is still unwell,' Helen told them.

'I do hope it isn't anything serious?' The sister settled herself comfortably, not looking at all sincere about Alice's health.

'A slight chill.' Beth smiled at the maid who had just wheeled in the trolley of refreshments. 'Thank you, Jenny; we will look after ourselves.'

'Very good, Miss Langton.'

Beth busied herself pouring the tea while Helen handed round the sandwiches.

'Is Lord Sharland not joining us, either?'

'He is away at the moment. He will be sorry to have missed you again.'

'He doesn't appear to be around much.' Sir Peter's smile was forced as he glanced towards his sister. 'We shall have to call him the elusive guardian, eh, Dorinda?'

'Indeed we shall, Peter. I would not have expected a guardian to leave you to run this very large estate on your own, Miss Langton.'

It was on the tip of Beth's tongue to tell them to mind their own business, when Helen saved her from being rude.

'He doesn't need to do much. Beth has been trained by her father in all aspects of running the estate, and, with the help of an excellent manager, there is little for his lordship to do.'

Sir Peter Gresham studied Helen. 'And what about you, Lady Helen? How do you occupy your time?'

'I help by keeping the accounts,' she told him, her gaze unfaltering and defiant. 'As I am sure you are aware, I am quite expert at sorting out money.'

When their two visitors didn't answer, Beth could have laughed out loud. By referring to her father's debts, Helen had just put the Greshams firmly in their place, leaving them at a loss for a reply. If they had sought to make her uncomfortable by using her correct title, and thereby showing that they knew about her family scandal, then they had failed.

Changing the subject, Beth talked about the masked ball, and that filled the next half an hour. When their visitors finally took their leave, the friends heaved a sigh of relief, agreeing that Sir Peter and his sister were rude and not at all likeable.

'Where is James?' Beth asked Alice at dinner that evening.

'He has had to go to London and may be away for a few days.'

'And has Alex gone with him?'

'No,' she sipped her wine. 'One of the sows is about to produce, and he wanted to be present.'

Beth nodded. 'That should keep him out of trouble.'

'What do you mean?'

'I just thought that it would be better for him to remain here in case James is going to hold up another coach.' Beth was pleased when she saw Alice smile, for she was looking strained. The only one who did not seem to be concerned was Alex; he appeared to have complete trust in James. Beth wished she had!

'No, Beth, he has told us he will not do that again, and he never breaks his word, thank heavens.'

'That is an admirable trait.' She knew it was useless to probe further.

'Did you enjoy tea with the Greshams?' Alice changed the subject.

Beth grimaced. 'It was not pleasant, for it was quite a task to keep the conversation going so they would not ask probing questions. I must confess that I don't care for either of them.'

'No, they are not the most endearing people. Did they say why they had called so soon after the ball?'

'They were concerned for your health,' Beth told her.

Alice snorted in disbelief. 'More likely they were trying to meet James. They must be getting quite desperate to see him. I don't believe he knows that James was born, and to have a son of Edward turn up must be causing him a great deal of worry. If Gresham is the man who caused our family so much trouble and heartache, then he must be nervous to find us so close to him.'

'Yes, they did ask after him and were not pleased to find him absent once more.' Beth smiled wryly. 'They are calling him my elusive guardian.'

'James could not hope to remain undiscovered for much longer. I believe Gresham will now keep turning up until he actually sees James.'

'From what you say, he hasn't met him before and therefore would not be able to recognize him.'

'No, but James doesn't want to take that chance.' Alice rose to her feet. 'Forgive me, Beth, but I have a dreadful headache and think it best if I retire.'

'Of course. Is there anything I can get you?'

'No, my dear. I just need to rest. The worry these boys are causing me is quite debilitating.'

They watched the lady leave the room. Beth pursed her lips. 'Well, another snippet of information, but it doesn't get us much nearer to the truth, does it?'

'I'm afraid not,' Helen agreed.

Fifteen

There was no sign of Alice at breakfast the next morning, and Beth thought it best to let her sleep on, but Alex arrived, full of smiles.

'You have eight beautiful piglets, Elizabeth,' he told her. 'Would you like to see them?'

She looked at him in horror. 'No, thank you!'

He chuckled. 'I know you have an aversion to the animals, but they really are quite adorable when first born. I am sure you would change your mind if you saw them. I'll take you now, if you want.'

'I shall decline your kind offer,' Beth told him, fighting to keep from grinning at his enthusiasm.

'Ah, you don't know what you are missing.' He consumed a hurried breakfast, and then he was up from the table and rushing to get back to his new babies.

As James was away, Beth decided to tour the estate and see how things were going, avoiding the pigs, of course, but Helen declared that she would love to see the piglets. Beth stayed well out of the way while her friend saw the new arrivals.

'They are adorable,' Helen declared, smiling when she returned.

'That is not a word I would use.' Beth pulled a face, making Helen laugh as they continued their ride.

Two hours later Elizabeth was well pleased with what they had seen. James had made quite a few changes, but everything was running smoothly, and Beth had to admit that he was taking good care of the estate and its workers. She had encountered only respect for him, and all the earlier worries seemed to have disappeared as they had come to know him. She really did hope he was not a criminal.

Helen tipped her head to one side and studied her friend intently. 'I believe you can put the worry of the estate out of your mind, Beth. All is in order, and he clearly knows what he's doing.'

'It does appear that way, and I do admit that it is occasionally pleasant not to have the burden of the day-to-day running of the estate on my shoulders. But I would dearly love to be free of this uncertainty about him.'

'Well, it is a pleasant day, so why don't we ride out to the Sharland mansion and see what is going on there. We may discover a little more about him.'

'That's a splendid idea! I would like to see what changes he is making.'

The young women turned their mounts and set off at a canter, smiling in anticipation.

They reached their destination, glowing and laughing after an invigorating ride.

The place was a hive of activity, with workmen everywhere, and when Becks and a hand they didn't know hurried to help them dismount and take charge of their horses, Beth exclaimed, 'My goodness! It looks as if extensive changes are being made here.'

'Water is being piped into the house, Miss Elizabeth,' Becks told her. 'It is quite a task, but his lordship insists that every bedroom has a sink with running water.'

'Really? May we have a look? We will not get in anyone's way.'

'I expect that would be all right, but it would be best to ask Lord Sharland's permission first.'

'Is he here?' Helen asked. 'We thought he was away.'

'He arrived here at early light, my lady. He's round the back.'

'Then we shall do as you say. Thank you, Becks.' Helen took hold of Beth's arm. 'I can't wait to see what is being planned for this school.'

When they reached the other side of the house, they both stopped in astonishment at the scene in front of them. A small field where men were working was a sea of mud, full of strange machinery, and right in the middle of it was James. His shirtsleeves were rolled up and he was pulling on a rope attached to a large pipe. And he was covered in mud!

'Oh my!' Beth clapped her hand over her mouth, unable to believe what she was seeing.

Helen was openly laughing and called out, 'You look as if you need more help, Lord Sharland.'

Only when the pipe was lowered into place did James turn. 'Are you offering, Lady Helen?'

'Oh, no, but I could go and find more men, if you wish.'

Beth gazed from her friend to the man covered in mud, and she was stunned. They were laughing and joking with each other like old friends.

Squelching his way over to them, James was still smiling broadly when he reached them. 'May I ask what brings you here?'

'We wondered if we might have a look at the work you are doing to turn this into a school?' Beth couldn't help smiling, joining in the light-hearted fun.

'Yes, of course, but, as you can see, I am in no state to give you a guided tour. I'm sure Becks will be happy to show you around, though.'

'Thank you. And I must say that this is a very worthy use for such a large mansion.'

'If you are interested, Lady Helen, I will show you the plans – when I'm in a more presentable state, of course.'

'I would like that.'

They found Mr Becks in the entrance hall, a smile on his face as he surveyed the work being carried out, and he eagerly agreed to show them round.

Helen was clearly enthralled by the idea of this rambling mansion being turned into a school, and she asked many questions, which Becks answered with enthusiasm.

Beth, however, was looking at the building with different eyes. She had always wondered why her godfather had bought this place, as it was far too large for a bachelor. He must have been quite a young man at the time, and he had never talked about it as a home; in fact, he spent as little time as possible here. Would he approve of it being turned into a school?

As they walked from room to room, she was overwhelmed with the certainty that he would be delighted. Yes, he would be happy to see his son putting it to such good use. That thought brought Beth up with a start. When had she started to accept that James was indeed Lord Sharland's legitimate son? And he must be or he would never have inherited the title. This realization had come upon her so suddenly, and it was clear that her fear had kept her from admitting this obvious truth. She must still be cautious, of course, until she could discover his motives.

'Isn't this exciting, Beth?' Helen said. 'I think Edward would approve, don't you?'

'Yes, I'm sure he would.' She smiled at Becks, who, along with his wife, had been with her godfather for many years. 'Will you and Mrs Becks have a role in this new venture?'

'Oh, yes, Miss Elizabeth. We're to be the caretakers and see that the young boys have everything they need.' His smile couldn't get any wider. 'We're to have our own quarters and a large increase in salary.'

'That is splendid.'

'Ah, it is. And his lordship has been taking an interest in our Charlie – teaching him things. He's a bright boy and loves books, and if he gets good enough, he might be able to attend the school. He's very excited about that prospect, and so are we.'

'Really?' Helen looked surprised. 'But surely the fees for a school like this will be high?'

'No, my lady.' Becks was shaking his head. 'His lordship isn't charging. He's going to take clever boys who can't afford to pay.'

'No fees at all?' Beth could hardly believe a school could be run like that.

'That's quite right, Elizabeth,' said a quiet voice from behind them. 'Crazy, isn't it?'

They spun round, and Beth gasped, 'Oh, Mr Edgemont, we didn't hear you approaching.'

'My apologies if I startled you.'

Mr Becks grinned. 'Mr Edgemont moves like a panther, my wife says.'

'I would agree with that.' Beth turned her attention to the tall man. 'And are you to become a part of this crazy venture?'

'I have promised to give James six months of my time when the school is up and running. Then we shall see.'

'Mr Edgemont is to teach the boys riding and other physical skills,' Mr Becks explained.

'Other skills?' said Beth, an amused expression on her face. 'That should be interesting.'

Dan tipped his head back and laughed. 'Nothing violent, I assure you, but the boys must learn how to take care of themselves.'

As Beth studied Daniel Edgemont intently for the first time, she realized that she was drawn to him. He was an impressive man, in a quiet way, and appeared to be someone you could depend upon. No wonder James had been pleased to have him here.

'Ah, good, you're back.' James reached them by taking the stairs two at a time. 'We need your strength for the next part of the work.'

Dan's glance swept over his friend's dishevelled state and he raised his eyebrows. 'Have you been taking a mud bath?'

'It's great fun. You'll enjoy it.'

'You've always had the strangest idea of fun – and it always involves hard work.'

They grinned at each other, obviously sharing a private joke. Dan had begun to unbutton his jacket when there was a commotion in the hall below them.

James glanced over the banister and cursed under his breath. 'Oh, hell, it's Gresham.'

The man James had been doing his best to avoid hurried up the stairs. 'Lady Helen, Miss Langton – what a pleasant surprise to find you here. I heard about the work going on and thought I might be lucky enough to catch Lord Sharland.'

'Sir Peter.' Beth inclined her head slightly, and out of the corner of her eye she noticed that Dan had disappeared. She also doubted that anyone would think the workman standing with them was James, and, as he remained silent, she took a chance. 'He was here a while ago, but I'm not sure where he is now.'

'Still being elusive,' he said, not hiding his disgusted tone.

'He has much to do.' Beth looked James straight in the eyes. 'Thank you for your report, George. I will tell his lordship that things are progressing well. Now, you had better get back to work.'

'Thank you, miss,' he replied in a rough accent and then hurried down the stairs.

Gresham watched James leave with a look of distaste on his florid face. 'I'm surprised you allow anyone in that state into the house.'

'The field he is working in is a sea of mud,' Helen explained sweetly. 'And, as you can see, there is dirt and rubble everywhere. It isn't possible to carry out major renovations like this without making a mess.'

'No, no, of course not.' Gresham turned his attention to Mr Becks, who had remained silent throughout this exchange. 'Do you know where I might find your master?'

'I couldn't say precisely, sir. He could be anywhere on the premises.' If Becks found this subterfuge puzzling, he didn't comment, and did not even offer to go and find James.

'Would you like us to show you round, Sir Peter?' Beth smiled with enthusiasm. 'It is going to be a splendid school when it is all finished.'

He brushed a speck of dust from his jacket sleeve. 'I don't have the time to spare at the moment. Perhaps another time.'

'Of course.'

'I will bid you good day.'

They waited in silence until they heard his horse gallop away, and then the three of them began to laugh.

'That was excellently done,' said a quiet voice behind them.

'It certainly was. You could use Elizabeth's and Helen's talents at times, Dan.'

At the sight of James standing beside Dan, Beth exclaimed, 'How did you get up here?'

'I used a ladder to reach the room Dan was hiding in. We were relieved Gresham didn't take you up on your offer to show him around; otherwise, we would both have had to climb down again.'

'I don't know how much longer you can keep this up,' Beth laughed. 'But I gambled on the hope that he hadn't recognized you under all that mud.'

'He isn't sure what I look like, so he's doing his best to meet me. However —' he glanced at his friend and grimaced — 'that was close, Dan.'

'Does he know *you*, Mr Edgemont?' Helen asked.

'Our paths have crossed once,' he replied dryly.

'And if he finds out you are with me, he might bolt again, and that's the last thing we want.'

'Then, James, I'd better get myself covered in mud as well,' Dan said, unbuttoning his jacket.

Smiling broadly, they both bowed. 'Ladies, if you will excuse us?'

As they made for the stairs, James turned, bowed again and said, 'Thank you.'

'What did you find out?' James asked Dan as soon as they left the house.

'Welland examined the handwriting carefully and stated that, in his opinion, it was written by the same hand as the one received by your grandfather, but that had been heavily disguised.'

'In his opinion? That doesn't sound very definite.'

'What did you expect, James? I told you from the start that you would not obtain the proof you needed in this way. The man was not going to make his demands in a letter that could easily be traced back to him. Welland is an expert and did his best, but the letter is thirty years old.'

'I know.' James rested his hands on the fence by the muddy field and took a deep breath. 'Sorry, Dan. Please thank Welland for me.'

'I have already done so.' Dan leant against the fence and studied his friend. 'What are we going to do now?'

'What do you suggest?'

'Leave the past where it belongs, and get on with your life.'

'I can't do that.' James shook his head. 'I made a promise.'

Dan swore under his breath. 'If your father was here now, I'd stick his head in that mud until he allowed you to withdraw that promise. What the hell was the man thinking? All he had was a suspicion that Gresham was the man he had been after, but he didn't have one tiny shred of proof.'

'Ah, but he didn't have you to help him.' James grinned. 'He told me to make sure I enlisted your services.'

'Oh, did he? And then he left me a letter just to make sure I did get involved.'

'He wasn't taking any chance that you would refuse,' James grinned. 'Impossible tasks are your speciality. So – seriously – what should we do next?'

'There's only one way open to you now, and that is to confront Gresham and get a confession from him.'

James stood upright, a look of utter disbelief on his face. 'You're not serious?'

Dan nodded.

'And while he's telling me he ruined my family for monetary gain, shall I ask him if he killed my mother's loyal coachman?'

'That would be helpful.'

'Helpful?' James tipped his head back and gave a harsh laugh. 'Oh, I'm sure he would send himself to the gallows, or add another victim to his list – me!'

'I'll be with you.'

'How comforting!'

'I've got one more piece of advice,' he said, ignoring his friend's sarcastic tone. 'You owe those two girls an explanation. For some odd reason, they are protecting you without knowing why it is necessary, and yet Elizabeth Langton is terrified you are here to ruin her. You should never have involved her in this.'

'I had no choice. My father made me Elizabeth's guardian and told me to move in here until she reached the age of twenty-one, or until this damned business had been finally dealt with. He wanted to make sure that once we started investigating she would be perfectly safe. Gresham is vindictive enough to turn his anger on anyone connected to the Sharlands. And Elizabeth's father knew the whole story, so Gresham might think he told his daughter.'

Dan nodded. 'I agree that does make a difference.'

James nodded. 'I can't tell them anything yet because that might put them in greater danger. What I've got to do is get them away from here. If Gresham suspects we are closing in, then things could get unpleasant. Somehow I've got to persuade them to stay in London with Alice.'

'Good luck with that,' Dan said dryly.

'I'll need it.' There was a call from the men in the field. 'Come on, Dan. Help is needed out there. Time to get you covered in mud.'

Sixteen

The next four weeks were peaceful, and Beth began to breathe more easily. After their meeting with Sir Peter Gresham at the Sharland mansion, the atmosphere had been almost friendly. Almost, she thought wryly, for James was still aloof, never allowing himself to unbend too much in her company. Helen was the only one able to make him relax. He appeared to gain great pleasure explaining to her his plans for the school, and she was showing a lot of enthusiasm for the scheme. He was a different man with Daniel and Alex, and they could often be heard joking and fooling together.

James was still a mystery to her, and she was becoming increasingly confused about his motives, but Daniel was also an enigma. No matter how she puzzled over it, she could not fathom what he was, or how he was involved in the Sharland mystery — for that was how she now labelled it.

'I miss Alice.' Helen came in and sat down, looking to see if there was still tea in the pot and then pouring herself a cup.

'So do I, but she must have been happy to leave her boys — as she calls them — to visit her friends in London. They have been quiet of late. The three of them have been spending most of their time working on the school, and there has been no sign of Gresham. Do you think they've given up on whatever they were trying to find out?'

'I doubt that.' Helen looked thoughtful. 'Whatever the problem is with the Sharland family, I don't think James will rest until it is settled.'

'No, of course you're right.' Beth sighed. 'I was beginning to hope that we might get through the next few months without any trouble. And no mention has been made of a season in London again, so perhaps that has been forgotten.'

Helen laughed at her friend's hopeful expression. 'Alice isn't only in London to visit friends, Beth. She's also there to make final arrangements for our stay and to start gathering invitations for social events.'

'Oh no!' Beth groaned. 'I will refuse to choose a husband in that way. If I ever marry, it will have to be to a man I love and respect, not someone who will court me for the estate I own.'

'I agree that it will be a very big enticement to many young gentlemen. With my situation being common knowledge, however, I am certain that I will not be besieged with offers.' Helen didn't look at all sorry about that prospect. 'But we can enjoy the dancing and social events. We shall give the gossips plenty to tattle about, for I am sure that the happenings here have been circulating for some time.'

The girls burst into laughter, and Beth said, 'You are quite right again, Helen. Our appearance in society will set the tongues wagging, and all will be consumed with curiosity.'

'We shall not be lacking invitations, I think.'

At that moment they heard a carriage arrive at speed — and then raised voices. They rushed down the stairs and out of the front entrance to see what all the fuss was about.

James was standing in front of an elderly gentleman who was leaning heavily on a cane. The two men were confronting each other angrily.

'Get back in your carriage. You are not welcome here!'

Beth couldn't believe her eyes. The elderly man was so weary he could hardly stand, and the horses were lathered after being driven to their limit. Alex had arrived and was looking equally angry. Daniel had also appeared as if out of nowhere and stood slightly back from the others, but his presence was immediately felt.

The man glared at him. 'So you're here as well! I might have guessed.'

Daniel simply inclined his head, giving a respectful bow and saying nothing.

'I told you to leave!' James growled, clearly furious.

When the man swayed slightly, Beth couldn't stand by any longer. She pushed her way forward and caught hold of the elderly man's arm. Helen was there at once as well, and they both steadied him.

Beth glared at James. 'This is still my house and I will say who can stay! This gentleman is clearly in need of rest, and those poor animals must have attention.'

Young Tom was already soothing the exhausted horses, and Beth's staff had gathered ready to help if needed. She gave orders for a room to be made ready, food and brandy supplied, and the animals taken care of.

With herself and Helen either side of the elderly visitor, Beth pushed the men aside. 'Out of my way!'

Stanley, the footman, had to help them up the stairs with their guest, and they soon had him settled in a comfortable chair, with a blanket over his legs and a large glass of brandy in his shaking hands.

Helen was making sure he was feeling better, and Beth was relieved to see some colour return to his face. He had been deadly white, and she had feared he was about to collapse. And that heartless guardian of hers had been ordering him to leave when neither the man nor the horses were in a fit state to take another step. It was unbelievable! There was no excuse for such callous behaviour. This man – whoever he was – had clearly been in need of help.

'You, girl!'

Beth had been checking that the bed was ready and turned her head to see who had spoken so rudely.

'Who the devil are you?'

She bristled with indignation at his tone of voice and was in no mood to endure more bad manners. She left what she was doing and walked over to him. 'I am Elizabeth Langton, and the devil has nothing to do with my identity, sir! You are in my house and you may call me Elizabeth or Beth – I answer to both. I shall not respond to "girl" again.'

He surveyed her through narrowed eyes, and then the corners of his mouth twitched just a fraction. 'Ah, you stood your ground against my grandsons. That shows me you have spirit. Admirable.'

He did not utter a word of thanks or apology, and Beth couldn't stop the next words tumbling out. 'It would seem, sir, that rudeness is a family trait. Now, may I ask what you are doing here, and why your grandsons are so angry?'

'I am here to take Alexander back where he belongs, and James hates me with a passion. Where's Alice?'

'Alice is in London with friends. What have you done to make James hate you so much?'

'None of your damned business! Send for Alice.'

'I will do no such thing, sir. You have just told me that your family squabbles are not my business, so, as soon as you are well enough, you might care to join her in London. Until then we will see to your needs, and you may stay until you are fully recovered. I will send for a physician to make sure you are not suffering from anything more than fatigue.'

'I don't need a blasted physician!'

'While you are in my care, you will do as I say, sir! Stanley, send Tom for the physician.'

'At once, Miss Langton.'

'The bed is ready and warmed for you. Have you brought a valet with you, or would you like one of my staff to help you, sir?'

'My driver, Hutton, will look after me. There is no need for you to put yourself out further,' he said sharply. 'And as you are so set on the correct forms of address, you may call me Your Grace.'

'Your Grace.' Beth didn't even bother to bow her head, showing no sign of shock or awe, for she knew that was exactly what this infuriating man was expecting. She'd had enough of this family, and titles meant nothing to her. Seething, she stormed out of the room and down to the study where she guessed she would find the men.

They were in deep discussion when she stormed in, and they stopped talking the moment the door flew open.

James spun round to face her, and she could see he was still furious, but so was she at this moment. In her shock at the loss of her dear godfather, she had allowed this man to take control over her life and estate, but this was about to end.

'It would have been polite to knock first,' James growled.

'Polite? This is my house, and if I want to enter a room, I will do so without your permission!' She walked over and faced him, standing toe to toe. 'That cantankerous old man upstairs is sick. He couldn't have taken another step, and neither could the horses. How dare you treat man and beasts in that cruel manner?'

'He isn't welcome here.' James had also raised his voice.

'Neither are you!' she shouted back. 'And as soon as your grandfather is fit to travel, you will all leave this house. You will have no more say in my affairs.'

'The law says otherwise.'

'I don't give a damn about the law! You are finished here. You can leave and take your blasted family with you.'

There was a throaty chuckle behind her. 'That's right, girl – you tell him.'

She turned and glared at the elderly man who had just entered the room, and saw Helen and the footman rush in right behind him and take hold of his arm. 'I told you not to address me in that derogatory way. Get back to your room and wait for the physician. You need rest.'

'A man can't do that with the two of you shouting at each other. And I want to talk to my grandsons.'

'Well, you can't until you are in a fit state to face them without collapsing.'

Stanley had a firm grip on the elderly man now and looked apologetic. 'I'm sorry, Miss Langton. Her ladyship and I turned our backs for a moment and he was gone. We didn't catch him in time to stop him coming in here.'

'I'm not surprised,' she said. 'He's unpredictable – like the rest of his family. Take him back upstairs and lock him in if you have to.'

A smothered laugh came from Alex whose eyes were dancing with amusement. James was still scowling, and Daniel was impassive, as usual.

'I think I had better do as you say, Elizabeth; I do still feel a little shaky.' Before leaving the room, he nodded to James. 'And I think you had better do as she says. It looks as if you have met your match at last. I'll talk to you later. And stop shouting, the pair of you. I need my rest. The train to London was unbearable, so I finished the journey by coach, and that is exhausting for a man of my age.'

There was silence while the grandfather left the room and the door was closed behind him. Only then did Alex roar with laughter. He gave Beth a smile of respect. 'That was priceless!'

James glared at him. 'What's so damned amusing?'

'Oh, come on, James. That was the funniest thing I've seen for some time. Have you ever seen anyone order Grandfather around like that and get away with it?'

'I doubt Elizabeth will get away with it. That nasty old man will find a way to get even with her.'

'He won't be staying long enough to cause me any more trouble – and neither will you!' She turned her attention to Daniel, who, as usual, was standing silently in the background. 'I do not include you in any of this, Mr Edgemont. You have behaved impeccably, and you are welcome in my house.'

He inclined his head and smiled. 'Thank you, Elizabeth.'

Without another word, Beth spun on her heel and walked out of the room. She had had her say, something she should have done in the beginning, and, to her immense satisfaction, it had given them plenty to think about.

Helen was waiting in Beth's sitting room and handed her a cup of strong tea as soon as she came in. 'I think you need that.'

'I do.' Beth collapsed into an armchair and drank the hot brew gratefully. 'I've told them to leave.'

'So I heard.' Helen looked doubtful. 'Do you think they will?'

'No, but it felt good to let my anger spill out. I have been docile for far too long, and I am determined to take back control of the estate.' Beth's hand shook as she put the cup back on the tray. 'Has the physician arrived yet?'

'Yes, he's examining His Grace at this moment. He's a duke, by the way.'

'I don't care what title he has, Helen. While he is in my house, he will do as he is told.'

Helen hugged her friend, smiling broadly. 'That's the girl I grew up with! You've been in shock – we've both been in shock – but now we are back to normal. Let's show them they can't boss us around!'

'Yes, they are not going to get their own way any longer,' Beth agreed.

There was a knock on the door and Stanley looked in. 'Doctor Gregson, Miss Langton.'

She knew the man who walked in very well; he had been their family doctor for many years. 'How is he?' she asked.

'He's tired after a long journey, that's all. Apart from that he seems to be in good health. A couple of days of rest and he will be fine.'

'That is good news. Thank you for coming so quickly, Doctor Gregson.'

'My pleasure, Miss Langton. Call me again if you have any concerns, but I don't anticipate any problems. Although he's quite advanced in years, he is still a strong man.'

'And very determined, from what I've seen of him,' Beth remarked.

The doctor grinned. 'That is obvious.'

When he had left, Beth sighed and rubbed her temple. 'What a day!'

'Why don't you go for a walk outside, Beth? I'll see to everything here. A quiet stroll in the fresh air will clear your head.'

'That's a lovely idea. I won't be long, Helen.'

Relieved to be out of the house and away from all the tension vibrating through it, Beth climbed on to the fence, just as she had done as a child, and gazed at the horses in the paddock. It was late afternoon, with a soft breeze ruffling the grass, and she sighed contentedly. How she loved this place! It would break her heart to lose it, and she wondered, not for the first time, how Helen had survived the disaster that had befallen her. But she had, and her courage was undeniable. She had no wealth or material possessions now, but she had the love and respect of those around her, and that was worth more than gold.

One of the horses rolled on the ground and kicked its legs in the air, clearly enjoying the sunshine. Beth laughed and whistled softly in greeting, catching its joyful mood. When it stood up again and began to prance around the field, she called, 'That's the idea, Starlight – enjoy yourself.'

The animal finished playing and went back to grazing, and Beth let the peace of the scene wrap around her, content just to sit and watch.

'This is a lovely spot.'

Beth nearly fell off the fence, startled by the quiet voice behind her. Steadying herself, she turned her head. 'Mr Edgemont, I didn't hear you coming, as usual.'

'Dan – please. Am I disturbing you?'

'Not at all.' She smiled and patted the fence beside her. 'Why don't you join me?'

'Thank you.' In one smooth movement he was sitting next to her. 'Like you, I have come seeking a little tranquillity.'

'Are they still arguing?'

Dan's laugh was amused. 'James is walking around with a face like thunder, Alex is trying to calm him down – without much success – and Helen is threatening to lock their grandfather in without dinner if he doesn't behave himself.'

'And he had better heed her words,' Beth laughed, 'because she won't put up with too much nonsense from him. What on earth did he do to make James hate him so much?'

'It's a long story.' Dan cast a steady glance at her. 'But it isn't mine to tell, Elizabeth.'

'No, of course not. I shouldn't have asked. But there is one thing I am desperate to know, and I would be grateful if you could give me a truthful answer. This land has been in my family for generations. Could whatever James is involved in be a danger to the estate?'

There was a brief pause before Dan said, with conviction, 'No, Elizabeth. I will not allow it. James is determined to honour his promise to his father and will not let anything, or anyone, stand in his way. But you can rest assured that I am watching him carefully, as is Alex. If there is the slightest indication that he is neglecting his duty to you, I will forcibly drag him away and Alex will take over. You will not lose your estate.'

Beth was stunned but also heartened by this declaration. She studied the tall man beside her intently. 'Thank you. That eases my mind, but do you have the power to stop him from acting recklessly?'

'I do,' was all he said.

Those two words were said with such conviction that for a moment she was speechless. For some reason she had liked this man from the moment he had arrived; she had felt he could be trusted, although she had nothing to base that conclusion on. But he appeared calm, solid and dependable, whereas James was volatile and unpredictable. 'Who are you?' she asked quietly.

He cast her a sideways glance, the corners of his mouth twitching in amusement. 'Daniel William George Edgemont, from London, twenty-nine years of age and six feet two inches tall.'

'That wasn't what I meant,' she laughed, 'and you know it. It is very noticeable that you move almost silently and disappear from time to time. And everyone turns to you for advice. So, what do you do? I've heard tales.'

'Ah, you've been listening to Charlie and Tom.'

'They are convinced you are a spy. Are you?'

'Young boys have vivid imaginations.'

When he didn't say anything else, Beth shook her head, still smiling. 'You're not going to tell me, are you?'

He chuckled. 'I am here to help a friend, and also at the request of one other person.'

'Oh, and who was that?'

'A man I held in high regard. Your godfather.'

Beth nearly fell off the fence in shock. 'You knew him?'

'Very well.' Dan jumped off the fence and swung her down. 'Time we got ready for dinner. Did you think your godfather would leave you completely at the mercy of his volatile son, Elizabeth?'

The relief at this unexpected news was so overwhelming that Beth swayed alarmingly, causing Dan to reach out and catch her quickly.

'Rest easy, Elizabeth. You are not alone.'

Seventeen

'I have some news!' Beth rushed into her sitting room, out of breath from running up the stairs. She caught Helen by the arms and danced her around the room. 'It's going to be all right!'

'Whoa!' Helen made her friend sit down. 'Tell me, calmly, what has happened to remove that worried frown from your face.'

After taking several deep breaths, she told Helen about her conversation with Dan, unable to stop tears of relief from running down her cheeks. 'I haven't only been worried about the estate and the livelihoods of all those who depend upon us,' she admitted. 'I loved my godfather very much, and I was hurt that he should place me under the control of someone I didn't know, even if it was his son. But a son I never knew existed. Over the last few weeks that sense of betrayal has grown. It hurt, Helen. It hurt so much I couldn't talk about it. But that dear man put safeguards in place to protect me.'

'Do you think James is aware that Dan and Alex are watching him closely?'

'I'm sure he is, but he has a mission to complete for his father, and he wants Dan here. James is a very determined man, but I have come to believe that he has been given a task he cannot carry out on his own.'

'I agree.' Helen nodded. 'But I do feel he is also an honourable man, Beth. I have come to know him better over the last few weeks, and I have become increasingly convinced that he will do all he can to see you come to no harm.'

Beth gave a friend a curious look. 'You like him, don't you?'

'Yes, I do. He is passionate about his school to help clever but underprivileged boys. Setting up such an organization is not the action of a selfish man.'

'It does seem out of character for the man who walked in here giving orders and threatening me with ruin if I didn't do as he says. What I don't understand is why he acted like that.'

'Perhaps because he didn't want you to get in his way and come to any harm while he sorted out this mess your godfather was in?'

'Oh, I never thought of that. It makes sense.'

'I think so, but only time will tell if that assumption is correct. However, the other man I find puzzling is Daniel. Did he give any hint about what he does?'

'I did ask, but he turned it into a joke and didn't give me an answer. But he did say that he had known and respected Edward.'

'Hmm.' Helen looked thoughtful. 'I wonder how close they were. Did your godfather ever mention a Daniel Edgemont?'

'Not that I can recall. He never talked about himself or his life, but now I come to think about it, he used to disappear from time to time on business. He never said what his business was, and I never asked. I can see now that I never really knew him, only that he was my father's lifelong friend and a man I loved and trusted.'

'Perhaps he was a spy, like Dan,' Helen joked.

'Oh, do you think so?' Beth looked at her friend and they burst into helpless laughter. 'We are sounding just like Charlie and Tom. I did ask Dan if he was a spy, but he avoided answering – again.'

'He seems to be very good at that,' Helen said.

'Indeed, but I do trust him, and even more now that I know he knew Edward.' Beth drew in a deep breath, a look of determination on her face. 'It is time I took some action against this very unsatisfactory arrangement. I shall take over the running of the estate again, starting tomorrow. I feel on stronger ground now that I have a few answers.'

There was a quiet tap on the door. It opened a few inches, and Tom looked in. 'Psst!'

'Come in, Tom.' Beth fought to control her expression, but she could hear Helen spluttering with suppressed laughter behind her.

Easing the door open just enough to allow him to slide his thin body into the room, he then closed it behind him ever so gently. 'Mr Jenkins told me to come right up, Miss Langton. Mr Greenway sent me.'

Beth's amusement fled. 'You have a message for me?'

'Er . . . yes, miss. He didn't write it down.' Tom's face screwed up in concentration. 'He said . . . something odd is going on. A few of our regular buyers are unwilling to do business with us. They are nervous and edgy. He's having a job to sell the harvest this year.'

Tom drew in a deep breath and nodded, looking relieved he'd managed to remember the message.

'That's serious.' Beth turned to Helen. 'We've supplied local businesses with grain, fruit and vegetables for years. What do you think is going on?'

Helen looked equally puzzled. 'I don't know, but at a guess I would say it sounds as if some kind of pressure is being put on the buyers. Perhaps someone is moving in and offering lower prices.'

'You could be right.' Beth turned back to the boy. 'Thank you, Tom. Would you tell Mr Greenway that I'll find out what is going on?'

'Yes, miss, I'll do that. Er . . . I got another message for Mr Edgemont from Charlie. Would you please tell him that a couple of strangers are skulking around the pig farm? Mr Edgemont asked us to let him know if that happened.'

'Tell Charlie I'll let Mr Edgemont know at once.' Beth took some coins out of her purse and gave them to Tom. 'Share that with Charlie, and thank you for being so vigilant. We are grateful.'

He quickly slid the coins into his trouser pocket and bobbed his head. 'We'll keep watching.'

He disappeared as quietly as he had arrived, and Beth said, 'We've got to find out what this is all about. The men are bound to be in the study enjoying pre-dinner drinks. So let's see what they have to say about this.'

They made their way quickly downstairs.

'Good, you are all here,' Beth said as soon as they entered the study. 'James, I have just received some disquieting news. Some of our regular buyers are not willing to take our harvest this year. Do you know why?'

Putting his glass down with a thud, James frowned. 'No, I don't. The estate manager was dealing with that. Why didn't he let me know?'

'He came to me first because I have known these customers

all my life, and the estate and its workers are my responsibility. Your presence here is only temporary.'

James dipped his head slightly in agreement. 'I will see Greenway in the morning and deal with this.'

'No, you will not! Mr Greenway had the impression that the buyers are under some kind of pressure. If that is so, it might be connected to you. In that case it would be wiser if you stayed out of this. They could have been made a better offer, of course, though I cannot think from whom. I will talk to them.'

After a pause while he took a deep swallow of the whisky, he nodded again. 'That might be wise. They will be more likely to open up to you. If someone is interfering, you could let it be known that you are in complete charge, and my role here is just a legal formality until you reach the age of twenty-one.'

Her breath was taken away by this concession from him, and for a moment she was speechless. She had been prepared for a fight, and this was the last thing she expected. Was he handing everything back to her? She cleared her throat quietly and asked, 'And is that true?'

'From now on. But I will expect regular reports, and any problems are to be brought to me at once. Is that understood?'

'I will do as you say.' Beth could have thrown her arms around him in gratitude, but she held back, knowing that he probably wouldn't appreciate such a show of emotion. Instead, she said softly, 'Thank you. I will talk to the buyers tomorrow.'

James gave a tight smile. 'I believe you have missed running the estate.'

'I have. It has been my life, and I do dislike being idle.'

'Dan –' he turned to his friend – 'would you accompany Elizabeth tomorrow?'

'I was going to suggest the same thing.'

'Oh, that won't be necessary,' Beth exclaimed. 'I am quite capable of dealing with this myself.'

'I will not interfere, and you will not know I am there,' Dan told her. 'But if things should become difficult, I might be able to find out why they are reluctant to buy from you this year.'

'Oh, yes. I hadn't thought of that.' Beth smiled at Daniel, recognizing the wisdom of having him with her.

At that moment the study door opened with a crash, and all heads turned to see who had entered.

'A man can't get a damned decent drink in this place. Pour me a whisky, Alex.'

'Grandfather Beaufort!' Helen faced the elderly man. 'I thought the physician told you to stay in bed and rest?'

'Don't take any notice of them, girl! They don't know what they're talking about. I came here to see my grandsons, but you're not allowing me near them. I'm not staying in that bloody room.'

'Watch your language!' Beth declared, hands on hips. 'And don't you dare talk to us like that. You were close to collapse when you arrived, and we have been trying to help you. So you moderate your language, sir!'

'Show some respect, Grandfather, or they will certainly turn you out. In fact, we are all in danger of being thrown out.' There was amusement in James's voice and a slight smile on his face.

'Elizabeth won't do that,' the grandfather declared with confidence. 'She won't turn a duke away.'

There was a stunned silence, and then the three men burst into laughter, even Daniel.

'Did he tell you to call him Your Grace?'

They nodded, and Helen said, 'But we ignored him.'

'Good for you.' James nodded in approval. 'He's a terrible liar.'

The grandfather snorted, but his mouth twitched in amusement as he studied his eldest grandson. 'I thought it might impress the girls, but it didn't. They still locked me in my room.'

That caused a ripple of amusement in the room.

'So, will you tell us why you are really here?' Alex asked.

'I came all this way to take you both back home, where you belong, of course.'

James sighed. 'I've already told you I'm opening a school here. I am not coming back!'

'Damned fool idea,' the old man muttered before fixing his gaze on Alex. 'You're not involved in this crazy scheme, I hope.'

'No, Grandfather. I will be coming home, but not yet.'

'How long?'

Alex shrugged. 'When James doesn't need me any more. But I've promised Jeannie I won't stay away for more than six months.'

'Oh, you've promised her, have you? I had hoped that this trip would knock all thought of that girl out of your head.'

'Of course not. We are going to get married a year from now.'

'Over my dead body!'

'That can be arranged,' James muttered under his breath.

The old man spun round to face James. 'There's nothing wrong with my hearing, young man, so watch your tongue. And keep out of this.'

'It's no good you shouting at us,' Alex told him. 'You ruined James's mother's life and deprived him of his true father. You are not going to rule our lives. James is opening his school, and I'm going to marry Jeannie. So, as soon as you are well enough, you can return to Scotland and leave us alone.'

Beth and Helen were still in the room, watching with great interest as the two grandsons struggled with this difficult man.

James glanced over at them. 'Would you please lock him in his room again and keep him out of our way? We've got work to do, and if he interferes, as he always does, then he will ruin everything we've managed to achieve so far.'

'They can't!' the grandfather declared triumphantly. 'I've hidden the bloody keys.'

'There's a spare one in the butler's pantry,' Beth said, highly amused.

'Not any more. I've hidden that one as well.' The grandfather grinned at them. 'You've been watching me – but not closely enough.'

This was too much for the girls and they broke into helpless laughter.

'You're a crafty gentleman,' Helen said, wiping away tears of amusement.

'Of course I am.'

'You'll tell us where you've hidden the keys before you leave, won't you?' Beth was still smiling. Suddenly, this family she had been so frightened of appeared to be very human.

'I might.' He tipped his head to one side, studying them carefully. 'It depends how well you treat me while I'm here.'

'You'll be treated like every other *uninvited* guest in my house, so don't expect any special favours.'

He gave a deep throaty chuckle and turned back to his

grandsons. 'Why don't you two marry these girls? There's a real spark to them.'

Expressions of utter disbelief were on the young men's faces, and James was the first to find his voice. 'I can't believe you just said that! They don't like or trust us, and we had the impression that nothing lower than a duchess would be acceptable to you.'

'I can change my mind, can't I?'

'Heaven preserve us!' James raised his eyes to the ceiling. When he looked down again, he bowed to the girls. 'Please accept our apologies for our grandfather's behaviour. He must be going soft in the head.'

'Don't you be so sure, my boy. I can still outwit you any day.'

'You could be right,' James conceded dryly.

Helen nudged Beth and whispered in her ear. 'They might fight fiercely, but they're obviously fond of each other.'

Beth nodded as the elderly man spun round to face them. 'If you've got something to say, then say it out loud. I don't tolerate whispering.'

'I said that although you all fight and shout, you are clearly fond of each other.'

'Of course we are, girl. Why the hell do you think I'm here? These two boys mean the world to me. That's why they get away with so much. I'm not as firm as I should be with them.'

'Now we've heard it all!' Alex declared as both brothers burst into helpless laughter. 'We have to fight you every step of the way, or we won't have a life of our own.'

The grandfather gave a mischievous grin and chuckled. 'The pair of you have been a handful from the moment you were born. However, if you both refuse to come home, then I'm staying as well. I can help with this little problem you have, James. Though why the devil Edward asked you to deal with this, I really don't know.'

'My father,' James said pointedly, 'wanted this cleared up. A man should be made to pay for his evil deeds, even if he has got away with it for thirty years. And you stay out of it, Grandfather. It could be dangerous.'

'Nonsense! No one's going to hurt a confused old man. I can put on a good act when necessary, and people talk freely when they think you're daft.'

'Absolutely not!'

'James –' Dan spoke for the first time – 'he has a point. We are at an impasse at the moment.'

'There, you see: you do need me. Listen to Dan. He knows what he's talking about.'

Alex was nodding agreement, and James raised his hands in surrender. 'I'm outnumbered. We'll discuss it after dinner.'

'Good.' The grandfather turned to Beth and Helen, a look of satisfaction on his face, and held out his arms for them to hold. 'Come on – I'm starving. I hope you've got a good cook.'

Eighteen

When it became clear that the men had no intention of discussing the recent events in front of them, Beth and Helen reluctantly retired to their own sitting room. It had been a tense dinner that evening, and if it hadn't been for Dan keeping the conversation flowing, it would have been a silent one as well. They were enjoying a cup of tea and laughing about the tussle they had witnessed between the elderly man and his grandsons when there was a tap on the door.

It opened immediately and Alice swept in looking flustered and angry. 'Elizabeth! I am so sorry you have had to put up with yet another member of my family. I really didn't believe my father would make such a long journey at his age. I returned as soon as I heard the news. Where is the old fool?'

'He's in the library with his grandsons and Daniel.' Beth led her to a chair. 'Sit down and have a cup of tea. You look exhausted.'

'Oh, that would be welcome, and perhaps a touch of brandy wouldn't come amiss.'

Beth poured the tea while Helen handed her a brandy.

The brandy disappeared in two large gulps, and Alice grimaced. 'I don't usually drink spirits, but hearing that my father has arrived and will certainly interfere is enough to make anyone turn to drink. Tell me what havoc he has caused since he arrived.'

Beth and Helen took turns in relating everything, and they couldn't stop laughing when they told Alice that her father had hidden all the keys to his room so they couldn't lock him in. Their account of the fight before dinner had Alice shaking her head in dismay.

'You are both very kind to take this so well, but –' she stood up – 'I had better go and act as referee or they will tear each other apart.'

'No, they won't.' Helen made her sit down again. 'They were

on amicable terms during dinner. I think James is going to let him help with their problem – whatever it is.'

'What?' Alice surged to her feet again. 'That would be a disaster! Oh, my dears, I've got to get you away from here. Start packing. We'll leave for London in the morning.'

'I can't do that,' Beth told her, and she explained about the problem with some of their buyers. 'That must be dealt with, or we might not be able to sell our harvest this year.'

'Yes, of course you must stay.' Alice rubbed her temples wearily. 'But why isn't James dealing with this?'

'The buyers know me, and have done since I was little, so we thought they might be more willing to talk to me.'

'That's sensible, but you mustn't go alone, Beth. If this has happened because James is stirring up trouble, you must have a man with you.'

'Dan is coming with me.'

'Ah, that's all right, then. He'll know how to handle the problem. He doesn't intimidate people. Now, I had better go and pick up the pieces. Heaven knows what mad schemes they are hatching together.'

It wasn't long before they heard raised voices, and they went on to the landing to see what was happening. Alice and her father were coming up the stairs, arguing fiercely.

'You can stop shouting at me, Father; it won't make any difference. You are going to bed – now!'

'If you're going to order me around like this, then I'm sorry I sent for you to come back here. Helen was looking after me well enough.' He gave a throaty chuckle. 'Even had the nerve to lock me in my room. Fine girl.'

'I thank you for the compliment, sir.' Helen stepped down to help him up the last few steps. Despite all his protestations, he was obviously very tired.

'You shouldn't be eavesdropping, girl.'

'I didn't need to. I should think the entire estate can hear you,' Helen remarked. 'And Alice is right. You should have been in bed ages ago.'

'Humph! Now I've got two of you ordering me about.' When they reached Beth, he winked at her. 'Fine table you have here, girl. Thank your cook for a very enjoyable meal, and tell her I'll have some of that fine ham for breakfast with two lightly fried eggs. I suppose it's too much to ask if you have any porridge.'

'That I can't promise, but I'm sure Cook will do her best for you. Sleep well.'

He nodded and allowed himself to be guided to his room.

Hearing her name called, Beth looked over the banister and saw the men standing at the bottom of the stairs. Alex was mopping his brow in mock relief, James was looking grim, and Dan's expression was – as usual – unreadable.

James looked up and beckoned her down.

Puzzled, she descended the stairs and followed him into the library. Alex and Dan didn't come with them.

James was silent for a while, gazing out at the moonlit garden, and then he turned. 'Things appear to have got out of hand. It wasn't my intention to cause you all this trouble. My father left me certain instructions. I was to move in here while I carried out my investigation.'

When she opened her mouth to speak, he held up his hand to stop her and then continued. 'On no account was I to tell you what I was doing here. You were only to know that I was your temporary guardian, and you – and everyone else – were to believe that. My father loved you dearly and made me promise that no harm would come to you.' He grimaced. 'I had believed that if I came here, took over and kept you in the background, all would run smoothly. Then, when I had successfully kept my promise, I could leave and you would be none the wiser. However, the man we are trying to prove committed a serious crime years ago has become suspicious of us and he is beginning to retaliate. If this problem with the buyers is his doing, then let Dan handle it. He knows what he's doing.'

When he paused, she said quickly, 'Dan told me he'd known Edward, but my godfather never mentioned him.'

'They worked together at times – and don't ask, Elizabeth; I can't tell you more than that.' James walked over and stood right in front of her, his expression serious. 'I want you to know I will never break a promise, and my promise to you is that I will tell you the whole story once this is over.'

She nodded, took a deep breath and said, 'Thank you. Perhaps you could answer one question for me?'

'Ask.'

'My godfather appears to have made extensive arrangements before going to India. Did he know he might not be coming back?'

'His health was failing, Elizabeth, and he knew that the journey would be a strain for him.'

'Then why did he go?' she asked, upset by this news. 'I would have looked after him!'

'Of course you would, but he had urgent business to deal with and he wanted to handle it himself. Unfortunately, he didn't live long enough. His estate is being wound up and I have a representative out there now. It was his request that the business be sold, along with everything else – except his house. Now, I've made you a solemn promise, and I want you to make one. Promise me that when the trouble with the buyers is sorted out, you and Helen will go to London with Alice.'

'I promise,' she said, and she meant it. He had been as forthcoming as he was able to be at this point, and she had gained a glimpse of what he was up against. Her godfather had left his son a heavy burden.

'Thank you.' He smiled. 'We'll try and keep Grandfather from causing too much mayhem while he's here.'

'That might be difficult,' she laughed. 'See if you can find out where he's hidden the keys to his room, if you can.'

'We'll do that. Goodnight, Elizabeth. Sleep well.'

'I think I might. Thank you for talking to me, James. I'll let you know what happens tomorrow with the buyers.'

'Trust Dan.'

'I do.' She smiled, knowing that was true. The more she got to know Daniel Edgemont, the more she liked him. 'Goodnight, James.'

The next morning Beth and Dan made an early start, intent on catching the largest buyers before they began work for the day and disappeared somewhere. The first one they visited was John Masters, the main supplier of grain in the area. Beth had known John and his family since she was a small child, and she was anxious to find out what had gone wrong with their long-term business arrangement.

When they arrived, the door was opened by Hannah Masters. 'Oh, I'm so glad you're here, Miss Langton. I told John it isn't right what he's doing and he should've come to you straight away. But he wouldn't listen to sense. Come in.'

Mrs Masters led them into the kitchen where her husband was just finishing his breakfast. He stood up quickly, eyeing Dan with suspicion.

'I know why you're here, and I'm sorry, but I haven't got a choice. I've got to think of my family, so it's no good you bringing a strong man to persuade me otherwise!'

Beth was shocked by his outburst. What was going on? 'We are not here to put any pressure on you, Mr Masters. You have every right to buy from someone else, and we are only here to find out if we have let you down in some way. If our grain is not of the usual high quality, then we need to know, so we can do something about it. This is Mr Daniel Edgemont, a friend of mine.'

'Tell Miss Langton, John,' his wife demanded. 'You owe her that at least after all these years. Sit down, both of you. Would you like some breakfast?'

'No, thank you.' Beth smiled as they sat down, relieved to see that Hannah Masters wanted her husband to talk to them.

'Doesn't say much, does he?' John was still uneasy about Dan being there.

'He speaks when he has something to say.' Beth cast Dan an amused glance and then turned her attention back to John Masters. 'But I would trust him with my life, and you can as well. Now, will you tell me what is wrong?'

He ran a hand through his thinning hair and sighed deeply. 'It seems you have an enemy. A couple of weeks ago two tough-looking men visited me. Never seen them before. They said I wasn't to buy from the Langton estate any more. When I told them to bugger off – pardon my language, Miss Langton – they began telling me the names of all our children and grandchildren. They said that if I wanted them to stay healthy, I had better do as they say. Well, what was I to do?'

'I understand.' Beth was furious but fought not to show it. 'Did they say who had sent them?'

'Not exactly, but they did say I could buy my supplies from the Gresham estate.'

Beth drew in a deep breath. So this *was* connected to James. 'Do you know if others have been threatened?'

He nodded. 'They seem to have targeted the largest suppliers.'

'Dan?' Beth frowned. 'This is outrageous. Innocent people are being hurt and it can't be allowed.'

'It will be dealt with.' Dan surged to his feet. 'Mr and Mrs Masters, thank for talking to us. I will see that you have no more trouble from these men.'

'I don't know what you can do, sir, but we'd be mighty relieved to be free from this threat. We've all dealt with the Langton estate for a long time. Not only because we consider them friends, but because their produce is the best quality. They've always dealt fairly and honestly with us.'

'If these men should come again, let them believe you are heeding their threat, but would you tell the others concerned that I will see the intimidation is stopped?'

'Thank you for your time,' Beth said. 'I will let you know what happens, and please don't do anything to endanger your family.'

Once outside, Beth turned to Dan and caught his arm, her stomach churning. Her life up to now had been protected and peaceful. She had never come across anything like this before, and it was frightening. 'How can you promise there won't be any more trouble? I'm now sick with worry for these families. How can this man be stopped?'

'I will persuade him that this is not a good idea.' Dan helped Beth on to her horse and then swung into the saddle with fluid ease.

'Is that possible?'

'Well, let's see if he's at home, shall we?'

His calm, confident manner heartened Beth. James had told her to trust Dan, and she would do that. She nodded, and they turned their horses in the direction of the Gresham estate.

They rode in silence, and the first time Dan spoke was when they reached the Gresham mansion. 'Leave the talking to me, Elizabeth.'

'Gladly,' she replied, having no idea how he intended to handle this, but more than happy to let him take charge.

Grooms ran over to take their horses. Then the main door opened and Sir Peter Gresham appeared.

'Miss Langton. If you wished to visit my sister, I'm sorry, but she has returned to London. The country is too quiet for her.'

Beth smiled politely. 'I hope your sister is in good health, but we have come to see you.'

'How thoughtful of you. Do you have a new estate manager?' he asked, eyeing Daniel with interest. 'Have we met before?'

'No,' Beth shook her head when Dan didn't answer the question. 'Mr Edgemont is a friend of the family.'

Dan stepped forward, dwarfing Gresham. 'Our apology for calling unexpectedly, but a grave situation has arisen, and we felt you should know about it. May we ask for a few moments of your time?'

'That sounds serious. Please come in; you must be thirsty after your ride.'

Gresham looked as if the last thing he wanted to do was invite them in, but Dan had asked so politely that he must have felt he couldn't refuse.

They followed him to the drawing room and were offered drinks, which they refused.

'Perhaps you would prefer tea?' he asked.

'No, thank you, sir. We won't take much of your time.'

Beth watched Gresham carefully. He appeared wary, giving Dan suspicious glances from time to time, and she couldn't help wondering if that was a guilty conscience. She was now sitting and so was Gresham, but Dan remained standing. He was a quiet man and could disappear into the background when needed, but at this moment she was seeing a different side to him. He was dominating the room, and there was something in his manner that said it would not be wise to make an enemy of him. She was extremely glad to have him on her side.

'Well?' Gresham cleared his throat. 'What is it you felt I should know?'

'Miss Langton has been told that a few of her regular buyers and their families have been threatened and told not to take her produce this year.' Dan paused for just a brief moment and then said, 'And the threats have been made in your name.'

Colour drained from Gresham's face. 'That is preposterous!'

Dan inclined his head. 'That is why we have come to you. There are two men involved, and they have suggested that your estate will be able to supply everything needed. That does appear strange, does it not? Your estate is less than half the size of the Langtons', and therefore could not produce enough to satisfy these buyers.'

'Do you know who these men are?' Gresham asked.

The man was putting on a show of being shocked by the news, but Beth could see it was false. He was not a good actor.

'Not yet, but we will track them down. I will see that they are quickly put in gaol – and the man who hired them. Miss Langton has known these families all her life and considers them friends.'

Dan glanced at her; somehow she immediately knew what he wanted her to do.

'Indeed, Sir Peter. Mr Edgemont is correct. They have always been a part of the Langton estate family, but not bound to us. They are free to trade wherever is best for them. That is not the problem. What I do not like – and will not tolerate – is that they are being forced to do something against their will in order to protect their families from harm. That is criminal.' She sat back, feeling that she had said enough, leaving Dan to take over again.

'So, you see our dilemma. This must be stopped for everyone's sake – including yours, if you do not wish to be accused of this crime. Do you have any idea who these men might be?'

'No, no! And what can be done about it if their identities are unknown?'

'I will find them; have no fear about that.' Dan smiled at Gresham. 'That is my job.'

'Oh, are you with the law?' Gresham finished his drink in one gulp.

'Something like that.' Dan helped Beth out of her chair. 'We have taken enough of Sir Peter's time, Elizabeth.'

'Thank you for seeing us,' Beth said politely as they left the house.

'Always a pleasure, Miss Langton.'

'Do you think our visit will help to resolve this unpleasant business?' Beth asked Dan as they cantered towards the gates.

'We've made him aware that we are not going to let this matter drop, and that is enough for the moment. He will now have to be very careful, and I hope that will give us the time we need to catch these men.'

'Don't you believe he will now be frightened enough to withdraw his men?'

'No. We shook him today, but he is sure we have no proof of his involvement.'

'But that is true, surely? We are only surmising he is responsible.'

'Are we, Elizabeth?'

She sighed, knowing she wasn't going to get a full answer from Dan. 'I have a house full of secretive men. Do you have any idea how frustrating and worrying that is?'

'I know it is difficult, but I am asking you to curb your curiosity for a while longer, Elizabeth. This business with the buyers might turn out to be just what we need to put an end to James's problem.'

'I'll try, but I will not tolerate anything that interferes with the smooth running of the estate. So, will you tell me what you want me to do next?'

'We are going back to your house now. There is no point in visiting the other buyers; Masters will spread the word of our interest. We have to catch these men, because it will be the only way to remove this threat – and the only way to stop Gresham.'

Beth opened her mouth to ask another question, but Dan stopped her by pulling the horses to a halt. 'Leave this to us. Just wait, Elizabeth.'

She sighed loudly in exasperation. 'You are asking a great deal, Dan.'

'Most young ladies would be grateful to be shielded from any unpleasantness.'

'I am not most young ladies!'

'Indeed you are not,' he said, urging his horse forward into a gallop.

Nineteen

'I thought the ladies would never leave us tonight,' James exclaimed, closing the library door firmly and locking it. 'That will stop them coming back in here while we talk. I thought I was going to have to carry Alice upstairs and make her retire for the night. The girls went reluctantly, but they didn't make a fuss.'

'What did you expect, James? They want to know what the hell is going on.'

'So do we, Grandfather,' Alex said, looking enquiringly at Daniel. 'Tell us what your plan is, Dan.'

'To catch these men and make them tell us who is paying them. Once we have proof it is Gresham, we will then be able to have him arrested. And then your promise to Edward will have been honoured, James.'

'Not good enough!' James exploded. 'He'll receive a mild rebuke and be set free. He's guilty of blackmail and murder, Dan.'

'That was thirty years ago,' Daniel said firmly. 'I told Edward it would be impossible to charge him with that now. In my opinion, the best we can do is to completely ruin his reputation.'

James was shaking his head. 'From what I've heard, he doesn't have a reputation of high enough standing to ruin. I won't settle for that. There must be more we can do.'

'Why not take his estate from him? It borders the Sharland acres. Be useful for your school, wouldn't it?'

All eyes turned towards the elderly man sitting comfortably and swirling a large brandy around in his glass.

'And how are we going to do that, Grandfather?' James asked softly.

'Catch these men, like Dan said, persuade them to talk and then make Gresham an offer he couldn't possibly refuse. Once you have done that, I will take Alice and the girls to London, and we will spread rumours he will never be able to recover from.'

'You're a devious old man,' Alex said, laughing and shaking his head in disbelief.

'So you've said frequently. What do you think, James? Would you settle for ruining Gresham that way?'

James looked up at his friend. 'What about it, Dan?'

'I think Edward would approve.'

'He would. But is it possible?'

'It's worth a try. We'll all have to work together.' Daniel let his gaze rest on each man in turn. 'I'll set out a plan, and you will have to do as I say. Our first task will be to catch these men.'

'Absolutely.' Alex raised his glass. 'You give us the orders, and we'll obey them, won't we, Grandfather?'

'I wouldn't dream of doing anything else. Just as long as you include me in this, young man,' the grandfather said to Dan. 'I have a debt to settle with Gresham as well. If the blasted man hadn't disappeared, this would have been settled years ago.'

There was a tap on the door, and the handle rattled as someone tried to open it. The men frowned, wondering if the women had decided to join them after all.

'Your lordship!' the butler called. 'Mr Greenway would like to speak with you urgently.'

James hurriedly unlocked the door and opened it. 'Sorry you couldn't get in, Jenkins, but we didn't want to be disturbed. Come in, Henry.'

As soon as the estate manager entered, Alex asked anxiously, 'Are the pigs all right?'

'Yes, sir, but Charlie came to me and said those two men are sneaking around again. They came just as the light was fading, and he followed them. They spent some time examining the barns and stables. When it got too dark to see clearly, he lost them. They might still be on the estate.'

'Ah, hell! Where's the boy now?'

'I made him go home, my lord.'

'Good.' James sighed with relief. 'I wouldn't want him to get hurt. We'll have to make a thorough search of every building. There's no telling what they could be up to. It looks as if Gresham has stepped up his campaign against us.'

Dan nodded. 'That's what I thought he would do. A desperate man acts in haste and can make mistakes. This could be our chance. We are going to need every man we can muster for the search.'

'Stanley, the footman, will help, I'm sure. Shall I fetch him?'

'Please, Henry, but give him the choice. He doesn't have to put himself in danger if he doesn't want to.'

'Understood, your lordship.' The estate manager hurried out of the room.

Then Jenkins suddenly appeared. 'I'll help as well.'

'Thank you, Jenkins, but I have a very important task for you. These men could be dangerous and I don't want the ladies to be at risk should they enter the house while we are all outside. I need you and my grandfather to remain here and protect them. There are pistols in the desk drawer if you need them, Grandfather.'

'You take those, James. Jenkins and I will be all right.'

'We don't need them. Dan has guns with him.'

'Of course he has. How foolish of me to forget,' the elderly man remarked dryly.

Henry Greenway soon returned with the footman. 'I've explained the situation to Stanley, and he's eager to help.'

'Thank you.' James turned to Dan. 'What's the best way to tackle this?'

'We'll have to split up to cover as much ground as possible. Move quietly and don't call out to each other, and on no account are any of you to confront them on your own. Come to me and I'll deal with them. I'll stay in the area of the main barn.'

They all nodded agreement.

'Can you fire a gun, Stanley?'

'Yes, sir. I'm a reasonable shot.'

'Right, you have one of mine and Alex the other one. The rest of us can arm ourselves with anything to hand.' Dan glanced at each man. 'And be careful! Let's go.'

'What is all that noise?' Beth buried her head in the pillow and groaned.

'Wake up!' Helen ran into the room and pulled the covers from her. 'Please, Beth. I heard gunshots!'

The urgency in her friend's tone snapped Beth awake and she sat up. 'Gunshots! Is that what woke me?'

'Something serious has happened. I just know it!' An agitated Helen started dragging Beth out of bed. 'We might be needed.'

Beth opened her eyes wide for the first time and tumbled out of bed, hastily pulling on her clothes.

'Hurry!' Helen helped Beth fasten the buttons on her gown. 'From the noise and activity downstairs, something terrible has happened!'

That wiped away the last of Beth's sleepiness, and they both ran downstairs.

The scene that met them in the library was unbelievable. Dan, the grandfather and Jenkins were leaning over a man sprawled in an armchair – and there was blood everywhere. The man who had been hurt was James, and it looked very bad.

With a cry of distress, Helen pushed them all aside and placed her hands firmly over the injury in an effort to stop the bleeding.

'Take charge, Helen,' Dan said quickly. He turned and ran from the room.

'Stop standing around doing nothing!' Helen shouted at the men in the room. 'Someone go and fetch the physician. Now!'

'That hurts, woman!' James gasped. 'Get off me.'

'Shut up and keep still. Do you want to bleed to death?'

Alice ran into the room and straight up to James, her face bleached of all colour. 'Stupid, stupid!' she cried. 'Why couldn't you leave this alone? I told you it would lead to dangerous trouble.'

'Get out!' he growled as soon as he saw her. 'I don't need another female who is going to make a fuss.'

Beth pushed the men aside, ignoring his outburst, and snapped out her orders. 'Fetch me a pair of scissors, someone, and something to use as dressings. Has anyone gone for the physician?'

'Yes – Stanley,' the grandfather replied. He was standing beside his daughter and holding her hand to steady her. 'He'll be all right, my dear. I don't think the bullet has hit anything vital.'

James wiped the perspiration from his face with the uninjured hand. 'I don't want a bloody doctor.'

Scissors were thrust into Beth's hand. 'I don't care what you want. Let us tend you, or you are going to bleed to death.'

There was another muttered expletive.

'And you can moderate your language, your lordship,' Helen scolded.

'Oh, for heaven's sake, don't go all formal on me. You know my name.'

'Very well. Keep still, James, and let us cut away your shirt. We do not wish to add to your injuries.'

The scissors slice through the sleeve and across the shoulder of the elegant dress shirt.

'Oh!' gasped Alice. 'That bleeding must be stopped.'

Beth had already made a pad of linen from the shirt and placed it on his arm. 'All right, Helen, let us both press – hard!'

James clenched his teeth but said nothing.

Ten minutes later the bleeding had almost stopped, and Helen took the opportunity to inspect the wounds carefully, concentrating on what she had to do and not allowing fear for his life to come into her thinking. 'Whoever did this meant to kill you. There are two wounds, and a bullet might still be in the shoulder.'

'Then remove it!'

'That would be extremely dangerous and not necessary now I'm here.' The doctor hurried into the room. 'I'll need hot water, and everyone but her ladyship out of the room. I shall need her assistance.'

'I shall stay,' Alice declared.

'No.' Beth smiled to soften the refusal. 'You are already distressed, and this will not be pleasant.'

'Come, we must leave the doctor to do what is necessary.' Alice's father led her, still protesting, from the room.

'I'll see the hot water is sent in at once.' Beth went straight to the kitchen and was not surprised to see the entire staff there, anxious for news and eager to help. Pans of hot water were already bubbling on the stove.

'Oh, well done,' she praised. 'I'll take one now and come back if more are needed.'

The doctor made her put it on a small table beside James. As she did so, she heard Helen say gently, 'You may swear if you wish; I shall excuse you on this occasion.'

His fingers closed around Helen's. Then, with a grim expression, he said, 'Let's have done with this, doctor.'

★ ★ ★

Half an hour later Helen sank to her knees beside the chair and let out a ragged sigh. The bullet had been removed, and James had mercifully passed out. That had given the doctor the chance to stitch the wound and bind it without causing James any more pain.

The doctor checked his patient. 'There shouldn't be any permanent damage, but we must watch him carefully and hope he does not take a fever. You may allow the others to come back now; the men can help his lordship into bed.'

'I'm not going to bed! We still have work to do this night.'

'Ah, you are awake. I expected you to be unconscious for a while yet.' Helen wiped his face with a clean, cool cloth. 'You are a brave man; you did not curse at me once.'

He gave a weak smile. 'How did you know what to do to stop the bleeding?'

'I have been tending the estate workers and their families for some years, and I have received instruction from a physician.'

'I am grateful.' James tried to move and groaned.

'Stop that, young man,' the doctor admonished. 'You have lost a lot of blood and are going to need to rest.'

James leant his head back and closed his eyes. 'I thank you for what you have done for me, doctor, and you also, my dear Helen.'

Taken aback that he should call her that, Helen felt his brow in alarm, but he was quite cool.

It was difficult making James go to his bed, but the doctor was firm, and, with Stanley's help, they practically carried him up the stairs, as he continued to curse under his breath.

'He always has been fiercely independent,' Alice said. 'Even as a young child, he insisted on doing everything himself, and if he didn't know how to accomplish the task, he persisted until he got it right. He will hate being incapacitated and having to rely on others. Especially tonight. He will want to be out there with them.'

'He is too badly hurt to be able to do anything for a while, so he will just have to rely on us for a while.' Helen looked down at her stained gown and grimaced at Beth. 'We're both in a mess and ought to change our gowns.'

Before they had a chance to go to their rooms, the front door burst open and Henry Greenway rushed in. 'They've got one man cornered in the main barn. Alex and Daniel are dealing with him. The other one is heading for the stables, we believe.'

'Let's go and get him!' The grandfather actually ran, his age and infirmities forgotten for the moment.

'Father, come back!' Alice called desperately, but to no avail. Both men rushed for the back entrance of the house and disappeared.

The footman appeared at the top of the stairs and looked over the banister. 'What's going on, Miss Langton?'

'They think one of the men is heading for the stables. Mr Greenway and Lord Sharland's grandfather have gone after him. Would you go and help them, please?'

Without a word, Stanley came down, several steps at a time, and ran with great speed to catch up with the others.

Taking a deep breath, Alice took a moment to compose herself and control her fears for her family. 'I had better check that James is comfortable and ask the physician if he could stay a while longer. We might have need of him again before this night is over. If Edward was here now, I would give him the sharp end of my tongue for placing my family in such danger. I have told them time and time again to leave this in the past, but they would not listen to me.'

Still talking angrily to herself, Alice went up the stairs while the girls watched, not able to comfort Alice in this situation. One of her family had been shot, and the other two were in great danger. What could they do or say?

'What is happening is terrible for all of us, but for Alice it must be terrifying,' Helen said, shaking her head in dismay. She studied her ruined gown again. 'I was going to change into a clean gown, but I think I will wait and see what happens. Let us pray there are no more serious injuries, but this is a dangerous situation, Beth. Our men are determined to catch these villains.'

'And with no thought for their own safety.' Beth studied her friend thoughtfully. 'You have just referred to everyone involved as "our men".'

'Did I? Well, I suppose that is how I consider them now. They have become a part of our lives.'

'Yes, they have,' Beth admitted. 'When James began to fill the house, I was determined not to trust or like them, but slowly my feelings towards them have changed. Not only do I trust them – especially Dan – but I have grown to like them. And Alice is a dear.'

Helen gave a weary smile. 'How things have changed.'

'And they will change again, Helen. The time will soon come when they will all leave here, and it is unlikely we shall see any of them again.'

'That will be a sad time.'

'Yes, it will.' Beth forced the disquieting prospect from her head. 'We can't stand around doing nothing, so let's go to the kitchen and see refreshments are prepared for the men. They are going to need something later.'

Cook was already at work preparing enough food for a feast. The large stew pan was already bubbling away, giving off an appetizing aroma. Several large savoury and fruit pies were cooling on racks, and the scrubbed wooden table used by the staff had been set ready for use.

'We'll eat in here,' Cook announced. 'The men can come in when they've done with what they have to do this night. They won't mind eating in here for once.'

'That's very sensible, Mrs Howard,' Beth said. 'Is there anything we can do?'

'Well, if you wouldn't mind taking a tray up to his lordship. Poor man, he must have plenty of nourishment.'

Beth nodded agreement and couldn't help wondering just when everyone's opinion of James had changed. In the beginning they had all viewed him with fear and distrust, but now he was liked and respected. Somehow he had gradually crept into their hearts and minds.

Twenty

Cook insisted that the physician be fed as well, so Beth and Helen took a tray each. They had just reached the bedroom door when they heard soft footfalls behind them and turned in alarm, thinking one of the villains might have entered the house.

'Oh, Tom!' Beth gasped. 'You gave us a fright.'

'Sorry, Miss Langton.' His face was aglow with excitement. 'I got a message for his lordship.'

'I'm not sure he should be disturbed,' Helen told the boy. 'He has been hurt rather badly.'

'I know, but Mr Edgemont said I was to tell him they'd caught both the men. He might rest easy if he knows that, he said.'

'Ah, that's different – and good news indeed. Open the door for us, Tom, and you had better come in with us.'

'Yes, Miss Langton.' He slid in front of them and pushed the door open after knocking softly first.

The doctor and James were playing chess when they walked in. Beth shook her head. 'I thought your patient was supposed to be resting?'

The doctor shrugged. 'This was the only way I could keep him in bed. Good, you've brought us some food; we are very hungry.'

Tom edged forward, bobbing his head to the men. 'I got a message for you, sir. Mr Edgemont said to tell you they've caught both the men.'

'Thank the heavens for that!' James sighed with relief and rested his head back on the pillows piled up behind him. 'Has anyone else been hurt, Tom?'

'A few bumps and bruises, sir, but nothing serious, Mr Greenway said.' Tom was so excited he couldn't stand still. 'Mr Greenway said it was quite a scrap. Wish I'd seen it, but Cook wouldn't let me go out there.'

'And quite right, young man,' James told him sternly. 'Those men are dangerous, and they had guns.'

'Yes, sir. Er . . . we're all sorry you was hurt, and hope you get better quick.'

'Thank you, Tom. If you hear any more news, I want you to come straight up here and tell me. Will you do that?'

'Yes, sir!' The boy beamed with pleasure. 'I can do that, sir.'

'Good lad. Now you go and get something to eat. It smells wonderful.'

Thrilled to be included in these exciting events, Tom bobbed his head again and hurried out.

'Now eat.' Helen put her tray in front of James.

Beth put her tray on a small table which she pulled over to the doctor. 'It looks as if we won't be requiring your services again tonight, Doctor Gregson, thank heavens, but eat before you leave.' She then walked over to have a look at James, noting how pale he was. 'And you really must rest after you've finished your meal, James.'

He didn't have time to reply because the door swung open and Alice came in, followed by her father and Alex. 'My apologies for disturbing your patient, doctor, but these two insisted on seeing James. Just look at them!'

The girls gasped at the sight. They were filthy dirty; Alex had a cut lip and his grandfather had the beginnings of a black eye.

Doctor Gregson was immediately on his feet. 'Let me have a look at you.'

'We're all right,' the elderly man declared, grinning. 'You finish your meal. I haven't had so much fun for a long time. They put up quite a fight, James, but we were too much for them.'

'So I can see,' James said, his mouth twitching at the corners. 'Where are they now?'

'In the barn, tied up nice and tight. Dan is with them.'

'Have you sent for the constabulary?' Beth asked.

'Not yet.' Alex walked over to the bed, examined James's tray and pinched a piece of pie. 'Dan wants to talk to them first.'

The grandfather sniggered, helping himself to something from the doctor's tray.

'Leave that food alone! There's plenty in the kitchen for you.' Beth was watching the men with a frown on her face. They were all smiling at each other in a strange way, making her suspicious. 'What do you mean *Dan wants to talk to them first*?'

'He's just going to ask them who hired them.' The grandfather took something from his grandson's tray this time. 'Won't take him long. Our Dan's a very persuasive man.'

They were all laughing now. The doctor picked up his bag. 'I think it's time I left, Miss Langton. I'll come by in the morning to check on my patient.'

'Thank you for staying. I'll see you out.'

Beth opened the door and turned her head to look at the others in the room. It was quite crowded, and they didn't look as if they were going anywhere. 'I assume you are all remaining here?'

'We'll entertain James for a while,' Alex told her.

'He's supposed to be resting,' Helen sighed. 'But I'll have food sent up to you.'

'That would be welcome.' Alex gave them one of his engaging smiles and winced when his cut lip hurt. 'We are very hungry.'

'So I have noticed,' Beth said dryly. 'James has hardly had anything to eat. You have eaten most of it, and I don't believe you left much for Doctor Gregson, either.'

'Would you like to eat downstairs before you leave?' Helen asked the doctor. 'Cook has prepared plenty for everyone.'

'No, thank you, Miss Langton. I'll be on my way now my services are no longer needed. Try not to let Lord Sharland's family tire him too much.'

'We'll try, Doctor Gregson, but I doubt they will listen to us.'

'Do what you can,' the doctor said as they made their way downstairs. 'The bullet wounds and loss of blood would have left most men unconscious for hours, but he's a strong, determined man.'

'Don't you mean stubborn?' Beth asked.

'That too.' The doctor laughed quietly. 'Ah, splendid – my horse is ready and waiting for me. Thank you, young man.'

'We couldn't put him in the stables because of what's going on, sir,' Tom explained. 'But I rubbed him down, and fed and watered him, so he's been quite happy – and safe.'

'You've done well.' The doctor slipped a couple of coins to Tom, and then mounted and rode away.

Beth caught hold of the boy before he scampered away. 'Have you heard what is going on in the barn, Tom?'

He shook his head. 'We've all been told not to go there. Mr

Edgemont's with the men they caught. And they ain't sent for the law yet.'

Beth and Helen gave each other worried looks but said nothing. Tom tugged at Beth's sleeve, his fingers to his lips.

'He's a spy and trained in things like this – so Charlie says,' the boy whispered. 'Because he's quiet-spoken and a real gent, people think he's harmless – but he ain't. Wouldn't do to make an enemy of him, as I expect these men are finding out. Do you need me any more, Miss Langton?'

'No, thank you, Tom; you can go now.'

'Oh, dear,' Beth said, shaking her head as the boy tore off, eager not to miss anything. 'I do hope this is all the imaginings of young boys.'

'I'm sure it is,' Helen assured her. 'They've been building up stories ever since they arrived. A mystery excites them.'

'Of course you're right.' Beth linked her arm through Helen's. 'We had better see about the food. Then we really must change our gowns and have something to eat. I do declare I am feeling quite famished after all the excitement.'

An hour later, clean and with a substantial meal inside them, the girls were feeling drowsy in the warmth of the kitchen when Dan strolled in. They leapt to their feet, anxious for news.

'Is everything all right? Did they tell you anything? Have you sent for the police?'

A slow smile spread across Dan's face. 'The answer to all your questions is yes, Elizabeth. They are being taken off to gaol at this very moment.'

'Thank goodness for that!' Beth studied him, trying to find any signs of injury, but nothing was visible. He looked tired and strained around the eyes but was otherwise his usual self.

'You must be hungry.'

'I am.' Dan smiled at Cook. 'Would you mind if I took my food upstairs? I have to talk to the others.'

'That will be quite all right, sir.' Mrs Howard smiled back. 'They are all up there, so I'll send up trays with enough food for all of you. I expect they are still hungry.'

As Dan left the kitchen, Helen nudged Beth. 'Look at Tom's face. He's found a hero to worship.'

Beth nodded and turned away to hide her smile, not wanting the boy to see them amused by him. He was such an engaging youth, and she was very fond of him.

'We'll take the trays up, Mrs Howard,' Helen said.

'Me too! I can help, please, Miss Langton!'

'Thank you, Tom. That will be a great help.'

The moment Dan entered the bedroom he was bombarded with questions, with everyone talking at once. He held up his hand to stop them. 'I'll tell you everything; just give me a chance. First, I want to know how James is.'

'I'm all right. The doctor doesn't believe there will be any permanent damage, but I'm going to be out of things for a couple of days.'

'More than that,' Alice declared. 'You are to stay in that bed until the doctor declares you fit enough to move around again.'

'I can't! The school is nearing completion, and we've still got Gresham to deal with.' James sighed in exasperation and turned his attention to Dan. 'Please tell me it is Gresham, and we haven't been pursuing the wrong man.'

'Yes, it's him. Edward was right to suspect him.' Dan handed James a sheet of paper. 'Those men didn't want to talk at first, but I was patient, and after a while they began to talk freely. Their orders were to set fire to the smaller outbuildings and scatter the horses. Gresham told them that they could sell any animals they stole and keep the proceeds. I wrote down everything they said, but they refused to sign it, I'm sorry to say. It won't be a great deal of use to us in court, but it is something we can hold against Gresham.'

'And it does confirm our suspicions about the man. It took you more than an hour, Dan, and perhaps another hour might have made them eager to sign.' The grandfather was smirking as he peered at the paper his grandson was holding. 'Their confession is rather short.'

'Long enough for what we want.' Dan took the paper and slipped it back into his pocket.

'Can we have Gresham arrested?' Alex asked, looking doubtful. 'After all, he didn't shoot James.'

'True, but he paid someone else to do it, and we would have to prove that. If that's what we want to do.'

'What do you mean by that, Dan?'

'I think we should try your grandfather's plan first, James, and if that doesn't work, we can have him arrested. But we'll have to move fast.'

'Splendid! We can hold the threat of gaol over his head.' Grandfather gave Dan a respectful glance. 'You're a clever boy, but we'll have to watch Gresham carefully or he will run again. He's obviously got a good hiding place, because we couldn't find the rogue all these years, and we know Edward never gave up looking for him. We wouldn't have caught up with him now if he hadn't inherited that estate from a relative. Wonder where the devil went?'

'Australia.'

'What?' everyone exclaimed together, staring at Dan in astonishment.

'How do you know that?' Alex asked.

Dan merely smiled.

'Daft question – of course you won't tell us. So, he was on the other side of the world,' the grandfather muttered. 'No wonder we couldn't find the bugger.'

'What do we do next, Dan?' James leant his head back and closed his eyes for a moment, and then opened them again. 'I'll be glad when this is all over and I can settle down to running my school.'

'Won't be long now,' Dan assured him. 'You leave everything to us.'

'I'll have to.' James started when there was a loud thump on the door. 'What the devil is that?'

'Open the door, please!' they heard Beth call.

Alex rushed over to the door, swung it open and grinned at the sight, calling over his shoulder, 'Food – and lots of it.'

A dressing table and chest were quickly cleared and the trays put on them, with sighs of relief from Beth, Helen and Tom.

'My goodness!' Alice exclaimed when she saw the amount of food loaded on the trays. How did you manage to carry those up the stairs?'

'It wasn't easy,' Helen laughed, 'but Cook insisted that you would all be very hungry. You must help yourselves; the only one we are serving is James. Tom, will you hand round the plates, please?'

They were soon happily eating, and Beth took the opportunity to ask Dan, 'Is it all over?'

'Not yet, but it shouldn't be long now.' He smiled kindly. 'But you can tell your buyers that they will not be troubled by these men again.'

'They will be relieved – thank you.' Noticing that Tom was still in the room, obviously eager to stay, Beth was about to say he could go to bed now when James called the boy over.

'Yes, sir.' He hurried to the bedside. 'Can I do something for you, sir?'

'Indeed you can. I am going to be stuck in this bed for a couple of days and will need some company. I'd like you to come and visit me every afternoon for an hour or so. Do you think you could do that?'

The boy shot Beth a beseeching look, and when she nodded, he said excitedly, 'Yes, sir. I'd like that, sir.'

'Good.' James nodded his thanks to Beth for giving the boy permission. 'I'm sure we can find plenty to talk about. What are you interested in?'

'Horses, sir.' Tom was now leaning on the bed. 'My dad was the stable master here before he died, and that's what I want to do when I'm old enough.'

'He's excellent with the animals,' Beth told James, 'and seems to know if they are not feeling right. I think they know he loves and cares about them.'

'They tell me if they ain't happy.' He gave a bashful smile. 'Sounds daft, but they do.'

'I believe you, Tom. Can you read and write?'

'Oh, yes, sir. Miss Langton insisted I learn my letters, but I ain't as good as Charlie. He's clever. He can run his finger along a line of numbers and he's added them up.' Tom shook his head. 'Don't know how he does that. He told me you've been teaching him lots of things.'

James nodded. 'It's true Charlie has promising abilities, Tom, but everyone has different talents. Charlie is good at reading and arithmetic, but he can't care for horses and talk to them like you do. That's a talent to be proud of, young man.'

'Gosh! I never thought of it like that. So, you mean we're all different?'

'That's right, and everyone's talents should be cherished.'

'Cor, you mean Charlie's good at some things, and I'm good at others.' Tom shot Beth a wide grin, and there was a gleam of confidence there she had not seen before.

'That's right. So, when you come and see me tomorrow, I'll tell you about the history of horses. And it would be helpful for you to know more about their anatomy.'

When Tom gave him a puzzled look, James explained. 'Their inner workings and bone structure'

'Ah, yes, I'd like that, sir.' The boy's face was shining with pleasure and anticipation. 'What time do you want me to come?'

'Let's say two o'clock, shall we? Can you manage that?'

'Yes, sir. Two o'clock – I'll be here.'

'Good.' James smiled at him. 'Now, I believe it is past your bedtime, don't you?'

Tom pulled a face. 'Suppose so, but I don't think I'll be able to sleep, with all the excitement going on tonight.'

'I agree it might be difficult, but I think you should try.'

'Yes, sir.' He beamed at everyone in the room, nodded his head and practically ran out of the room, eager to tell the others downstairs what he was going to do.

'Tell me about him? Where are his family?'

'His mother died when he was born, and his father was killed in a riding accident five years ago. They had both been with us for many years. We are Tom's family now. Mrs Howard took the place of his mother and Jenkins of his father. He's a good boy, and we try to see he is brought up well and is happy.'

James nodded. 'I'll see what I can do for him.'

Beth studied James carefully, seeing a different side of his character. This man had had an upbringing of wealth and privilege, and yet he was going to open a school for boys from a poor background. 'You care about children like Charlie and Tom, don't you?'

'I do. Why should only the wealthy have access to a good education? There are hundreds of bright children who have their education cut short because they are poor. I can't help all of them, but I'll give as many as I can the opportunity of a better life.' He leant his head back and closed his eyes. 'I'm so damned tired.'

'It's time you rested.' Alice came over and took the tray from him. 'I'll sleep in the chair tonight in case you need anything. Now, everyone out!' she ordered.

'Helen, before you go, would you do something for me?'

'Of course.'

'The inside rooms of the school are to be finished this week, so would you oversee the work for me? I want a comfortable, bright look to the rooms. Don't let the men turn it into a bleak place.'

'I will be delighted to do that, James.'

'Thank you.' He opened his eyes and gave a slight smile. 'I'll expect a full report every evening.'

'Of course.'

Twenty-One

'How are you this morning, James?' Dan asked.

'I hurt and I'm feeling helpless, frustrated and worried, Dan. Don't you think we should get Gresham locked up so he can't do any more harm?'

'We can, if that's what you want. But he will serve a short sentence, if that, and then he will be around again. And he will be even more determined to cause you as much trouble as possible. Remember, I told you it will be just about impossible to send him to the gallows for a crime committed thirty years ago. We haven't any witnesses or hard proof. The only two people who could have testified are dead, so all we can get him for now will be hiring those men.'

'And he might not even be put in prison for that?'

'A very real possibility. It will only be his word against the two men we caught. We can prosecute him, but I cannot guarantee success.'

James shook his head and ran a hand over his face. 'I can't risk that, Dan. You know why I'm here, and what my father feared as soon as Gresham appeared again.'

'And it looks as if Edward was right. Gresham has already made a couple of clumsy attempts to undermine the Langton estate so that he could step in when things were desperate and buy for a ridiculously low price. Thank goodness we've managed to put a stop to him. He must want this land very desperately. All the time Edward was alive, Elizabeth was safe, because he dealt quickly with any attempts to disrupt the smooth running of the estate. He told me that had happened more than once since Gresham turned up as a neighbour.' Dan perched on the edge of the bed. 'This man is evil, James. He'll try again if we don't stop him once and for all.'

'We've got to! My father loved Elizabeth like a daughter, and if his fears are proved correct, then I'll never be able to forgive myself.'

'Neither will I.' Dan stood up. 'You can only stay until Elizabeth's next birthday, and then we will all move out. Those two lovely girls won't stand a chance.'

'And Helen has suffered enough already. If her friend finds herself in the same situation, what will happen to them?' James looked up at his friend imploringly. 'What are we going to do, Dan?'

'I believe the best way to stop him is to strip him of his wealth and ruin his reputation in a way he will never be able to recover, as your grandfather suggested. Then we'll see if we can have him put in prison for a while.'

'It seems the best way,' James agreed. 'I'll have to leave that to you. So, how are you going to do it?'

'My first task will be to see that these men are tried – very publicly – so Gresham is forced to attend the trial. Once I've arranged that, I'm going to have a long talk with the man.'

'Good, I'll come with you.' The grandfather walked into the bedroom, Alex right behind him, and studied his grandson. 'You look terrible.'

'I feel it! You can't go with Dan, Grandfather; it could get nasty.'

'Of course it could, with Dan doing the . . . talking.'

'I do wish you'd stop that,' Dan sighed. 'You're ruining my reputation. I expect everyone on the estate believes I'm an assassin!'

'No,' the grandfather laughed. 'They are probably thinking those two boys are right and you're a spy. And it's no good you protesting. You are not facing Gresham alone. This man threatened my daughter's life, and I had to hide her away not knowing when he would strike.'

'If you'd paid him, he might have left you alone,' James said.

'I did pay him! He wasn't satisfied and kept coming back for more. What was I to do – keep handing over money to him? He only disappeared when I sent the law after him. It was years before I felt he really had gone. Call me a nasty old man all you like, James, but I did what I thought was right for you and your mother.'

James sighed. 'I'll never believe it was the right way to handle it, and I have never understood why Mother never contacted her husband. She could have done so quite easily without you knowing about it.'

'She thought he was dead.'

'What did you say?' James sat straight up in bed, eyes narrowed on his grandfather.

'Now, don't fly into a rage! Ever since I sent for your father, you have never allowed me to talk to you about the past, but now you are captive in that bed it's time you heard the truth. You already know that your mother and Edward ran away to get married because I disapproved. Gresham must have found out and thought it was a good way to make money. However, things went wrong and the coachmen opened fire on him. Edward was shot and was thought unlikely to live, so I told my daughter he had died. But Gresham wasn't prepared to give up and threatened your mother's life if I didn't pay him a substantial amount of money, so I sent her to safety. You had been born when Edward came to me; it had taken him that long to recover. Your mother was not strong after your birth, so I told him she had died.'

'How could you have done such a thing? You denied them nearly ten years together,' James remarked through gritted teeth.

'I am very aware of that, but I kept you both safe. That was enough for me. When it became clear that your mother was dying, I sent for Edward. After the way I had behaved, the least I could do for him was give him his son. He was a sensible man and, seeing you were happy with Alice and Alex, he decided not to take you away from the home you had always known.'

'Why the hell didn't you tell me all this before?'

'Because after that you only ever spoke to me to hurl insults. You weren't ready to listen, and how the devil could I excuse what I had done? I couldn't, James, and I shall have to live with that for the rest of my life!'

'My father never said a word about any of this, but you should have, Grandfather.'

'I should have done a lot of things, James, but when the people you love are in danger, you don't always act rationally.' His grandfather grimaced and looked at Dan. 'But for now we have this mess to deal with. When are we going to see Gresham?'

'I have to go to the court this morning, but if I'm back in time, I'll visit him this afternoon. You can come only if you agree to be quiet and let me handle everything.'

'I'll be as quiet as a mouse.'

James gave a dry laugh. 'And if you believe that, Dan, you'll believe anything.'

'Ah, an insult! You're feeling better.'

'No, I'm not! I need to get out of this bloody bed and help Dan.'

'Language,' his grandfather admonished.

'Ha! You're a fine one to talk.'

'Stop it, you two!' Alex glared at them. 'If we're going to sort out this mess, then we've all got to work together – in harmony. What do you want me to do, Dan?'

'Stay on the estate. See Henry Greenwood and work with him to keep a lookout for anything unusual. Has anyone seen Elizabeth and Helen this morning?'

'They both came to see me about an hour ago,' James told Dan. 'Helen has gone to the school, and Elizabeth rode out to visit her buyers.'

'They are up and out already?' Alex showed his surprise. 'It's only eight o'clock now.'

'I doubt those girls have ever had a life of ease, or wanted it,' his grandfather remarked. 'From what I've heard, Elizabeth has been involved in running this large estate from an early age, and I expect Helen's life has been much the same. Damned fine girls.'

'In that case, Alex, I'm changing your task. I want you to find out if Elizabeth has taken one of the staff with her. If not, try to catch up with her and stay with her until she returns here.'

'I'll go at once.' Alex left quickly.

'Good thinking,' the grandfather said, nodding his approval. 'That beast likes to use women. It's his way of getting us men to do what he wants.'

'If he touches either of them, I'll kill him and gladly hang for the crime!' James threw back the covers and struggled to sit on the edge of the bed, sweat pouring down his face.

'Oh, no, you don't!' In two strides, Dan was by the bed and lifting James with ease to put him back in the bed. If you open those wounds again, you could be in this bed for weeks, not days. Now, you listen to me. It is highly unlikely Gresham will try anything for a few days. He'll wait and see what we are going to do now we've caught those men. I'm just being cautious; we don't want to be taken by surprise again. Relax and get well,

James, because there are enough of us to deal with this at the moment. If it looks as if we are going to have more trouble than we can handle, I'll bring in more men.'

'Damned fool!' His grandfather had a cloth and was wiping his grandson's face. 'If you kill yourself, Alice will never forgive me. We didn't expect those men to be armed and ready to kill, so we won't make the same mistake again. Trust Dan. Hell, why do you think Edward brought him into this?'

'I know, but it is agony being stuck here and wondering what the devil is happening!'

'Of course it is, my boy, but you've got to remain in bed. Where's Alice?'

'Retired to get some rest. She was here all night.'

'Ah, then we won't disturb her until the afternoon. I'll stay with you for now.'

James didn't protest but rested his head back, almost as white as the sheets covering him. He nodded and closed his eyes.

'Off you go, Dan,' the grandfather said softly. 'Would you ask Cook to send us up some breakfast? I'll see James eats something.'

Dan nodded and left silently.

It was a busy morning for Dan. Once the court officials knew of his profession and family, he was given access to the prisoners and anyone else he needed to talk to. Satisfied that he had done all he could that morning, he returned to the Langton estate and went straight up to see James. He was much relieved to see him looking brighter and calmer.

'How did you get on?' James asked the moment he walked into the room.

'We will have to wait for the judge to arrive, but the good news is that they are expecting one within the next week. They have a list of cases waiting to be heard. The men are being held in the local gaol until then. All we can do now is wait.'

'Will you act as prosecutor?' the grandfather asked.

'No, but I will be called as a witness, and so will Henry Greenway.'

'What about me?'

Dan shook his head. 'You are too badly injured to attend court.

That's what I will tell them, and I'm sure the doctor will confirm that. I believe it would be for the best.'

'In other words, you want me to stay out of it. Well, I will do as you say. As a barrister, you know what you're doing.'

'I bet you didn't tell them what else you do.'

'Don't you start that again, Grandfather Beaufort, or I won't take you with me this afternoon.'

The elderly man gave a deep rumbling laugh of amusement just as Alice walked into the room, carrying a tray for James.

'Oh, Dan, you're back. Lunch is being served in the dining room for you. The doctor has been and was pleased with James. He said if he continues to rest and eat well, he should have healed enough to get up in a few days' time. But he will have to do very little for another two weeks.'

'I'm relieved to hear that, Alice,' Dan said, ignoring the scowl on his friend's face.

'Yes, it is good news.' Alice studied her father. 'And what are you looking so pleased about?'

'The old devil is enjoying himself,' James told her. 'Do you know where Alex is?'

'He's still out accompanying Elizabeth; so Mr Greenway told me.'

'I'll leave you to have your lunch, James. I'm starving. Come on,' Dan said to the grandfather. 'I'll tell you what I intend to do this afternoon.'

'Are you still going to see Gresham today?'

'Yes. It would be impolite not to let him know we have caught the men causing all the trouble. Don't you think?'

'Absolutely. I wish I could come with you.'

'Never mind. I shall have your grandfather to protect me.' Dan kept a perfectly straight face, making James and Alice laugh at the ridiculous thought. The elderly man just smirked.

'You'll have to watch him,' James warned. 'He could ruin everything for you.'

'No, he won't.' Dan tipped his head on one side and studied the grandfather. 'You can put on your confused old man act, and then if you say something I don't want mentioned, I can dismiss it as the ramblings of a confused old man. Of course, it will be better if you say nothing at all, but I expect that is asking too much?'

'We'll have to wait and see, won't we?' He was grinning broadly now. 'Come on, let's eat. I'm hungry.'

'The best of luck, Dan.' James said as they left the room.

'Now, you know what you've got to do?' Dan asked the grandfather as they dismounted in front of the Gresham home. I want him unsettled so that the shock I'm about to give him will be even greater. I'm relying on you to play your part. It is unlikely he will remember you after all these years, but it doesn't matter if he does. Don't let your personal feelings get in the way.'

The elderly man nodded. 'We'll have him so jumpy he won't know which way to turn.'

'Good. Let's start making this man pay for his crimes, recent and past.'

They were shown into the library without delay.

'Good afternoon, Mr Edgemont.' Gresham stood as soon as they entered. 'I don't believe I've had the honour of meeting this gentleman.'

Grandfather Beaufort had seemed to shrink in size and now had a vague expression on his face. He started shaking Gresham's hand vigorously. 'The Earl of Renton, sir, but you can call me Your Grace.'

Dan drew in a deep breath rather loudly. 'Now then, you know that isn't true.'

'Isn't it? Oh, well, it's a nice name anyway. What are we doing here, Daniel?'

'We're visiting Sir Peter Gresham because I have some news for him,' Dan explained patiently.

'Lots of books here. I like books.'

'I'm sure Sir Peter wouldn't mind you looking at them while we talk. Would you, sir?'

'Er . . . No, but be careful. Some of them are very valuable.'

'You must excuse him, sir,' Dan said quietly, his eyes never leaving the elderly man as he ambled around the room. 'He's a little confused and has been upset today.'

'Who is he?' Gresham didn't look very happy to have this unpredictable man roaming around and touching his possessions.

'A friend of Miss Langton. His grandson usually looks after him, but I'm sorry to say that isn't possible now. That's why I'm here. Last night we caught two intruders who were intent on causing damage. Unfortunately, they were armed, and the grandson was shot.'

'I'm sorry to hear that. Did you kill the men?' Gresham asked quickly.

Dan shook his head. 'We captured them unharmed. They are now residing in the local gaol; by the time they come to trial, they could be facing a murder charge.'

At that moment a loud cackle of laughter came from across the room and, distracted, Gresham glanced over at Grandfather. 'What's he doing? Be careful with that!'

'Daniel, have a look at this. It's full of pretty pictures. I like this one. I think I'll keep this.'

'No!' Gresham rushed over and took the book out of the elderly man's hand. 'You mustn't tear out pages!'

Grandfather looked upset and even more confused. 'I don't like this man, Daniel. I want to go home. Where's my grandson? I want to see my grandson! He wouldn't talk to me this morning.' A tear began to trickle down his cheek.

'Don't get upset again,' Dan comforted. 'He was asleep, that's all. I won't be long now, and then we'll go home.'

'Oh, good,' he said, beginning to wander around the room again, this time looking at the paintings and ornaments.

'Don't touch anything.'

'I won't . . . they are all fakes anyway. Er . . .' He studied Dan, frowning. 'What's your name? Why am I here with you?'

'I'm Daniel, your grandson's friend – remember?'

'You tell him to talk to me.'

Seeing that Grandfather had now wandered over to look out of the window, Dan turned his attention back to Gresham, but his attitude had changed dramatically. Instead of the affable man he had appeared to be, he was now stern and towering over Gresham. 'The men have been eager to talk, and they have implicated you in this crime.'

'Then they are lying!' Gresham exploded. 'I was at home last night, and my servants will confirm that.'

'I'm sure they will, but these men have said that you were the person who hired them, and if that is proved, you could be found as guilty as them.' Dan reached into his pocket and pulled out an official document. 'That is a summons ordering you to appear at the trial. I will inform you of the date when the judge arrives, but it will be within the next week.'

'But this has nothing to do with me!' Gresham waved the paper at Dan, agitated and clearly alarmed. 'Surely you can't take their word against mine?'

'That will be up to the court, sir.' Dan walked over and took Grandfather by the arm, then turned back to Gresham. 'Oh, and please don't think of disappearing. I know you've escaped the law more than once before, but you won't be able to do that again. I have made arrangements for you to be watched – day and night.'

'Who are you?' Gresham was visibly shaking now.

'I'm a barrister by profession, sir.'

'Among other things,' Grandfather cackled. 'Can we go home now, Daniel?'

'Of course. Our business here is now finished – for the moment.'

Twenty-Two

Alice, Elizabeth and Alex were in the kitchen sampling Mrs Howard's cherry cake when Daniel and Grandfather arrived back at the house.

'Two more cups and plates,' Cook called as soon as they walked in. 'Sit down – you must be hungry.'

'How did everything go?' Alex asked Dan. 'Any problems?'

'It's early yet, but so far so good.'

'How is James, Alice?' her father wanted to know, edging towards the door.

'He's looking better, but you can't go up there yet. He's got Tom with him. Sit down, Father, and have tea and a piece of the delicious cake.'

'How did you get on with the buyers, Elizabeth?' Dan took a bite of cake and smiled at Mrs Howard in approval.

'They were all very relieved to hear that the men had been captured and were now in gaol, but they were upset to hear about James being shot.' She smiled at Dan. 'Mrs Masters said to thank you, and said she knew you were a fine man the moment she set eyes on you.'

'Well, I'm glad we didn't let her down then, but I hope you told her that I didn't do this on my own.'

Just then all conversation stopped as Tom burst into the kitchen clutching a book to his chest, his face rosy with pleasure.

'I've learned such a lot about horses, and I can go up again tomorrow. Gosh, he knows so much, and he's easy to understand.'

'That's because James is a first-class teacher,' Alex informed Tom.

'What's that you're holding on to so tightly, Tom?' Mrs Howard asked.

'It's a book about horses I've got to read. There are lots of beautiful pictures in it. Not just of the horses, but all their bones and everything.' Tom looked down at the book and then back to Mrs Howard, a slightly worried expression on his face. 'His lordship said I can keep it for my own, always. Is it all right to do that? It must have cost a lot of money. Can I keep it, please?'

Cook smiled and ruffled his hair affectionately. 'If his lordship said you can have it, then it's all right. Why don't you go and put it in your room? You don't want to get cherry cake all over it, do you?'

'That's my favourite.' He grinned, happy now that Mrs Howard had said it was all right for him to keep the book. 'I'll be back in a minute.'

'That was kind of his lordship,' Mrs Howard said as she watched the boy tear out of the room.

'James believes every child should receive a good education, whatever their abilities. Everyone has a talent of some kind, and it just has to be recognized and then expanded. It's his passion, and opening his school for the underprivileged is his way of helping a few.'

'It sounds a crazy idea to me, but I do hope it is a success for him.' The grandfather stood up. 'You coming, Dan? He'll be anxious to hear about your talk with Gresham.'

'You go and tell him. I'll be up when I've finished my tea.'

James was resting, his head back on the pillows and his eyes closed. He didn't move when the door opened.

'Are you all right, my boy?' his grandfather asked in alarm, rushing up to the bed.

'A little tired, that's all.' James opened his eyes and hauled himself upright, grimacing as he moved. 'Tell me the news.'

'He's really frightened now.' Then he gave James a moment-by-moment account of their visit to Gresham. 'He was so distracted by having this crazy old man poking through his possessions that he wasn't paying full attention to Dan. Then that clever boy changed – you know how he can do that – and he stepped in for the kill. I'll bet he's a demon in court. Not only did he hand Gresham an official summons to appear at the trial, but he let him know that he wouldn't be able to disappear this time.'

James was fully awake now. 'You mean he told him who we are and that we know all about his past?'

'Not in so many words, but Dan left him in no doubt that we

know more than we're saying and we intend to make him pay this time. We also hinted that you might not survive, and it could turn into a murder trial.'

'Ah, so that's why Dan wants me out of the way.'

'I would say so. Don't worry, my boy, we'll get him this time. Dan isn't going to let him go, whatever it takes, and he certainly isn't going to let him do anything to harm Elizabeth.'

James nodded. 'Dan has never told me exactly what my father asked him to do, but, like me, he won't break a promise.'

'It's more than that. Haven't you noticed?'

Frowning, James shook his head.

'I'd say our Dan has feelings for the girl.'

'Are you sure?'

Grandfather shrugged. 'I could be wrong. He hides his feelings well, but I've noticed one or two unguarded moments.'

'Ah, hell! I hope you're wrong because that could be awkward.'

'Maybe — maybe not. He won't do anything foolish, James — you can be sure of that. Whatever his feelings, when the time comes he will probably walk away from here and never come back.'

James fell silent and turned his head to gaze out of the window, and then he looked back at his grandfather. 'And talking about acting foolishly, I've been thinking over what you told me. I still believe you handled the situation badly, but I can understand your dilemma. I apologize for turning on you so savagely and refusing to listen when you tried to explain. What you did caused pain to others, but my actions were no better. I'm sorry for adding to your pain, Grandfather. I hope we can put the past behind us now.'

'Done, my boy!' There was a husky tone to his voice and he quickly brushed a hand over his eyes. 'We've had some grand fights over the years, haven't we?'

'We have indeed, and I expect we will still have a few.'

They looked at each other and laughed.

'What do you think, Mr Becks?' Helen surveyed the finished room with critical eyes. 'Is that deep cream colour suitable? His lordship doesn't want the place to look stark and uninviting, but neither does he want fancy wallpaper in the rooms.'

'It has a nice warm look about it, but if you're doubtful, why not paint that small piece of wood over there and let his lordship see the colour before the workmen do any more rooms.'

'That's an excellent idea!' Helen retrieved the wood from the corner of the room, picked up a brush and began painting it. When she had finished, she sat back on her heels and held it up. 'Does this look the same as the colour on the walls?'

'A very good match, my lady.' Becks hid a smile as he studied the girl sitting on the floor.

'Good, I'll take it and show him now; if he approves, the workers can carry on in the morning.'

'Be careful on your ride back. That paint is still wet.'

Helen laughed. 'I'm already a mess, Mr Becks, and a little more paint won't make any difference, but I'll try to keep as much off me as possible. And I won't gallop!'

The ride back proved more difficult than Helen had anticipated, but by the time Tom took her horse from her, she had only smudged a little on the end where she had been holding it.

'What on earth have you got there?' Alice exclaimed when she walked in.

'Be careful, it's still wet. I've brought this to see if James approves of the colour. How is he, Alice?'

'He's looking better and happier. Dan and my father are with him, and they appear to be in good spirits. And, surprisingly, James and his grandfather are not shouting at each other. In fact, I can't remember when I have seen them so friendly together.'

'That's lovely.' Helen smiled at Alice. 'I like your father.'

'The feeling is mutual, my dear. Locking him in his room was an inspired thing to do. He respected you for not trembling in his presence, and he thought it was great fun. But he still won't tell Beth where he's hidden the keys.'

'Ah, he's a rascal.' Helen shook her head in amusement.

Alice laughed so much it was a few moments before she could speak. 'He's been called many things, but nothing as mild as rascal. Now, don't you think you should take that up to James before you get any more paint on you, Helen?'

'Should I interrupt them? They might have things to discuss in private.'

'They'll stop their planning for you.' Alex stood up, a huge smile on his face. 'Rascal indeed! Wait until grandfather hears that. He'll love it.'

'Well, if you're sure. I can't stand here all evening holding this sample.'

'I'll come with you because I want to hear what has been happening. I've been Elizabeth's chaperone all day, but she's in conference with her estate manager now. Let me carry that for you.'

'Thank you, but I'll manage. No point in you getting covered in paint as well.'

Alex chuckled. 'I hope that's an old dress you are wearing, because it isn't going to be much use after this.'

Helen glanced down. 'It is a mess. Never mind – it couldn't be helped.'

When they reached the bedroom, Alex rapped once on the door and flung it open for her to enter.

'What on earth have you got there?' James exclaimed. 'What have you been doing, Helen?'

'Overseeing the finishing of the school, as you requested.' She glanced round at the others in the room. 'I apologize for disturbing you, but I need James to see this.'

'A plank of wood?' The grandfather smothered a laugh. 'Oh, my girl, you are a delight.'

'Not the wood.' She held it up so James could see it clearly. 'What do you think of this colour for the boys' rooms? We've finished one, but I don't want to continue with the rest unless you approve.'

'So you painted a piece of wood for me?' James was looking from the colour and then back to Helen, lingering on her soiled clothes.

'There isn't any other way to show you what it looks like. The workmen wanted to paint them white, but I said no to that. It took me ages to settle on the colour, but if you don't like it, you must tell me. We can still put up wallpaper.'

'No.' James shook his head and studied the colour again. 'I would say you have made an excellent choice. That colour should be quite suitable.'

'I'm pleased. I'll tell the men they can go ahead and do the rest of the rooms, then. Do you have a date when the furniture will be arriving?'

'It has been promised for the day after tomorrow.'

'My goodness, we will have to get a move on. Have you settled on a date to open the school?'

'I have two teachers from London who will be joining the staff, and they are in the process of visiting various schools. Already eight pupils have been chosen, so we should have enough young boys to open the school in the new year.'

'That is excellent – and exciting.' Helen smiled at everyone. 'If you will excuse me, gentlemen, I need to clean myself up before dinner.'

'Helen!' James called as she reached the door. 'We do have workmen employed for the decorations. All you need to do is see that the work is carried out properly.'

'I know that, and they are quite excellent, but I do need to show them what is required sometimes.' She gave everyone a bright smile and left.

'Damn me!' Grandfather laughed and slapped his knee. 'She's thoroughly enjoying herself. A lady of breeding who doesn't mind getting her hands dirty. I've never come across the like before. No wonder she's such good friends with Elizabeth, for they are both the same. They are rare creatures indeed, and they will cause a sensation in London. The young gentlemen will be queuing up to meet them. We will have them married off in no time.'

'You won't be able to order them around, Father,' Alice said as she walked into the room. 'They are strong, determined women who will not easily hand their lives over to a man. Whoever marries them will have to respect their independence. And they are not our kin.'

'And that's a great shame.' He looked pointedly at his grandsons. 'Anyone would be proud to have that kind of spirit in their family line.'

'Father! You are interfering again.'

'No, I'm not. I'm only saying that the girls are worthy of good marriages.'

'We know exactly what you're saying, Grandfather.' Alex glared at the elderly man. 'And you can leave me out of your crafty plans. I've made my choice.'

'You could do better.'

'Grandfather!' James raised his voice, but there was a touch of a smile on his face. 'You have made it clear that you think Elizabeth and Helen are lovely girls, but we will all make our own choices in life. I thought we had negotiated a truce, but if you go on like this, we will ship you back to Scotland, and think of all the fun you will be missing.'

He held up his hands. 'I surrender. It's hard to break the habit of a lifetime. I accept that Alex is going to marry his girl back home, and that you and Dan will grow into crusty old bachelors.'

'Oh, you're including me as well, are you?' Dan remarked, shaking his head in amusement.

'Of course I am, dear boy. You're as good as one of the family.'

'Really? I'm not sure if I should be pleased or frightened by that.'

The teasing tone in Dan's voice had them all roaring with laughter.

'Don't make me laugh so much,' James gasped. 'It hurts. Why don't you all go and get ready for dinner and leave me to rest.'

'But I want to know how Dan got on today.'

'Dan and Grandfather will tell you over dinner, Alex. The girls and Alice will want to hear the news as well.'

'We most certainly do,' Alice agreed.

'Tell them the situation so far, Dan. They are as involved as us now and have a right to know. But don't say anything about the personal side of the story. That's mine to explain when Gresham has finally been dealt with.'

Twenty-Three

Beth and Helen arrived just in time for dinner. They had been so busy telling each other about their day that they had missed the bell.

They were well into the second course before Alex insisted that Dan tell them all the news.

The girls listened, enthralled by Dan's account of the arrangements made that day and his visit to Gresham. They were all laughing about Grandfather's antics, and the atmosphere was so relaxed Beth thought she would take a chance and ask a couple of questions.

'It sounds as if all went well, but I am still puzzled.'

'About what?' Dan asked.

'Well, how is it you appear to have some influence with the court?'

'It's part of my job, Elizabeth. I'm a barrister by profession.' Dan shot a warning glance at the elderly man when he opened his mouth to add his usual remark. Grandfather smirked, picked up his glass and took a sip of wine instead of speaking. Satisfied, Dan turned his attention back to Beth.

Her surprise showed clearly on her expressive face. 'I see. Will you be involved in the trial?'

'Only as a witness. Henry Greenway will also be called to testify. You have another question?'

She nodded. 'I don't understand why Gresham threatened my buyers and then sent villains here to damage the estate. If he wanted to harm James, why didn't he attack the school he is building?'

'Because Gresham wants this estate, and his plan was to weaken it so he could buy it for a reduced price.'

'What?' Beth shot out of her chair, alarmed by this news. 'How long have you known about this?'

'Sit down, Elizabeth, and I'll explain.' Dan waited until she was seated and then continued. 'When Gresham returned to this country and took up residence nearby, he began to see if he could get his hands on your land. He had evidently inherited a lot of money and wanted to add to his property. It seems likely he thought if he became a large property owner, then society would accept him, and that was something he greatly desired. On his return from abroad, rumours spread about him and he was shunned. While Edward was here, he refused every offer, but, after hearing of his death, Gresham renewed his efforts, as we have witnessed. Edward knew you would be vulnerable, so he made James your temporary guardian and ordered him to move in here. He also left a letter asking me to join James here. I have already explained this to your estate manager. So, you see, we both had reasons for invading your home.'

Beth was stunned, and it took a few moments to compose herself. 'So James moved in here to investigate Gresham, and to protect me at my godfather's request. Why didn't he tell me?'

'Edward didn't want you to know in case his suspicions were unfounded; if that had been the case, you would have been worried unnecessarily.'

'I thought he knew me better than that, but I can see now that I never really knew him very well. He was a dear man and I loved him, but I never guessed he was hiding so many secrets.'

'He loved you also, and only did what he thought was best for you, Elizabeth.'

'I can see that, and he was right. If he hadn't asked you both to come here, I could have been in dire straits by now, because I would not have been able to deal with that man on my own.' She looked at the men around the table, her eyes misted with unshed tears. 'Thank you.'

'We are only doing a favour for a man we all admired and respected.' Dan turned his attention to Helen. 'We are also deeply sorry that we were not in time to save your father and your estate. Edward was devastated about that.'

'What do you mean?' Helen had turned quite pale. 'My father gambled everything away. You could not have done anything about his losses.'

'That is true, but we could have stopped Gresham from calling in the markers he had purchased from others. The fact that he made such a large demand all at once was more than your father could handle.'

Helen shook her head, confused. 'I don't understand. I repaid everyone, but Gresham was not among them. The largest payment was to a man by the name of Walton. I never saw him, but most of them sent a representative to collect.'

'He would have done the same, Helen, in order to keep his involvement a secret. When Edward found out what had happened to you, he asked me to investigate, and it didn't take me long to uncover Gresham's part in the tragedy. The name he had been using was Walton. That also confirmed our suspicions that he was the man we had been trying to trace for another crime years ago. The need to protect the Langton estate then became urgent, because that man now had far more money and he wanted this desirable land with a passion.'

'Oh, my –' Helen grasped Beth's hand – 'what would we have done if James and Dan hadn't taken over here?'

'We would have found ourselves in a very sorry position. I need to apologize to everyone, and especially to James for the way I have treated him.'

James was alone when Beth went to see him, and she entered the room hesitantly, not sure what to say to him. He looked tired and strained as if in some discomfort from his wounds.

'I beg your pardon for interrupting your rest,' she said, standing just inside the door, 'but I need to speak to you alone. May I come in?'

He pulled himself upright and grimaced. 'That sounds ominous, Elizabeth. Has Grandfather been up to mischief again, or is it something I have done?'

'Oh, no, neither of you has done anything to upset me. I am the one who has behaved badly, and I must apologize. Dan told us what Gresham has been doing, and how my godfather asked both of you to come here to protect me and the estate. I hope you will accept my apologies for the hostile way I treated you. I am very sorry, and I thank you for what you have done. You put your own life in danger, and . . .' The words tailed off, and Beth swallowed back the emotion clogging her throat.

'You have no need to apologize, Elizabeth. My approach at

first was ill-advised. I arrived expecting a meek country girl who would bow to a firm hand and stay in the background out of all harm.' James shook his head and said wryly, 'How wrong I was. I found an intelligent young lady who was prepared to fight for her independence – two young ladies, in fact. That was surprising, but admirable. You have nothing to apologize for, Elizabeth.'

She smiled with relief. 'That is gracious of you.'

'Not at all. Dan urged me to explain these things to you and Helen, but I refused at the time. He was right, of course.'

'I wish you had told us of the danger facing the Langton estate. We would have helped you in any way we could.' When James rested his head back and sighed deeply, Beth moved towards the bed, concerned. 'I have exhausted you. Are you in pain? Shall I send for Doctor Gregson?'

'He's already called today and declared that I am healing well. I find this inactivity frustrating, that's all.' He turned his head to look at her. 'There is something you can do for me, though.'

'Just tell me.'

'When I am back on my feet again and the trial of those villains is over, will you and Helen go to London with Alice? I know you are not very enthusiastic about it, but I want you both to have the opportunity to mix in society for a while.'

'Do you still want us to do that? I thought it was merely a ploy to get us away from here. It is not necessary now, surely?'

'You are both attractive young women, and I feel it is right you should have this chance.' He smiled. 'It means a lot to me, and Alice has been looking forward to showing you and Helen off to London society. Will you go – to please us?'

Sensing that this really was important to James, Beth nodded and grinned. 'I suppose we can't let all those clothes you made us purchase go to waste, but neither of us has any interest in seeking a husband in that way. From what I have heard, it is nothing more than a market where the young men seek out a suitable filly. We will not demean ourselves in that way. Is that understood?'

'Perfectly,' he laughed. 'But you will enjoy the dancing and social gatherings, won't you?'

'The dancing, maybe, but I shall reserve my judgement on the social gatherings.'

'Alice is going to enjoy every function you attend, and so is Grandfather, for I believe he has appointed himself as your protector.'

'That should be fun! Now, I must leave you to rest. Thank you for allowing me to talk to you.'

'It's always a pleasure, Elizabeth. Would you ask Helen to come and see me? I have something to discuss with her about the school.'

'All right, but you can rest assured she is doing an excellent job for you. I had a quick look round today and everything is beginning to look good. The finish should be pleasing and practical, but not too overwhelming for your pupils.'

'I can't wait to see it.'

'I do not think that will be long,' she said wryly, knowing how difficult it was for this vital man to be tied to a bed for any length of time.

Beth went straight back to her sitting room where she knew Alice and Helen would be waiting.

'Is everything all right, my dear?' Alice asked the moment she walked in.

'He was very understanding and insisted that I had no reason to apologize.'

'And you didn't. Your reaction to finding an unknown guardian thrust upon you was perfectly reasonable. James could have handled it better.'

'That's what he said.' Beth sat down and sighed deeply. 'He looks very tired and drawn, Alice. He insists he is fine, but do you think I should call the doctor again, just as a precaution?'

'I'll go and stay with him for the night. If I think he needs the physician at any time, I will send for him.'

'You are not getting much sleep, Alice,' Helen told her. 'I would be happy to watch for a few hours.'

'And so would I,' Beth said.

'Thank you.' Alice smiled at both the girls. 'But I am quite used to sleepless nights with my boys.'

'Alice, may I ask you something?'

'Of course, Beth. What is puzzling you?'

'No one has ever explained what your relationship is to Alex and James. You always refer to them as your boys, but we know you are not the mother of James, and Alex does not have the same name as you. They both address you as Alice.'

'Alex is the son of my brother, Alexander; both his parents died when he was six years old. And James is the son of my sister, Gertrude. She was never strong following his birth and died after a long illness when he was ten. I took them both into my home, but I never tried to take the place of their mothers, and it was agreed from the start that they would call me Alice.' She smiled, affection showing in her eyes. 'But I couldn't love them more if they were my own flesh and blood.'

'That's very clear,' Helen remarked, 'but you do appear to have had a great deal of tragedy in your family.'

She nodded. 'Unfortunately, that is true. We have had a lot of sorrow in our lives, as have the two of you, and the sooner this wretched business is over, the happier we shall all be.'

'Let us hope it is soon,' Beth agreed. She gave a mischievous smile. 'James wants us still to go to London once he is on his feet and Gresham is no longer a danger to any of us. I told him we would, but we would not demean ourselves by choosing a husband at frivolous social gatherings.'

'We shall see,' Alice laughed. 'And I am delighted I shall have the chance to show off two such beautiful and charming young ladies. I must go and tell Father the good news.'

When they were alone, Beth turned to her friend. 'I hope you didn't mind me agreeing to this ridiculous idea of us joining the social scene, but it does seem important to James. As he has done so much for us, I didn't feel I could refuse.'

'I would have done the same, and I am quite looking forward to spending time in London. Did you notice how pleased Alice was?'

Beth laughed quietly. 'I did. With Grandfather joining us, it should be a lively time. He appears to have adopted us.'

'I expect he thinks we are in need of a father figure with a firm guiding hand.'

'Then I am afraid he will find us quite uncontrollable,' Beth said, laughing. 'Oh, I nearly forgot: James would like to see you, Helen. Something to do with the school, I believe, but don't let him exhaust himself too much.'

'I won't stay long.'

When her friend had gone, Beth checked the teapot and found it cold. Rather than call for a fresh pot, she picked up the tray and headed for the kitchen.

'Miss Langton!' Cook exclaimed, taking the tray from her. 'Why didn't you ring for us to collect this?'

'I thought I would bring it myself.' She looked around the crowded kitchen and smiled. This was a warm, friendly meeting place for everyone, and Mrs Howard encouraged them all to come and sample her little treats, as she called them. 'May I join you?'

Alex pulled out a chair for her. 'We would be delighted to have your company, Elizabeth. Dan and I are having an interesting talk with Tom and Charlie, and enjoying Mrs Howard's excellent biscuits.'

'Where is your grandfather?'

'He's just gone to see James, so we don't think he is up to any mischief at the moment.' There was a glint of amusement in Alex's eyes. 'Has he given you back the keys to his room yet?'

'No, and we haven't been able to discover where he's hidden them.'

The two young boys stifled giggles, having heard the full story of the elderly man's antics.

Beth took a biscuit from the plate, sipped her tea and then turned her attention to the boys. 'Have you been reading your book, Tom?'

'Yes, Miss Langton, and I've learnt ever such a lot already. I now look at the horses and know where all the muscles and tendons are, and how they're made. I'm able to do more for them, and they're happy about that.'

'I'm sure they are.' Beth never ceased to marvel at the rapport the young boy had with the animals. And it didn't stop at horses; she had seen the farm dogs and cats go to him when they were hurt, as if they knew he could help. James was right to encourage him. It was a rare talent indeed.

'His lordship talks to me when he can.' Tom bounced around on his chair in excitement. 'He's ever so kind, and Charlie's going to his school next year, aren't you, Charlie?'

Charlie nodded and glanced anxiously at Alex.

'Ah, yes, we haven't told you about this yet, Elizabeth. When the school opens, Charlie will be attending full-time, but we've been able to engage a local man to tend the pigs. He's been on a pig farm fifty miles from here but has had to return to look after his ailing mother. He has a wife and two small children, so they will be happy to move into the cottage we built. He's a good man and knows pigs, but we've told him that the final decision rests with you. The family's name is Anderson. Would you like to see him?'

'No, Alex, that won't be necessary. I know Mrs Anderson, and if you are happy that he will be suitable, then you can go ahead and employ him. I'll see them when they move into the cottage.' Beth then smiled at Charlie's relieved face. He had clearly thought she might refuse to let him go. 'Congratulations, Charlie. This will be a wonderful opportunity for you.'

His face lit up with a broad smile. 'I know it is, Miss Langton, and thank you for not minding about me leaving the pigs.'

'I wouldn't dream of stopping you from taking the chance of an excellent education. When something good like this comes along, it would be very foolish to turn our backs on it. I'm sure you'll make us all proud of you.'

'I'll do my best. I like learning, and I might even be able to become a barrister like Mr Edgemont.' He cast Dan an admiring glance.

'That is something to reach for,' Dan told him, 'but whatever you decide to do later in life, Charlie, make sure it's something you enjoy.'

'I will, sir.' The boy nodded vigorously.

'And now I think it's time you boys were in your beds,' Cook told them firmly.

Alex stood up at once. 'I agree. Come on, Charlie, I'll take you home.'

It took a little more urging to make Tom go to his room, but he was an obedient boy and left, if reluctantly.

'Do you think we will have any more trouble from Gresham?' Beth asked Dan when they were the only two left at the table.

'I really can't answer that, Elizabeth, but don't worry; he is being watched day and night. He won't be able to do anything without me knowing.'

'That is a comfort. Do you have any idea when the trial of those men will begin?'

'Not yet.'

'I wish it was all over. It's going to be a worrying week or two.' Beth looked at Dan imploringly. 'Or will it be longer than that?'

'That is another question I don't have an answer for. I won't lie to you: we have a difficult time ahead of us.'

Twenty-Four

'What the hell is happening?' James spun round to face Dan. 'How much longer is this going to last?'

'Stop pacing. And should you be up?'

'Stop evading the questions – heaven knows you're good at that! Another day like this and I'll be out of my mind. Tell me the damned news!'

'The two men have been convicted of attempted murder, but Gresham goes free. You know that when we caught them, they told me Gresham had employed them, but in court they refused to implicate him, and, without solid proof, it wasn't possible to prove his involvement.'

The stream of bad language coming from his friend made Dan grimace. 'I didn't think you knew language like that. Calm down, James, and, for goodness' sake, sit! I did explain that this was a real possibility, and Gresham is feeling jubilant at the moment. Something has come to my notice, however, but I need to investigate it thoroughly before taking action. If it turns out to be true, then I'm going to rock the comfortable world he's built up for himself. Do you still want his land to expand your school?'

Nodding, James eased himself into an armchair. 'It would be useful, but most of all I want Gresham to pay for his sins, past and present. I don't just want his world rocked, Dan; I want it torn apart.'

'Then I hope the information I have received from one of my associates is correct.'

At that moment the door burst open and Grandfather, Alex and the estate manager erupted into the room.

'Tom told us you were back at last and that the trial was over. That boy seems to know more of what is happening than we do.' Alex took one look at James's furious expression. 'Ah, it doesn't look as if the news is good.'

'Good or bad, tell us, my boy,' Grandfather demanded.

Dan explained, and the disappointment was felt by them all.

Henry Greenway shook his head. 'I'll alert everyone on the estate to be vigilant in case he starts to cause trouble again.'

'And we mustn't let our girls go around unescorted. He could decide to take out his revenge on them. Can't have that!'

'The problem will be getting Elizabeth and Helen to agree, Grandfather. They are used to roaming free without asking anyone.' James ran a hand over his eyes. 'Anyway, Dan might have a way to deal with that evil man once and for all.'

Chairs were hastily pulled into a circle. All eyes focused on Dan, waiting expectantly.

'So, what are we going to do?' the elderly man asked when Dan remained silent.

'*We* are not going to do anything. I'll manage him on my own.'

There was a roar of protest, and James was on his feet again. 'You've kept me cooped up right through the trial – for no good reason, as it has turned out. I am not being left out of this, Dan, so you can forget about working on your own.'

'With respect, sir,' Henry Greenway declared, 'if Miss Langton and her estate are in danger, then I must insist on being involved in anything to do with this estate.'

'The same applies to us.' Alex pointed to himself and his grandfather.

Dan raised his eyes to the ceiling. After taking a deep breath, he looked back at the men in the room, noting their stubborn expressions. 'You'll only get in the way. It would be better and safer for all concerned if you let me deal with this myself.'

'No!' The men all spoke as one voice.

'It's like this, my boy, I know you are only thinking of our safety, but you can't exclude any of us. This isn't only a family business now; it's reaching out to touch these lovely, innocent girls, and I won't stand by and see them hurt. We'll let you do what you do best without hindering you, but you have got to let us stand with you. Let this evil villain see what he's up against.'

'Grandfather's right.' Alex leant forward, elbows resting on his knees. 'We'll follow your orders, but let us help.'

Walking over to the window, Dan gazed out, silent. After a moment he faced them again. 'All right. I understand your concerns. Gresham is unpredictable, Henry, so it will be your job to see the girls and Lady Trenchard are protected at all times. I don't care how much they protest; I need you to see they are escorted wherever they go.'

'I'll do that, sir.'

Dan flicked open his pocket watch. 'I must leave now or I'll miss my train to London. I hope the answer to all this is to be found there.'

'You're leaving now? But what are we to do while you're away?'

'Behave yourself,' Dan told Grandfather. 'Stay away from Gresham and remain vigilant. A few quiet days should lull him into feeling safe, and then, if I find what we need, we'll go after him.'

'Are you going to tell us what information you have received, Dan?'

'I'll tell you when I'm sure, James. No point in raising your hopes when it might not come to anything.'

'And you're afraid we might confront Gresham too soon.'

Dan nodded to Alex, already heading for the door. 'I wouldn't put it past your grandfather to become impatient, so it's best if you don't know yet.'

'Anyone would think that boy doesn't trust me,' Grandfather grumbled. 'He never tells us a damned thing, but I wouldn't be surprised if he is going to look into the name of Walton.'

'Oh, that will just be a name Gresham decided to use for his illegal activities.'

Alex shrugged. 'Probably, James, but we must trust Dan. Let's hope he discovers something we can use to finish this blasted man. You are going to be living here once the school is open, and this is where the girls belong, so if Gresham is still around, none of you will be safe.'

'Aye, that's true,' Grandfather agreed, his expression grim. 'One way or another, he's got to be stopped.'

'Legally, Grandfather,' James warned.

The next morning the girls were surprised to see James already in the breakfast room and dressed for riding.

'I'm coming with you today, Helen, and you can show me what has been done at the school during the last week.'

'Has the doctor said you are fit to ride?' she asked.

'Of course he hasn't, but it's a waste of breath trying to stop him, Helen. I've argued with him until I have exhausted myself.'

'Well, if you've failed, Alice, I won't say another word.'

'I'm coming with you as well, because he's too heavy for you to manage on your own if he collapses.'

James glared at Alice and Helen. 'Will you two stop this nonsense? I am quite fit enough for a gentle ride to the school. It isn't far and the fresh air will do me good.'

'You make sure it is a gentle ride, my boy.' Grandfather sat down with a plate full of his choice from the many silver dishes. 'And I've arranged for Stanley the footman to stay with you all day. I hope that's all right with you, Elizabeth? He's a capable lad.'

'Er . . . yes, if you think it necessary.'

'It is, my dear. That leaves Alex and me to be your escort for the day.'

The girls shot each other a startled glance.

'What's going on?' Beth demanded. 'Where's Dan?'

'He's gone to London, and his instructions are to behave ourselves and be vigilant,' the elderly man told them dryly. 'So that's what we're doing.'

'It's sensible, Beth,' Helen told her. 'We don't want anyone else to be hurt.'

'No, of course we don't.' She sighed. 'And if Dan thinks we should take these precautions, then I'm not about to dismiss his advice.'

'Sensible girl.' Grandfather was on his feet, his breakfast only half finished. 'Let's get on with the day, then.'

Helen watched anxiously as James swung himself into the saddle without his usual fluid grace. No matter how he protested that he was fully recovered, he was clearly still suffering some discomfort.

They set off at a walking pace, and Helen was pleased to note that Stanley was right behind and armed. There was a rifle on the saddle, and she could see a pistol in his jacket. Whatever Dan had told the men last night, it was obvious they weren't going to give Gresham a chance to catch them unawares.

Although it was still early in the morning when they reached the school, the men were already working hard as more furniture was being delivered.

'I wasn't expecting that until tomorrow,' Helen exclaimed, dismounting quickly and almost running into the school, giving orders as she moved through the workers. 'When did this arrive?' she asked Mr Becks.

'An hour ago, my lady.' He smiled, rubbing his hands together with pleasure. 'The boys' rooms are completely furnished now, and so is the library. I've checked the consignment, and it contains all the tables and chairs for the dining room. What we need now are the linens and kitchen utensils. We haven't touched the master's quarters yet. His lordship has still to decide on the furnishings there, but he should be delighted when he sees the progress we've made in a week.'

'I can't wait to inspect it.'

Becks swung round. 'Your lordship! How good to see you on your feet again. Thank you so much for giving our Charlie a place in your splendid school.'

'He's earned that place and deserves it. He's a bright boy and shows promise.' James was turning and looking everywhere as he spoke, his expression unreadable. 'Helen, show me what has been done to the rooms upstairs.'

His inspection was carried out in silence, giving Helen no indication of his opinion. She was tense, desperately wanting him to like what she had done while he had been unable to come here.

When they had been in every room, checked every cupboard and chair and the suitability of every piece of furniture, they walked on to the landing. James gazed at the activity below him and finally said, 'You have worked miracles, Helen. I couldn't have done better myself. Thank you.'

Relief swept through her and she began to breathe more easily. 'I've loved doing it.'

He turned his head and smiled. 'That's good because I am going to ask you if you would continue for a while. There is still a lot to do and I need the help.'

'I would be delighted to, James.' She drew in a silent breath and hesitated.

'You have a question?'

'You are well aware of my situation, and I will eventually have to find some way to support myself. I can't stay with Beth for the rest of my life, so if there should be a position in your school for a woman, would you consider me for the post? I don't care what it is. I'll do anything.'

He studied her thoughtfully and nodded. 'I'll consider it, Helen, but I can't make any promises.'

'I understand.' She hid her disappointment. It had been foolish to hope he would be able to offer her a job at the school, but her future was a concern, and it would have been a perfect solution to her problem. His vision for the school excited her, and she loved being here. And it would have kept her near James, but that was another foolish idea!

The same routine was followed for the next two days without a sign of trouble. Being involved in the final stages of the school, James seemed to regain much of his former vigour and vitality.

Christmas was now only two months away, and James was planning to have a huge celebration before then to declare the school officially open. Alice, Alex and Grandfather intended to be present for that, and if Gresham had been dealt with by then, they would be returning to their home in Scotland for Christmas.

Beth and Helen understood their desire to leave, but they were going to miss them so much. Then, in early March, Beth would reach her twenty-first birthday and James would no longer be her guardian. Although he would still be in the area, she doubted that she would ever see much of him again, and Dan would also disappear from their lives.

The girls were discussing this at the end of another busy day, neither of them happy about the prospect of finding themselves alone again. In the past they had never found this isolation troubling or unusual, but things had changed now. *They* had changed.

'I have become accustomed to having the house full of people.' Beth sighed. 'I find myself fond of all of them.'

'Yes,' Helen agreed. 'It is going to be hard to see them leave, and you know, Beth, that I will then have to think about my future. I shall have to seek a position somewhere in order to support myself.'

'I know you need to feel independent, but you can stay here for the rest of your life. I would be happy to have you with me.'

'That's more than generous of you, but I would not be happy

taking advantage of our friendship. If our situations were reversed, can you tell me you would not feel the same?'

'You know we are too much alike, and I would indeed feel the same, but the thought makes me sad.'

'We must not be sad, because we have a few weeks to join the London social scene with Alice and Grandfather. That should be an enjoyable experience. After that, the future will be what it will be.'

'You are right! We will enjoy the short time we all have left together and let the future take care of itself!'

Twenty-Five

'I wonder when Dan will return,' Beth said at breakfast. 'This will be the third day he has been away. Did he say his business would take this long?'

'He didn't know,' Alex replied before rushing over to the window at the sound of a horse clattering to a halt. 'Ah, this could be news.'

Before any of them could reach the door, it opened, and the butler ushered in a travel-stained man. 'This gentleman insists on seeing you at once, Lord Sharland.'

'I have a message from Mr Edgemont. He asks that you meet him at the Gresham house as soon as you can.'

'We'll leave at once. Jenkins, will you ask Tom to saddle our horses, please.'

Jenkins nodded and left immediately.

'You appear to have ridden hard,' Beth said to the messenger. 'Will you rest a moment and take refreshments?'

'No, thank you kindly, miss, but I must be on my way again.' He bowed slightly, turned and left with the men right behind him.

'That man was a soldier.' Beth looked at her friend, a deep frown on her face. 'What have the military to do with this?'

Helen shook her head, perplexed. 'It is a mystery.'

'Do you know who that man was?' Beth asked Jenkins, who had just returned to the breakfast room.

'He did not give his name, Miss Langton. Do you intend to ride out today? If so, Stanley will escort you.'

'I am not sure what we should do. What do you think, Helen? Should we stay here in case we are needed, or go about our day as usual?'

'There is still rather a lot to do at the school.'

The sound of running feet caught their attention. After a quick rap on the door, it swung open and Tom ran in, skidding to a halt, flushed with excitement. He gave a slight bow to Helen.

'His lordship told me to come at once. He said if you are going to the school today, I was to be your escort, my lady. Are you going?' he asked hopefully.

'You might as well,' Beth told her friend. 'We will only become anxious if we stay here with nothing to occupy us.'

Tom was fidgeting from one foot to the other. 'We don't need to worry about the gentlemen. There's a whole crowd of them. Mr Edgemont rode in briefly and he had a lot of soldiers with him. No one's going to mess with them.'

Beth groaned. 'I do wish they had stopped long enough to explain what was happening.'

'It wouldn't have entered their minds to do so, especially the men of my family.'

'But Dan could have sent a message, Alice.'

'Oh, he's worse than any of them for keeping information to himself. And when I mention my family, Dan is included. My father jokes about him, but I know he greatly admires that complex man and looks upon him as another grandson. I think it would be best if you go about your business today, and I will stay here to do the worrying.'

Helen nodded. 'You're right. Tom, I will be ready to leave in half an hour.'

'Yes, my lady. I'll get Honey ready. She told me she's looking forward to a gallop this morning.'

'In that case I had better not disappoint her.'

Grinning broadly, Tom spun on his heels and tore out of the room.

As they approached the Gresham home, all but one of the soldiers peeled off and disappeared to various positions around the home.

Dismounting, Alex went to James, concerned. 'They were in a hell of a hurry. Are you all right after such a frantic ride?'

'I'm fine, but I wish they had taken the time to tell us what this is all about. Whatever Dan's up to, he doesn't intend to let Gresham escape. That must mean he has some damning evidence against him.'

'Of course he has!' Grandfather leant over, trying to catch his breath. 'And he's damned determined about it.'

Dan had remained in the saddle, as had the man who was clearly an officer, and it was only when the door opened and Gresham appeared that they dismounted.

'Well, well, what's all this? Come to apologize, have you?'

Dan gave a smile that made Gresham take an involuntary step back. 'I would like to introduce you to Major Andrew Gresham, the rightful owner of this desirable property.'

'I don't believe you. I am the only living relative of this branch of the Gresham family. Leave here this instant!'

'You are the one who will leave, Mr Peter Walton.' Dan removed documents from his jacket. 'I have here all the proof we need. The woman you have been presenting as your sister is indeed your wife. I visited her in London and she is already packing to leave the Major's house. You have used many names to carry out your criminal activities, but you were foolish enough to use your real name for a crime many years ago, and more recently here. That is how we tracked you down.'

'Uh, oh.' Alex moved closer to James and whispered. 'Look, he's not alone.'

When four men began to emerge from the side of the house, Dan nodded to the Major, who let out a piercing whistle. His men rode out of their hiding places, forming a circle around Gresham's men. 'Thinking of fighting your way out of this, were you?'

Seeing there was no escape, Walton glared at Dan and then focused on the Major. 'Where the hell did you come from? I went into the Gresham line carefully, and there wasn't anyone left to claim the inheritance.'

'So you thought you would have it?'

'Why not? And you haven't answered my question. Why has it taken you so long to appear?'

'I have been in India for the last three years and didn't realize that the estate should have come to me until Mr Edgemont informed me of the situation. Now, Mr Walton, my men will escort you.'

'Where to?'

'Gaol, of course. Mr Edgemont informs me that you have rather a long list of charges to face, dating back some thirty years. The London constabulary are also anxious to question you. I believe a charge of murder was mentioned, as well as fraud, embezzlement and blackmail, to mention but a few.'

'By all that's merciful, we've got him at last, James.' Grandfather gripped his grandson's arm, a tear trickling down his cheeks. 'Not for his crimes against us perhaps, but he'll surely go the gallows now.'

Walton was already mounted on a horse with his hands tied in front of him, and there was no sign of his men.

The Major turned to James. 'Lord Sharland, I will leave you four of my men, and you have my permission to clear the property of all staff. Tell the regular workers to present themselves to me at the village in two days from now and I will see they receive any money owing them.'

'It will be my pleasure, sir.' James shook his hand. 'And thank you.'

With only a slight nod of his head, the Major swung into the saddle. 'Once this man is safely locked away, I shall meet you at the Langton estate with Mr Edgemont. We have things to discuss.'

'What did he mean by that?' Alex watched as they cantered away.

'No idea.'

One of the soldiers came up to James. 'I'm Sergeant Dickins, your lordship, at your service.'

'Well, your officer wants everyone off his property, so let's carry out his orders.'

It was late afternoon when they arrived back at the house, where they found Alice and the girls anxiously waiting for them.

Alice breathed a sigh of relief when she saw them. 'Thank goodness you all look cheerful. I'm guessing everything went all right.'

'We've got him!' her father laughed, giving her a hug. 'He won't get away this time. Dan's made sure of that. What a day! I could have kissed that boy for the way he handled the situation.'

'I'm glad you didn't; it would have ruined the whole thing.' Dan strode into the room, followed by the Major. 'Allow me to introduce your hostess, Miss Elizabeth Langton, and her friend,

Lady Helen Denton. The other charming lady is Lady Trenchard, Mr Beaufort's daughter. Ladies – Major Andrew Gresham.'

The Major bowed respectfully to each of them.

The name had startled Beth, but, although bursting with curiosity, she maintained her poise. 'Welcome to Langton house, Major Gresham. Would you join us for dinner?'

'It would be my pleasure.'

'What about your men, sir? I would not wish them to go hungry.'

'They are already comfortably settled in the local hostelry.' His eyes shone with amusement. 'I can assure you that they will not go short of anything.'

'In that case I will go and let Cook know that we have a guest for dinner.'

Beth had just reached the kitchen when Tom burst in excitedly. 'I've got a warhorse in the stable! Wow! You ought to see the size of him. He likes carrots and apples. Can I have some, please, Mrs Howard?'

'In the store cupboard, but don't take too many. And Tom,' she called as he made for the stores, 'you be careful of that animal. I've been told they can be quite vicious.'

When he emerged clutching the treats for his new charge in his arms, he had a look of utter disbelief on his face. 'He won't hurt me.'

Cook sighed. 'I suppose he told you that?'

He nodded, then turned and ran, eager to get back to the stables.

'That boy's got no fear when it comes to animals. What are we doing with a horse like that in the stables, Miss Langton?'

'It must belong to the Major. I've come to tell you we have a guest for dinner.'

'Ah, I thought that might be the case. We've more than enough for an extra one. Shall I have a room prepared for him as well?'

'I don't know yet if he's staying the night, but it would be wise to have it ready. Tom's going to be very disappointed if the warhorse doesn't stay for a while,' Beth joked.

'He'll be in the stables all night.' Mrs Howard lowered her voice. 'Any news about what happened today?'

Beth shook her head. 'No details yet, but Grandfather is jubilant. He said they'd got him, and that was all.'

'Ah, well, that's something, and it was good to know they had all come back unharmed.'

'Indeed it was. I must return to our guest.'

The only occupants of the sitting room when she arrived were Alice and Helen. 'Where have they gone?'

'They've withdrawn to the library with a large bottle of brandy.' Alice pulled a face. 'They have things to discuss. Men's talk.'

'Did they say any more about today?'

Helen sighed. 'What do you think?'

'Of course they didn't!' Beth sat down and folded her arms. 'So, we are to be left in suspense – again.'

The Major sipped his brandy appreciatively. 'Dan has told me about your plans for a school for underprivileged boys, Lord Sharland.'

'James, please. I am going to open the school in the new year. At least it will give a few children the chance of a good education.'

'An admirable project. And you would find extra land useful?'

'Not essential at this point, but it could become so if I decide to expand the school. That will depend upon its success, of course.'

Andrew Gresham nodded. 'With your qualifications, I am sure that success is assured. I also agree that all children should receive a sound education, and I would like to make a donation towards your work. The Gresham estate, and everything it contains, is yours.'

The brandy glass in James's hand nearly went flying as he leapt to his feet. 'But you can't just give it away! I will be happy to pay a fair price for the property.'

'I neither want nor need a country home, but I shall keep the London house as that could be useful. In two months I shall be returning to India.' He shook his head. 'What would I do with the place? And before you argue further, James, I do not need the money, and it would please me to know it will be helping such a worthy cause. I am a very distant relative of the Greshams and can't ever remember having met them. The place means nothing to me, and I would be honoured if you would accept it as my gift to your school.'

'What can I say but thank you?' James bowed his head. 'I am overwhelmed by your generosity, and I hope you will be able to visit us when you are home on leave next time?'

'That is an invitation I shall accept with pleasure. I will have the transfer documents prepared as quickly as possible, but from this moment you may consider the property yours.'

They shook hands to seal the arrangement.

'This is cause for a celebration.' Grandfather began refilling their glasses. 'Dan, all we need now is your assurance that Walton will go to prison for a very long time.'

'Now he has been exposed, the London police want him for many serious crimes. He will be transferred there tomorrow, and I am confident that it will either be the gallows or transportation for him. I will be involved in the trial.'

'Good.' Grandfather raised his glass. 'It has taken thirty years, but at last we can look forward to justice being done.'

Dinner that evening was a lively meal, with everyone in high spirits, and although they heard some details of the day's events, the girls were still awaiting the full story.

The Major had accepted Beth's invitation to stay the night, and the men retired to the library as soon as the meal was over.

Alice, Beth and Helen retired then, knowing from the laughter coming from the library that the men would be talking and drinking well into the night.

Twenty-Six

A commotion coming from the paddock the next morning had them all running outside to see what the noise was about.

Beth and Helen were the first to arrive, with the men close behind. The sight of Tom running as fast as his legs would carry him and the enormous warhorse in hot pursuit made Beth wrench the gate open. 'Tom, come out – quickly!'

The boy turned in their direction and skidded to a halt to slam the gate shut. 'No, no, don't let him out!' Then he tore off again.

'Help him!' Beth turned to the men gathered along the fence.

The Major was about to vault the fence when Jenkins stopped him. 'You don't need to, sir. Our Tom knows what he's doing.'

'But what *is* he doing?'

'Don't know, sir, but *he* does. Look at him; he's laughing.'

'He has a great understanding of horses,' James told the Major. 'It's quite remarkable. He isn't running scared; he's playing with the animal.'

They all watched in astonishment as the animal caught up with Tom and pushed him just hard enough to knock him off his feet. The boy sprung up and stood on tiptoe to reach the horse's head, pulling it down so he could say something in his ear. That sent the warhorse into a mad gallop around the field. Then he stopped in front of Tom and dipped his head.

'I don't believe I have just seen that.' The Major shook his head in disbelief. 'That animal is trained to kill, not play games with young boys. I did explain this to him when he was so eager to take charge of Zeus. Tom!' he called.

'Yes, sir.' He arrived flushed and grinning.

'What was that all about? And why have you put him in the paddock?'

'Ah, well, I had to, sir. He's a handsome beast and er . . .' He shuffled his feet in embarrassment, casting a quick glance at Helen. 'Er . . . you see, Honey fell in love with him, and when she kept talking to him, I couldn't stop her. I tried, my lady, but she wouldn't listen to me. Well, Zeus could see her over the partition, and well . . . I had to separate them. Zeus thought I was going to bring Honey out as well, and when I told him she wasn't coming, he decided to give me the run-around. In the end we was both laughing and having fun. He's calmed down now, sir.'

'Zeus didn't get near Honey, did he?'

'Oh, no, Major, sir. I wouldn't have allowed that without her ladyship's permission. Honey's just a bit cross at the moment, but I'll go and have a little talk to her. She's a good girl and will understand.'

Muffled laughter quickly turned into coughs from the men gathered there. The Major was controlling his expression with difficulty. 'You did well, Tom.'

'Thank you, sir.' The boy looked shyly at the soldier. 'Zeus would do anything for you, sir. He told me, and he also said that it's too cold here, so can you both go back to the warm?'

'Really? Can you tell him we will only be here for a short stay?'

'I'll do that, sir.' Tom bounded off towards Zeus again.

Grandfather was openly laughing now. 'That boy is a treasure.'

Before anyone else could comment, a soldier galloped up to them. 'Sir! We're needed.'

'What's happened, Sergeant?'

'The police were getting ready to take Walton to London when he tried to escape. Don't have more details, sir.'

Tom had anticipated the need and Zeus was already standing near the Major, almost saddled and ready to ride. Another stable hand was leading Dan's horse out in case it was needed.

The major nodded his approval. 'Excellent staff you have, Miss Langton.'

It only took a few minutes, and the Major and Dan were galloping away.

It was several hours before Dan arrived back, alone. Unable to stand the suspense, they all hurried out to the yard.

'What's happened?' James asked.

'Did he escape?' Alex wanted to know.

'Give me a chance to draw breath.' Dan dismounted and nodded to Tom, who was already there to take the horse. 'Thank you, Tom. He'll need a rub down.'

'I'll see to him, sir.' Tom led the animal away, talking to him all the time.

'I need a drink!' Dan strode into the library, and they all followed.

After pouring himself a large whisky, Dan took a generous mouthful, swallowed and then faced them.

'Well?' James demanded. 'If it's bad news, then, for heaven's sake, tell us.'

'It's all over. He must have known he was facing the gallows and was desperate. While he was being taken to the train, he tried to overpower one of those guarding him. Somehow he had a knife concealed on him, and the constable was injured, but not seriously. There was quite a fight, and it looked as if he might get away. They said he fought like a madman, and when they finally managed to subdue him, he had a heart attack and died.'

'He's dead?' James looked as if he couldn't believe what he was hearing.

'How do you know it was a heart attack, Dan?' Grandfather looked equally shocked.

'A doctor confirmed it. That's why I've been such a long time. I've been waiting for the results of the examination.'

'I can't believe it is really over.' James sat down heavily and ran a hand over his eyes. 'Walton must have been out of his mind with fear to try such a risky escape attempt.'

Alex poured all the men a whisky, and they drank in silence, the atmosphere subdued.

Beth, Helen and Alice were as shocked as everyone else. There wasn't any jubilation at the news, just a feeling of numbness that, after all the tension and danger, it had ended in this way.

Grandfather was the first to break the stunned silence. After draining his glass, he turned to his daughter. 'You can start packing now, Alice. There's nothing to stop us taking our lovely girls to London. I'll have to get my dancing shoes polished to a bright shine.' He winked at Beth and Helen.

'Are you sure you can dance?' Helen teased, sensing that the elderly man was trying to break the tension.

Without a word, he walked towards her, bowed elegantly and

then began to waltz her around the library, skilfully avoiding the various tables and chairs.

'I think that answers your question.' He released her and bowed again.

His antics had the desired effect, and everyone in the room was smiling now.

'Right!' James stood up. 'We can put the past behind us at last and think about the future. Elizabeth and Helen, you deserve a few frivolous weeks in London. You have both been splendid during this difficult time. Alice, how quickly can you be ready to leave?'

'Two days should be enough – don't you agree?' She smiled happily at the girls. 'I can't wait to see you dancing in those beautiful gowns.'

Beth looked doubtful. 'I'm not sure we are good enough dancers for the London scene; I think Grandfather had better give us a few dancing lessons before then. Oh, and are you going to tell me where you've hidden the keys to your room before we leave?'

'I'll consider it.' The elderly man grinned. 'I'm surprised you haven't found them yet. They've been right under your nose, behind something you use all the time.'

'Where?'

'I've given you a clue, and that's all I'm saying at the moment.'

'Father, you're an old rascal. I hope you are going to behave yourself in London, or we shall disown you.'

'Now, Alice, when have you ever known me to behave?' He looked at his grandsons and Dan. 'I hope you are going to show your faces at a few functions?'

'We might consider it.' James winked at Alice. 'Just tell us which ones he won't be attending.'

Laughter filled the room, and Beth and Helen smiled at each other. They were going to make the most of the short time they all had together, and secretly hoping that certain gentlemen would indeed show their faces in London.

The next two days passed in a flurry of activity as they prepared for London. When the packing was complete, Beth declared, 'My goodness, I cannot imagine how we are ever going to wear so many clothes.'

'I agree we have far too much, but Alice doesn't think so. She even said we could buy anything else we need while we are there.'

'Then we will have to convince her that we have more than we shall need. Our stay will only be for a short time, and we cannot allow James to incur more expense for us. He has already been more than generous.'

'You are the only young girls I have met who do not relish spending a gentleman's money,' Alice joked as she walked in, nodding when she saw the mountain of luggage. 'Splendid – we are almost ready. James would like to see you both in the library, please.'

'Oh, do you know why?'

'Some last minute details, I expect, Helen. Off you go.'

When they entered the library, they were surprised to see not only James, but Dan, Alex and Grandfather as well.

Beth's heart plummeted. Had they called them to say goodbye? She knew that day wasn't far off, but she had hoped it wouldn't be so soon.

James appeared tense when he asked them to sit down. He remained standing. 'I promised to give you an explanation when this troubled time was over, and I keep my promises.'

The girls sat upright in their chairs, waiting eagerly, but knowing that this was not going to be easy for him.

James walked over to the window, eased the tension in his shoulders and then turned to face them. 'We have to go back to before I was born. Edward Sharland and my mother, Gertrude, met and fell in love, but her father was opposed to the marriage. They eloped and married in secret, but an unscrupulous young man found out and contacted her father, who was desperately searching for his daughter. The man offered information about their whereabouts for a price. Her father paid, but Edward and Gertrude had moved on, and when more money was demanded, he refused.'

'I told him to go to hell,' Grandfather explained. 'That was the most terrible mistake I have ever made, and it will haunt me to my dying day. I underestimated the villain, and, in the circumstances, that was stupid.'

Walking over to his grandfather, James rested a hand on the elderly man's shoulder, giving him a brief understanding smile.

Then he continued. 'Angry with the refusal, the man caught up with the newlyweds while they were travelling to return and face her father. The blackmailer killed the driver in his attempt to kidnap Gertrude, and Edward was so severely injured it was thought impossible for him to survive. Other travellers on the road came to their aid, and, seeing he was outnumbered, the attacker ran. Gertrude was in a state of shock when she reached home, and when her father told her that Edward was dead, she believed it. And when she was told by a physician that she was not strong enough to attend a funeral, she was too sick, physically and mentally, to question that decision too. But Edward did not die. When he finally regained consciousness, his full recovery took more than a year, and by that time I had been born.'

Grandfather stood up then, grief and shame etched clearly on his face. 'As soon as he was able to, Edward came to see me, and I was shocked and panicked, for I had been convinced that he could not possibly survive. My daughter believed her husband was dead, and after the birth she was not strong. I was certain she could not survive the shock of discovering that Edward was alive, so I told him she had died that day. He left and I never saw him again for some years. The cruelty of my decisions at that time would not let me rest, and when my daughter died, I contacted Edward. It was a terrible meeting and I wouldn't have blamed Edward if he had killed me for what I had done.'

The elderly man sat down again, looking exhausted, and James took up the story once more.

'When I met my father, we liked each other from the start, and I wanted to stay with him. However, after much discussion it was agreed by us all that I would be happier remaining with Alice and Alex. My father came to Scotland often and we spent as much time together as possible. At that time I hated my grandfather, and we fought each other fiercely. It was only when he came here that I began to understand the terrible situation he had faced.' James nodded to his grandfather to take up the story at this point.

'Edward was determined to track down the villain who had caused us so much pain. The only evidence I had was a letter from him demanding money. The signature on the letter was Walton, but we assumed it was a false name. Edward never intended to stop looking for him, and that was when Dan came into our lives. He'll tell you about that.'

'Edward and I were involved in carrying out investigations for the police and sometimes the government, so we combined our efforts to try to find Walton, but it seemed a hopeless task – until Gresham turned up here. When Edward discovered that the man with the largest claim in Helen's family tragedy was calling himself Walton, we felt we had something to go on at last. It didn't take me long to discover that it was Gresham, but we needed proof before we could take any action against him. The rest you know.'

Bowing her head, Beth didn't try to hide her distress. How this family had suffered – she couldn't bear to imagine the anguish her dear godfather had gone through. She had known him all her life, and not once had he said a word about his past. Wiping the moisture from her eyes, she looked up. 'I wish I had known. Thank you for telling us.'

Helen was also overcome, but managed to say, 'That was a harrowing story, but I also thank you. At least now I feel as if my father's death was not entirely in vain, for it helped to uncover that evil man.'

'It did indeed,' James told her gently. 'We are desperately sorry that it happened in such a tragic way.'

'I think we all need a strong drink.' Grandfather began pouring brandy in enough glasses for all of them and then handed them round. 'Drink that, my girls; it will help.'

James raised his glass. 'It is now time to put the past behind us. My mother and father would have wanted that. Let us drink to a happier future.'

Twenty-Seven

'I've spoken to Henry and he's satisfied with the new man. He knows his pigs, so I'm going home, James, but I'll come back for the opening of the school.' Alex looked at Dan. 'What are you going to do now?'

'I have promised James six months of my time to teach at the school, but there is something important I must do before that.'

'Any point me asking what it is?'

'None at all.'

Alex grinned and shrugged. 'Nothing changes there, then. What are you going to do when you're running the school full-time, James? There won't be much time left for you to spend here as Elizabeth's guardian, surely?'

'I will legally be her guardian until March, but I've talked this over with Henry. He's a reliable estate manager, and Elizabeth is trained to run the estate – and does so very efficiently. They will only need to come to me if a problem arises and they require help, but that is unlikely now.'

'No, thank heavens. We can all relax at last and get on with our lives. It's sad that Edward never lived long enough to see this day.'

James sighed. 'Yes, it is. However, we managed to do what he wanted, and if he's looking down on us now, I'm sure he will be smiling. When are you leaving, Alex?'

'Tomorrow morning, if that's all right with you.'

'Perfectly – and thank you for coming. You have been a great help. Tell your lovely girl that I apologize for keeping you so long.'

'I'll do that – and thanks, though I'm not so sure I've been a help. You two are the brains – I'm just a farmer. But it's been an experience. I'll expect you both at our wedding in the summer.'

'Wouldn't miss it.' James slapped Alex on the back. 'And you tell your future wife she had better look after you or she'll have me to deal with.'

Alex tipped his head back and roared with laughter. 'I wouldn't dare tell her that. She's already frightened of you – the stern professor, she calls you.'

'Me?' James said in mock disbelief.

'Yes, you. The only two girls who weren't cowed by your powerful personality were Elizabeth and Helen.' Alex studied the two men in front of him. 'Just what are you going to do about them? And don't either of you tell me you're not interested in them. I've got eyes in my head.'

'What's he talking about?' Dan asked James.

'I haven't the faintest idea.'

'You two will never change,' Alex said, shaking his head in amusement. 'I think I'll go and say goodbye to my pigs.'

They watched Alex leave, laughing softly to himself.

'He's really happy about going back to his farm and his girl. And I think I'll go and pack.'

'Thinking of going somewhere, Dan?'

'Your grandfather did order us to show our faces in London.'

'So he did, and we had better obey him, I suppose.'

'He'd be furious if we didn't.'

'Ah,' James pretended to shudder. 'That would not be a good thing.'

Both men headed for the stairs, their expressions unreadable.

The London house was impressive, and the girls didn't have to lift a finger to help themselves. This was something they were not used to, and they had great difficulty remembering to send for a maid each time they needed something.

'What do the ladies find to occupy themselves?' Beth asked Helen.

'I expect some do embroidery, and all seem to spend a great deal of time visiting and gossiping.' Helen pulled a face. 'And we are not skilled in either of those things.'

'Perhaps coming to London was not such a good idea.' Beth paced the sitting room. 'What are we going to do? No one is going to send us invitations, and the weather is too wet for sightseeing. I can't sit around doing nothing. I'm not used to it, and neither are you.'

'Patience, my dears; we only arrived yesterday. But word travels fast.'

There was a soft knock on the door and the butler entered, bowed before Alice and held out a silver tray. She took the cards and he left, just as quietly.

Beth watched the door close. 'Does he ever speak or smile?'

'Sometimes,' Alice laughed. 'You run a very informal house, Beth, but it is different here. You treat your staff like old friends or a part of your family.'

'They have all been with me for as long as I can remember, so, yes, they are like family to me.'

'I realize that, but don't try to become too familiar with the staff here. They wouldn't understand.'

'No, I can see that.'

'Anyway, you can both cheer up because I have lots of invitations here. We shall now be very busy. I'll sort out which ones to accept.'

Over the next week they went to concerts, afternoon tea and dinners where they endured entertainment during which the singers made them wince in pain and the pianists were little better. They also had many callers who were only visiting to prise information out of them after hearing rumours about the shooting in Hampshire. The girls were very relieved to have Alice and Grandfather with them, both experts at being evasive and giving very little away. Society was beginning to buzz with speculation about them, and they didn't enjoy that at all.

'We cannot stand any more of this!' Helen declared after another distasteful visit during which they had been quizzed about their lives.

'Now, now, my girls, don't let them upset you,' Grandfather soothed. 'Those two ladies have marriageable sons who have been taking an interest in you. They were trying to find out if you would be suitable wives for them.'

'What?' Beth's expression was one of horror. 'I was not aware that anyone was showing an interest in us like that. You must point them out to us, for we would not want them in the family. I agree with Helen: we have had enough and wish to return home.'

'You don't want to leave and miss the grand ball to be given by the Earl of Huntswood and his charming lady, do you? If you disappear now, then society will say you are running away. That would keep them in gossip for weeks. They would consider you cowards, and I know you most certainly are not. Anyway, I hear that Alex has gone back to Scotland to see his girl, but James and Dan have arrived in town and are staying at their club.' Grandfather smiled slyly after giving them this piece of news. 'I think it quite likely they will be invited to such a prestigious occasion.'

'Why have they not called?'

'No doubt they have had business to attend to first, Helen.'

The girls looked at each other, sending a silent message, and then Beth said, 'We will stay a while longer, for we would not want to be the cause of more gossip. When is this ball?'

'Tomorrow evening.' Alice walked around the girls, surveying them from every angle. 'You must have the hairdresser tomorrow and decide on your gowns. We shall see that you outshine everyone else there.'

'Oh, dear.' Helen relaxed, amused now. 'I fear you will have a hopeless task on your hands.'

'You both have more beauty and grace than any of the other girls. Haven't they, Father?'

'Indeed. I shall be the envy of every man there when I arrive with you on my arms.'

'You are a tease,' Beth told him. 'Oh, and you never did tell me where you hid those keys.'

'I gave you a clue.'

She nodded. 'That they were under my nose. Not much of a clue. It's a large house.'

'There's a mirror on the landing just outside your rooms. You always check that you are tidy and your nose isn't too shiny before going downstairs. They are behind that.'

'I don't recall that is what I do,' she laughed. 'But we never thought of looking there, though we have searched all the rooms.'

He grinned. 'Now that is settled and you are staying for a while longer, I think we should have tea. Don't you, Alice?'

The evening of the ball arrived, and the girls had to admit they were rather excited. Helen looked stunning in a pale green gown which brought out the green in her eyes. Beth was wearing a light shining shade of blue, also to match her eyes. Alice looked regal in dark red, and Grandfather elegant in full evening dress. He had been missing for most of the day and seemed very pleased about something.

'Heads up, my dears,' he told them when they arrived at the ball. 'This is going to be a night to remember.'

The girls silently agreed, knowing that the gossip about them was going to be rife as soon as they entered the ballroom.

Alice shot her father a suspicious glance, then fixed a smile on her face, murmuring softly under her breath, 'You behave yourself, Father, or we shall send you home at once.'

'Stop worrying, Alice. I'm just a spectator tonight. All I'm going to do is dance with three lovely ladies, and a man of my age doesn't often get to enjoy such a pleasure.'

The girls listened, but they were too nervous to wonder what they were talking about. They had little hope of having many names on their dance cards, and they could already sense that their entrance had caused a stir.

Suddenly, Beth lost all her nervousness as defiance swept through her. What right did some of these people have to whisper about them behind their fans? They had probably never done anything useful in their entire lives. She knew that was not a kind thought, but at the moment that was how she felt.

Grandfather led them to chairs in a prominent position where they could see – and be seen – by the whole room. Before sitting, Beth turned slowly and swept her gaze over the room.

Helen stood beside her and they remained standing for a couple of minutes, then smiled at each other and sat down.

'Well done, my dears, you've just shown them you are not afraid of any of them.' Grandfather grinned smugly. 'Let the show begin.'

The orchestra was about to get the dancing underway, and Helen looked at her empty dance card. 'I think those dancing lessons you gave us are going to be wasted. I doubt anyone is going to approach us.'

'You'll have partners,' Grandfather announced with confidence and a wink. 'You'll see.'

'Father, you are in a strange mood tonight, and I don't trust you.'

The only reply she received from him was a deep rumbling laugh.

Suddenly, the noise in the room stilled and the girls looked around quickly to see the cause of the interest. Two tall, elegant men were striding across the middle of the dance floor and heading straight for them.

'Right on time,' the elderly man muttered.

Beth and Helen leapt to their feet, smiling with delight. They curtsied gracefully when the men reached them.

'We hope your dance cards are not full,' James said, taking Helen's card from her.

Dan took Beth's card and began to write his name in every space. She watched him, wide-eyed, looking from Dan to the card and back again. 'I don't believe it's proper to dance all evening with the same partner. People will talk.'

The orchestra starting playing and he held out his hand. 'Do you care?'

'No,' she laughed, feeling quite light-headed with pleasure as he led her into the first dance. 'Has James claimed all Helen's dances as well?'

'That was his intention.'

'Did Grandfather know about this?'

'We saw him today.' Dan smiled down at her. 'You dance beautifully, Beth.'

The use of her shortened name jolted her because he had always been quite formal when speaking to her, but he was a different man tonight, and she felt completely at ease with him. 'It is easy to dance well with such an accomplished partner.'

Alice and her father danced close to them. 'Told you you'd have partners, didn't I?'

The evening became a blur of happiness for the girls. As expected, they caused quite a stir, but they didn't care. They were spending a few hours in the company of the two men they had become far too fond of. They would not admit to more than that. It was going to be hard enough to say goodbye to them when the time came without examining their feelings too deeply. After all the tension and danger, the men were enjoying themselves, and so were they.

Grandfather was finding the whole evening a delight. 'You're the envy of every female here. They're a couple of handsome devils, and to add to that there is an air of mystery about them. A potent mixture, don't you think?'

The girls agreed as they watched them make their way back after collecting drinks for all of them. This was going to be a night they would always remember.

'Are you going to let me dance with my girls?' the elderly man asked when the music began again.

'No,' both men said, leading their partners back on to the floor again.

The door to the garden was open to allow fresh air into the crowded ballroom, and Dan guided Beth outside. She shivered slightly in the cool evening. 'What are we doing out here? Has the heat in there become too much for you?'

'We are here because I have no intention of doing this with the curious eyes of London society on us.' Dan hesitated for a brief moment and then said, 'Elizabeth Langton, you are a remarkable young lady. I fell in love with you the moment we met and I cannot imagine my life without you. Would you do me the honour of becoming my wife?'

Beth felt so breathless she had to draw in air quickly. She had never heard such a long speech from this man of few words. She had felt that he liked her, but she had no idea his feelings for her were more than that.

When she didn't answer, he said, 'I am sure you must have concerns, for you know very little about me, so before you answer I will make some things clear. I will never interfere in the running of your estate. You have been in complete charge, and that is how it will stay. I will be by your side to help if needed. I will continue with my profession as a barrister, and I have already resigned from any investigative work. Will you consider my proposal?'

'I have already considered it.' Beth took a deep steadying breath. 'I love you, Dan, and accept your proposal of marriage. I never dared hope that this would happen. I am so happy!'

Dan drew her into a passionate embrace. After some time she gazed up at him.

'I would not want a long engagement.'

He swung her round, laughing. 'Oh, you are such a wise girl. We will marry quickly. But before that you will have to meet my family. My father is a judge and I have a younger brother who is a lawyer, but don't worry about them – they will love you as I do.'

'So that is why you had influence with the court officials.'

'It helped.'

James danced Helen around until they reached another room. He guided her through the door and closed it firmly, then leant against it. 'It's quieter in here so we can talk. I've been giving a lot of thought to your request for a job at the school. You said you would do anything – is that so?'

'Yes,' she nodded. 'I don't mind what it is, James.'

'The job I have in mind could be very demanding, but I'm convinced it would be perfect for you.'

'I don't care how demanding it is. I would love to be a part of your school. What is the job?'

'You would be helping me to run it as my wife.'

She stared at him, sure she hadn't heard correctly. 'Are you . . . are you asking me to marry you?'

'That was a clumsy proposal, but, yes, I am asking you to marry me, Helen. I've grown to love and admire you very much as I've watched you handle each crisis with courage and intelligence. I believe together we will make a success of the school – and be happy.' He studied her intently. 'Would you like me to go down on my knees and plead for your acceptance?'

'No!' she laughed, throwing her arms around him. 'The proposal was perfect; I just wasn't expecting it. James Sharland, I love you, and it would be a joy and honour to be your wife.'

'Thank heavens for that!' James breathed a sigh of relief, wrapping her in a strong embrace.

Helen looked up at James, her eyes shining with happiness. 'Grandfather said this was going to be a wonderful night. The rascal knew, didn't he?'

'I told him today. Now, we had better join the family as they will be on tenterhooks waiting for news.'

When they reached the others, Dan and Beth were already there, and when the girls saw only smiling faces, they hugged each other briefly.

Grandfather was so excited. 'We will have three weddings in the family. This is indeed a wonderful night and a fitting end to all of our troubles. My boys have found lovely wives, and I couldn't be happier about it.'

'I think Edward would have approved of the way things have worked out, don't you, Dan?' James asked his friend.

'Without a doubt. We have kept our promises to him, and all past debts have been paid.'

The two men smiled at each other and then led their future wives on to the floor to dance the rest of the night away.